SOMETHING HIDDEN

Kerry Wilkinson has been busy since turning thirty.

His first Jessica Daniel novel, *Locked In*, was a number
one ebook bestseller, while the series as a whole has sold
one million copies.

He has written a fantasy-adventure trilogy for young
adults, a second crime series featuring private investigator
Andrew Hunter, plus the standalone thriller, *Down Among
the Dead Men*. *Something Hidden* is the second in the Andrew
Hunter series.

Originally from the county of Somerset, Kerry has spent
far too long living in the north of England, picking up
words like 'barm' and 'ginnel'.

When he's short of ideas, he rides his bike or bakes
buns. When he's not, he writes it all down.

For more information about Kerry and his books visit:
www.kerrywilkinson.com or www.panmacmillan.com
www.twitter.com/kerrywk
www.facebook.com/JessicaDanielBooks
Or you can email Kerry at kerrywilkinson@live.com

Also by Kerry Wilkinson

The Jessica Daniel series

LOCKED IN

VIGILANTE

THE WOMAN IN BLACK

THINK OF THE CHILDREN

PLAYING WITH FIRE

THICKER THAN WATER

BEHIND CLOSED DOORS

CROSSING THE LINE

SCARRED FOR LIFE

FOR RICHER, FOR POORER

The Andrew Hunter series

SOMETHING WICKED

Standalone thriller

DOWN AMONG THE DEAD MEN

The Silver Blackthorn trilogy

RECKONING

RENEGADE

RESURGENCE

KERRY WILKINSON

SOMETHING HIDDEN

PAN BOOKS

First published 2016 by Pan Books
an imprint of Pan Macmillan
20 New Wharf Road, London N1 9RR
Associated companies throughout the world
www.panmacmillan.com

ISBN 978-1-5098-0663-8

1 3 5 7 9 8 6 4 2

A CIP catalogue record for this book is available from the British Library.

Typeset by Ellipsis Digital Limited, Glasgow
Printed and bound by CPI Group (UK) Ltd, Croydon, CR0 4YY

Visit **www.panmacmillan.com** to read more about all our books
and to buy them. You will also find features, author interviews and
news of any author events, and you can sign up for e-newsletters
so that you're always first to hear about our new releases.

SOMETHING HIDDEN

1

Owen glanced up as the bell above the door jangled its greeting.

Ding-a-ling-a-ling.

Nice. Very traditional. He liked that. None of this modern *nee-nar* nonsense that some of the shops had on the go when customers walked through the door. Newsagents were awful at it, especially on a Sunday morning when hungover people popped in for a paper.

Wendy half-turned as she led the way into the shop, offering him that wonderful grin of hers. Her green eyes met his for a fraction of a second before she twisted back to look where she was going.

Bloody hell, this was really happening.

Her slightly wavy black hair bounced across her shoulders as she offered a small giggle as if to indicate that she couldn't quite believe what they were doing either. As she continued inside, Owen wrestled the rain-swelled door back into place, standing directly underneath the heater and enjoying the gust of warm air that was battling the October squall.

They were too young to be doing this, weren't they? That's what everyone thought, even if they didn't say it.

1

He'd seen it on the faces of their old university friends when the news was delivered. On the surface it was all smiles, congratulations, and 'when's the engagement party?' Underneath, it was all 'they're only twenty-two, why are they getting married?' Either that, or 'I'd marry her sharpish too if I was punching above my weight that much.'

Only Owen's older brother possessed the guts to say what so many others were surely thinking, taking him aside in their old shared bedroom, nodding towards the stack of well-thumbed *FHM*s in the corner with that laddish smile of his, and asking if Owen was *really* going to spend the rest of his life sleeping only with Wendy. Or, in his own less-poetic terms, 'but there's so many women you haven't shagged yet . . .'

Despite the heat, Owen shivered as he turned. He was nervous. The whole room was a U-shape of varnished wooden cabinets and glass display cases polished to within millimetres of their existence, all surrounded by pristine green carpet. It was all very neat. Very professional. Very . . . not him. He'd never been into a jewellery shop before. Well, Argos, but that didn't count.

Wendy skipped her way across the floor and was bent over the cabinet directly across from the front door, peering towards the rows of items they probably couldn't afford. Owen watched her and broke into a smile of his own. Sod his stupid brother and those un-shagged women – Wendy was worth it. This was happening and, despite his worries over how much it would all cost, Owen was happy.

On the other side of the counter, a man turned away from a workbench to greet them. He smiled thinly, wiping his hands on his stripy red and white apron, then pushed back the remnants of his greying hair, before removing his glasses and allowing them to hang from the chain around his neck. On the bench behind him there were neat rows of tools next to something sparkling that he was fixing.

'Can I help you?' he asked.

Wendy looked up from the display case, reaching backwards to take Owen's hand. He could sense the excitement in her voice. 'We got engaged last weekend and we're looking for a ring.'

The man's grin widened, showing off a set of slightly crooked yellowing teeth. He was either full of the joy that comes when two people find their eternal soulmate, or he sensed a sale. Owen knew which scenario he believed.

'You've come to the right place,' he said, focusing on Wendy. 'This is my shop, Sampson's, and you'll always receive a personal service here. There's none of the staff merry-go-round you get in the chains, plus I can resize or reset anything on-site. Most of the other local places send their items out to be worked on externally but I always look after my customers. You'll also get the best prices. If there's something you've seen elsewhere, I can work with you to recreate any design.'

Wendy giggled again, spinning to face Owen and telling him with a raised eyebrow that she'd made her mind up to buy from here. She always liked the local places and personal touch thing. He was more of a 'wherever's cheapest' kind of guy.

'I'm Leyton, by the way,' the shop owner added. 'Leyton Sampson. Feel free to browse and ask anything you want.'

He stepped back, holding his arms out in pride to indicate the selection, before glancing sideways at the clock on the wall above him: 11.47. He was presumably eyeing a nice chunky sale before midday.

Wendy removed her hand from Owen's and pointed at the cabinet in front of her. 'I'm not really sure what I'm looking for. We've not got loads of money but I don't want something big anyway . . .'

Sampson nodded knowingly. 'Diamonds are my speciality. I've got personal contacts in Botswana. They mine things directly for this shop. I don't have to deal with middlemen, so you won't find better prices anywhere. Do you mind if I ask how much you're looking to spend . . . ?'

Botswana? There was sales spiel and there was taking the piss – this really walked the line. Next, he'd be telling them about a gold-mining expedition to the mountains of South America – or wherever it was gold came from. Owen had no idea.

Sampson tailed off, maintaining eye contact with Wendy, which was probably best considering Owen was staring at his shoes. This was the question he really didn't want to hear. He hoped for something ending in 'hundred', not 'thousand'. It was his own fault: Wendy had been the sensible one, saying that the ring didn't matter and it was all about the commitment to each other; he'd been the one insisting that he could afford whatever she might want and that she should pick something she really liked.

Wendy pointed towards a ring on the end of the row, with a sparkling rock that was, thankfully, small. 'I think I'd prefer something understated, like that one.'

Thank God.

Seven hundred quid: Owen could just about afford that. All those Saturday morning overtime shifts at the call centre were finally going to seem worth it. He hated that bloody job but it was a means to this end. All those people telling him to piss off meant he could actually afford something his girlfriend . . . no, fiancée . . . wanted.

The truth was that Wendy knew what they could afford and, despite Owen's bravado at the time of wanting to get the 'right' ring, she wasn't interested in expensive things anyway. She'd never gone for designer dresses or shoes, preferring something from the vintage shop on Oxford Road that was wedged between a run-down pub and a tanning place. They were both practical, sensible people, knowing the engagement had to be a long one and that finding somewhere to live where they were happy was more important than blowing thousands on a lavish ceremony they'd spend a decade paying for. Perhaps that would mean leaving Manchester? This was the city where they'd met at university but now they were in the real world and had to find proper jobs.

Distressingly, they were actually adults.

Owen's thoughts drifted as Sampson unlocked the cabinet and began banging on about 'white gold'. Whatever, mate. You do your thing, keep it to around seven hundred, make Wendy smile, and all's right with the world.

Owen began peering around, taking in the row of trophies on the wall and trying to figure out what the shop smelled of. It reminded him of when he'd cleaned out the attic at his parents' house a few years ago: dusty and . . . old. This place must have been here for years.

He wondered what they should do after picking a ring. Go out to celebrate? In typical understated fashion, they could go to the pub on the corner close to their flat. It'd be showing football via a dodgy satellite hook-up on a Saturday afternoon – a definite bonus – plus it was where he and Wendy first met, meaning he even had an excuse to suggest it. Of course, as soon as they sat down to eat and the match came on, she'd realise his slightly ulterior motive but he would've just spent a small fortune on an engagement ring, so should be able to get away with it.

Hmmm . . .

Oh, balls to the football. He was engaged and happy. They could go home and make their own entertainment.

As Owen grinned to himself, imagining exactly what entertainment they could come up with, there was a howling squeal of car tyres from the front of the shop. He turned in time to see the front door being rammed inwards as the silhouette of a figure burst through, sending the overhead bell into tinkling overdrive.

Suddenly, the room was spinning. Another man slammed through the door, all dark jacket, jeans and balaclava. Then there was a third man, wearing the exact same get-up. Someone was shouting – perhaps all three of them – but the words overlapped each other and Owen was left holding his arms out pathetically. He turned to Wendy but she was already on her knees, both hands on the ground, not daring to look up. When had she dropped? Her head

6

tilted slightly towards him, arms trembling as she crumpled into a ball.

'Get down!'

Owen heard the man's shout clearly this time but still his legs didn't obey. What was his body doing? He peered up to see the double barrel of a sawn-off shotgun pointing in his face, its owner bellowing a string of threats. He'd never seen a gun before, not a real one.

He heard the blow before he felt it and the next thing Owen knew, he was on his knees, a throbbing sensation burning through his head. One of the men had whacked him across the temple with the butt of the gun. It was only glancing but left him seeing stars as his legs finally gave way and he slumped to the floor, pushing himself up against one of the cabinets.

The man was shouting again: 'Look at the floor, not me.'

Owen blinked away the thudding in his head and tried to focus on Wendy, who was shuffling the short distance towards him. He risked a glance upwards but could see only three sets of heavy boots stomping around the shop. Wendy clasped his hand, her freezing fingers wrapping around his. She was staring at the floor, her hair a mess, as she continued to shake.

Her voice was barely a whisper: 'Okay?'

Owen squeezed her fingers to say yes, easing himself closer to the ground as the noise continued around them. This was the type of thing he'd seen on the news but had never really taken in. There were always interviews with witnesses who were so stupid, they'd not seen anything happening right in front of them. Only now did Owen understand it was no wonder: they were too busy trying to control their bowels.

The cabinet felt solid behind him and Owen could taste the harsh mustiness of the carpet. He released Wendy's hand and tilted his head slightly so he could see what was going on. All three men were now standing in front of the main counter he and Wendy had been at moments before. They were a similar height, five nine or ten, not fat, not thin, all dressed identically. One had a sawn-off shotgun hanging by his side as nonchalantly as if it was a shopping bag, another was pointing his at Leyton Sampson.

'Open it, then!'

There was a twang to his accent that Owen had missed initially. Something northern: not Mancunian, a bit harsher. It was hard to tell because he was shouting.

'What are you doing?' Wendy's whisper was so soft that only Owen could've heard it. He could sense the anguish in her voice. 'Don't look *at* them.'

Owen returned his eyes to the carpet, taking another mouthful of the dust-caked bristles, before twisting his face the other way again so he could see what was going on. The top of the cabinet was now open and one of the men was filling a Tesco carrier bag with the contents.

There was a smash of glass as another broke into a case on the far side of the store with the butt of his gun. He reached in, yanking out necklaces, bracelets and handfuls of other shiny things, before dropping them into a different Tesco bag. Every little really was helping.

Owen could feel Wendy's hand reaching for him again, thumping into his arm, silently asking why he wasn't staring at the floor as they'd been told. He didn't know: he wasn't a hero and definitely wasn't going to try something stupid, he simply felt an urge to watch.

He glanced over the front counter towards a trembling Sampson, who was resting on the workbench behind to keep himself upright. The owner kept peering down towards the bench and then back up at the man filling the bag in front of him. For a moment, Owen's eyes met Sampson's and then the shop owner turned away again. Owen couldn't read him but then he'd never stared into the face of someone who had a gun pointing at them before.

The third raider clumped back to the front door and gazed outside. 'We've gotta go.'

Definitely Scouse. One of Owen's mates at uni was an Everton fan and said 'go' in the exact same extended way, as if there was a succession of 'O's, instead of just the one. Usually he said 'we've gotta go' when Everton were losing at home to Liverpool again.

Crash!

Another cabinet on the far side was caved in, with the supermarket bag getting a final top-up of jewels.

'Come on.'

The bell clinked again as the door was heaved open and then three sets of boots boomed towards the exit. Owen pushed his face into the carpet, suddenly aware of how fast his heart was going. One-two-three-four-five-six-seven-eight. How many seconds had passed?

There was another screech of tyres, the beeping of car horns, an excited chatter of voices from the street, and a final tinkle from the bell as the door closed itself.

For a moment, there was silence, before it was broken by Sampson's quivering voice. 'I think you can get up now.'

Owen struggled to his knees, reaching for Wendy and helping her up until they were both standing. Her eyes were wide, taking in the carnage around them as she gripped his arm and continued to shake. He took a small step forward, crystals of glass crunching under his feet.

'Are you both okay?' Sampson asked. He had pushed himself up from the workbench, inspecting a cut on his wrist from where some of the shards had flown off at an angle. The floor was a mass of splintered wood and shattered glass, with two glittering rings and a necklace lying among the debris close to the door. Owen glanced at the clock: 11.49 – just two minutes had passed since he'd been standing with his fiancée ready to choose an engagement ring and now everything had changed.

'I think so,' Owen whispered.

The shop owner plucked something from his wound and dropped it on the floor as his gaze continued to flit between his workbench and the shop front, before finally settling on Owen. His tone was flat, emotionless, eyes unblinking.

'I should probably call the police.'

2

MONDAY

Andrew Hunter jammed his hands deep in his pockets, ducked his head down and bustled towards his office in a not-quite-running, not-quite-walking kind of way. The chilled wind bristled through his mousy definitely-not-ginger, definitely-not-thinning hair.

Seriously, what was the point of February? Somebody had obviously made the decision to ram Valentine's Day in there to give couples something to do but, apart from that, why bother? November was shite – everyone knew that. It got dark early, it was always cold, if you lived in Manchester – which he did – it would spend most of the time pissing down, but at least Christmas was around the corner. There'd be lights threaded through the city centre and a general sense of optimism as everyone looked forward to that golden week between Christmas and New Year, in which they could go on a seven-day drinkathon and not care about work. January was rubbish but at least it was a new year, with shops flogging anything they could on the cheap, something different on the telly and the memories of Christmas. But February? It was just there: a waste of every-one's time. Plus *this* February was colder than usual – which was saying something for the ice-ridden north of England.

Quite frankly, February could sod off. Bring on the spring, with bouncing baby bunnies, early blooming daffodils, and . . . okay, it rained a lot in spring too – but at least it was a degree or two warmer.

Frost clung to the shadows along the cobbled alley as Andrew hurried from his parking space to the office. It was only a few hundred metres but more than enough in this weather. A biting breeze sizzled around the tightly packed buildings, whistling into the minuscule gap between Andrew's shirt and coat and sending a new wave of shivers bristling through him.

Brrr.

Bloody February.

As he reached the corner and turned onto the street that housed his office, Andrew glanced up, spotting the hazy shape on the steps ahead. At first he thought it was a crumpled bin bag but then the outline moved, sending a thin spiral of breath into the atmosphere. It was a girl or a young woman, somebody small, with arms wrapped around her spindly legs, which were tucked into her chest. She was wearing a purple bobble hat, with long, dark hair peeping out at the bottom. All elbows and knees and seriously underfed.

Another breath disappeared into the ether as Andrew reached the front of his office, towering over the shrunken figure.

'Are you all right?' he asked.

She peered up at him through sleep-deprived half-closed eyes, her voice a harsh croak in the cold. There was a polite-ness to her tone that wasn't forced. 'Are you Mr Hunter?'

'Yeah, I, er . . . it's Andrew.'

Andrew stepped backwards as the girl clambered to her feet. She was young: twenty-one at the most but probably not even that. She was wearing a thin jacket and shivering uncontrollably under the northern onslaught. After stepping around her, Andrew unlocked the door and held it open, offering a thin smile as he turned off the alarm system. The girl was brushing grit from the back of her trousers, stretching her legs and suppressing a yawn. Her skin was white, almost grey. How long had she been outside? It had been below freezing the previous night and it looked as if she'd slept on the street.

She tried to smile but her jaw clicked and she winced as she wrapped her arms around herself. When she spoke, her teeth chattered. 'You investigate stuff, don't you?'

Andrew nodded towards the stairs beyond her. 'Let's get you upstairs first – the heating's on up there and you look, er . . .'

He didn't finish the sentence.

The office wasn't quite cosy but it was certainly warmer than the hallway. As Andrew fussed around putting the kettle on, the girl sat next to the radiator, splaying her fingers wide and taking deep breaths. Andrew wondered if she'd say anything else but she seemed happy to enjoy the temperature. He fished a pint of milk from the back of the mini-fridge and straightened the pile of cardboard folders next to his computer, before crossing to the other desk and taking a packet of Jammie Dodgers from the bottom drawer. He pulled apart the wrapper and passed the packet to the girl, offering a 'go on' as she asked silently if he was really giving them to her.

She ate slowly, nibbling at the layers and devouring one crumb by crumb, not allowing anything to fall.

'You can have another,' Andrew said. 'They're Jenny's . . . my assistant's. She's got packets and packets of the things in her drawer. I don't know how she eats so much.'

The girl nodded eagerly, eyes darting towards the open packet next to the radiator and taking a second biscuit as the kettle clicked off.

'Do you want a tea?' Andrew asked. 'Coffee?'

'Tea.'

'Milk? Sugar?'

'Just milk.'

Andrew made three identical teas – no sugar, don't go mental with the milk – plopping one on Jenny's unoccupied desk; resting one on the radiator next to the girl; and wheeling his chair over so that he was sitting next to her, before looping his fingers through the third. *This* is how you got through Mondays in February.

The girl smiled properly, holding the mug underneath her bottom lip and sucking on the warm fumes. 'I'm Fiona.'

'You look cold.'

She shrugged and took a sip of the tea. She wasn't looking at Andrew, more gazing through him. 'I saw your name in the paper the other month and got your office number from the operator.'

'Are you . . . homeless?'

Fiona shook her head. 'I can just about pay my rent but

that doesn't include bills, so I don't put the heating on. You know what it's like with British Gas.'

It wasn't just Andrew who knew – everyone did. In a public popularity poll, energy companies were ranked below the Nazis, Piers Morgan, and that bloke who answers his phone in a cinema.

'I've been saving,' she added.

'For what?'

She wriggled on the seat, thrusting a hand into her back pocket and pulling out a wad of crumpled five- and ten-pound notes, before dropping them on Andrew's lap. He put his tea on the floor and then picked up the money, flattening the notes between his fingers until he'd counted the sixty quid, and placing them on the radiator.

'I'm not going to take your money, Fiona.'

'But I need your help.'

'What do you need?'

Fiona opened her mouth to answer but the door rattled open. A bristle of chilled air followed and then Jenny came in, complete with a Morrison's bag for life. Her black ponytail swung from side to side as she closed the door, spinning on the spot, dimple on show.

'You'll never guess what this guy said to me on the bus . . . oh . . .'

Her brown eyes locked on Fiona, instantly examining the scene: freezing cold girl, sixty quid, mugs of tea, Jammie Dodgers.

She held up the bag, offering it to the other girl: 'I've got some choccie biscuits if you want – and some mini rolls. I'm Jenny, by the way.'

Andrew gave her a barely there nod to indicate all was well as Fiona held up her half-nibbled biscuit. 'I'm okay.'

Jenny motioned towards the door but Andrew shook his head, nodding at her chair. Plenty of room at the inn.

'What is it you need?' Andrew tried again.

Fiona stared into the tan-coloured tea. 'Everyone's saying my dad did something that he didn't. They all hate him, so everyone hates me. People spit at me in the street. I used to live in Oldham but my old landlord threw me out, so I'm living in this horrible place where I can't afford the heating. I had a job in this office but no one wanted to work with me – they wouldn't even talk to me. I thought that if I came to the city centre, there'd be more places to hide, more people, that they wouldn't know me.' She stopped, breathing and sniffling, then adding: 'But there's always someone . . .'

She stopped for another bite of the biscuit. Her sentences had come out so quickly that Andrew needed a few moments to take it all in. Before he could ask any follow-up questions, she was off again.

'I had to use a fake name to get the new flat just in case – and then I gave my neighbours a different name, not that we talk to each other anyway. Then my CV's all over the place. I can't use my actual name, which means none of my exams are going to show up if they check – plus I can't ask for a reference. I just . . .' She stopped again, exhaling heavily and blinking rapidly. 'I'm not sure what to do.'

Andrew met Jenny's eyes across the room but she shrugged in answer to the silent question. She didn't know who Fiona was either.

'Who's your father, Fiona?'

The girl shook her head, sloshing a drip of tea over the top of the mug onto her finger. She winced but didn't put it down. 'You don't understand – it wasn't him. I know how it looks . . . I know what everyone says happened but he wasn't like that. He was just a bit sad – anyone would be if they'd been through what he had.'

Fiona tried to drink from the mug but her hand was shaking so much that she spilled the tea across her chin. She gasped, rattling the chair backwards and dropping the almost-finished biscuit. She scrambled forward to make amends but Andrew already had a cloth in his hand. He took the tea from her, placing it on the table next to them and briefly rested a reassuring hand on her knee. It crossed his mind – as always – that this was rather creepy, but then Andrew always thought that. Accidentally glance at a girl on a bus: creepy. Give a homeless person who just happens to be female some change: creepy. Offer a girl directions when she's clearly lost: creepy. Ask a crying woman outside a club if she's all right: creepy. Sometimes – or a lot of times in his case – a man could try to be nice to a woman without there being any more to it than that.

Andrew tried to make eye contact but Fiona was doing all she could to avoid looking directly at him. She had found a spot on the wall behind him instead.

'You don't have to tell us anything you don't want to,' Andrew said, 'but if you want help, we're going to need to know.'

Fiona nodded pitifully, one arm hugging herself, the other dabbing at her chin.

'I'm sorry, it's just . . . my dad was Luke Methodist.'

3

Ishan Chopra was bored. There was no getting away from it: mathematics was really dull. It was one of those degree subjects he'd thought his parents would like him to take, something he didn't find too hard, a subject which would hopefully help him find fortune, if not fame. That might all be true but it was as interesting as watching paint dry, or staring at grass growing. The people were nice, but still . . .

He gazed down at the lecture amphitheatre from the back row as the screen flipped from one PowerPoint slide to the next. He would download the notes from the uni portal later and might get around to reading them at some point before the end-of-semester exams. There really was no reason to turn up, except to meet the attendance criteria.

Below, the lecturer was droning on in a monotonous tone of voice, hypnotic in the sense that it made a person feel sleepy . . . *very* sleepy . . .

A gut-wrenching yawn forced its way up from Ishan's stomach until it felt as if his head was going to split in two, not that anyone around him noticed he was on the brink of hibernation. A handful of maths nerds bashed away on their laptops and tablets, with a few others actually using a pen and paper to take notes.

Unbelievable.

Most of the class wallowed in their boredom, leaning back into their seats and strapping themselves in for at least another ninety minutes. Ishan often wondered what might happen if he smuggled in a small rodent. There were enough of them making a racket by the bins at the back of his flat for him to be able to catch one. He could wrestle it into a rucksack, wait until the lecturer started sending everyone to sleep, and then set it free. If that didn't liven up proceedings then nothing would. If not a rodent then how about—

Bang!

Bang!

Everyone turned as the sounds boomed from somewhere behind the theatre. The lecturer stopped speaking, mouth half-open as if he had forgotten what he was talking about. In an instant, Ishan was awake. He'd heard those noises a few months previously when he and his friend Vikram had been chased home from the city centre after dark. Vikram blamed a backfiring car, saying they shouldn't worry about contacting the police, but Ishan knew the truth.

One or two people near the back started to stand but Ishan was ahead of them, sliding along the aisle until he was next to the door. He opened it a sliver, peering out into the empty corridor.

Bang!

The third shot was louder than the first two, with a loud gasp ricocheting around the theatre. Ishan took a moment to compose himself, waiting to see if there would be a fourth noise, before pushing his way through the doors into the hallway and slowly approaching the front of the building.

Through the wire mesh glass, he could see the path beyond, with long rows of white paving slabs reflecting the October sun. The jeweller a couple of streets away had been robbed at gunpoint a few days previously and everyone was on edge.

Behind him, one of his classmates' voices hissed through the silence: 'Ish, where are you going?'

Ishan ignored him, continuing to edge towards the front door until he had a clear view of the scene beyond. He could reach up and lock the doors to keep out whoever was there but his eyes were drawn to the pooling patch of red staining the bright white fifty metres ahead.

There was a gurgle in his stomach that was nothing to do with food.

He knew he should stay back, think about himself, yet Ishan found himself opening the doors and stepping outside.

'Ish!'

The paths from the various lecture theatres converged in a courtyard that also served as a cut-through for students trying to get from Oxford Road to the halls of residence and flats beyond. Thousands of people would stream through at the top of each hour, yet it was almost always empty while lectures were going on. Now, the space was far from clear.

Ishan continued to move ahead, marvelling at how silent it now was. There was no distant chirp of birds, no hum of traffic or honking of car horns. Everything had stopped.

Forty metres. Thirty. Ishan could see all he needed to from where he was but he continued to edge forward a step at a time. To his left, there was a flicker of movement as another figure stepped out from the corner of the adjacent building, treading slowly, staggering even. It was a man in a dark blazer and trousers. He put his hand over his mouth as he approached the scene, knees wobbling.

Ishan was close enough to see what had happened, to smell it: the faint odour of burning, the coppery haze.

The other figure glanced up to catch Ishan's gaze, eyes wide as his arm flailed. 'He shot them both. I was on my way here and he . . .'

Ishan reached for the phone in his pocket, feeling unnervingly calm. The man was Professor Steyn: Ishan had studied an elective in his class during his first year.

Steyn dabbed at his forehead, eyes still bulging as he took another step. Ishan wanted to tell him to stay away but the professor was the grown-up, after all. Ishan was . . . well, he didn't know. The student. Shouldn't a professor know what to do? As if anyone knew what to do in a situation like this.

The expanding pool of blood seeped along the bright white tiles, nudging the edge of Steyn's shoe, and it was only then that Ishan saw the complete horror of it. A girl was slumped on the ground face-down, surrounded by the deep red, her wavy black hair soaking in the liquid that was oozing from the side of her face. Lying on his front next to her was a lad somewhere around Ishan's age, wearing a hoody and jeans, both arms trapped unnaturally underneath him. Ishan was sure he had the identical top somewhere in his wardrobe. Another day and he could have been walking around in the exact same get-up.

The third person was the only one facing upwards: a

man in a heavy green jacket with a pistol lying next to his hand and spurts of black and red exploding across the tiles where his head should have been.

As Ishan dialled 999, the background noise fizzed into focus again. Someone nearby was screaming and there was a hum of voices. The traffic was moving, there were footsteps, a door banging, windows opening. Chatter-chatter-chatter.

Professor Steyn reached forward to touch the girl's arm, trying to turn her over.

Ishan wanted to tell him that it was no good, that it was too late, but the voice was already speaking into his ear. 'Emergency. Which service?'

'Police.'

Professor Steyn gripped the girl's arm, turning her onto her back, but the sight was horrendous and he let her flop back into her lifeless state. He turned to face Ishan, skin colourless, mouth open, before emptying the contents of his stomach half onto his shoes, half onto the pool of blood.

More people drifted towards them, arms outstretched, hands over their mouths. Some screamed, some cried. Others turned and went back the way they'd come. Only a few stood and watched as Ishan somehow talked the operator through the sight in front of him.

The tremble in her voice matched his and she didn't even have to look at it. Professor Steyn was on his feet again but he was a mess, blood and vomit covering his lower half.

'Is there anything else?' the operator's voice asked.

Ishan blinked into the present. He'd been on autopilot

talking her through the scene, but it suddenly felt real now he could hear the sirens closing in.

'Sorry?' he said.

'Can you see anything else around you?'

Ishan wished he could close his eyes and make it all go away but he knew why the operator was asking – soon, this area would be swarming with police and crime scene experts. No one would see it as it was now and only himself and Steyn would be able to describe how things looked in the immediate aftermath. He forced himself to run his eyes across the bodies one final time, to search through the expanding mass of red for anything out of place. As he scanned the taller of the figures, Ishan noticed something he'd previously missed. It wasn't just a green jacket the man was wearing, it was an army jacket, or definitely something from the armed forces. There was a patch on the lapel, a name visible even through the dark smear of blood across it.

After a breath, Ishan closed his eyes and turned away, spelling the name out letter by letter.

'M-E-T-H-O-D-I-S-T,' he said. 'I think he shot them, then himself.'

4

There was a moment of silence in Andrew's office as he chewed on his bottom lip and wondered what to say. It wasn't right that she had to, but it was no wonder Fiona Methodist felt the need to change her name. As soon as she told anyone locally, there would have been a moment of hesitation, a second or two of recognition, and then . . .

'I get that a lot,' Fiona said with a humourless smile.

'Sorry,' Andrew replied.

She shrugged, reaching for another Jammie Dodger.

'When did you last eat?' Andrew asked.

Fiona shrugged again, nibbling away at the edge of the biscuit. 'It wasn't my dad.'

Andrew nodded, wanting to ask *how* she knew but knowing there was no point. It wasn't as if Luke Methodist had survived to tell anyone why he'd shot a young couple in the middle of the day two Octobers ago.

Fiona continued to eat, the scratching of her teeth the only noise in the room until she spoke again. 'I read everything they wrote. How he was a war vet scarred by what he saw, how he came home with post-traumatic stress, or PTSD as they kept saying. He never wanted to talk to me about what went on, so that part is probably true. Maybe he *was* a victim in a roadside bombing, like they said? Maybe he *did* see one of his friends shot? They had all those experts on the news and the analysts talking about his state of mind but they didn't know him. They can say all they want . . . but that doesn't mean he shot those two kids.' She paused, closing her eyes. 'They were only a couple of years older than me . . .'

Andrew glanced across to Jenny, who was sipping her tea in silence. Sometimes she knew exactly what to say but the blank look gave Andrew the answer he needed – she was as lost as he was but had enough self-awareness to keep quiet. He had no choice.

'I'm not sure what you want me to say.'

Fiona shivered again, her bony shoulders jutting through her thin coat as she tried to control herself. She soon finished the biscuit, clucking her tongue to the top of her mouth to clean the sticky bits away from her teeth. 'Dad left his sheltered accommodation without telling anyone and moved onto the street, so he was basically homeless. I didn't know where he was for a couple of months until he left a message on my phone. I tried to help but he wasn't interested. I don't know if it was because of that or because of what they said went on when he was in the army. They can say my dad approached that couple and shot them – but he wouldn't have dared to go near them. Apart from a couple of his street friends and me, he didn't talk to anyone. He was scared of people.'

'What about the drugs?'

Fiona met Andrew's eyes but this time she was angry, her nostrils flaring. 'They made that up. *If* he bought drugs from that Evans bloke, it was for his friends on the street. He didn't do drugs. When they tested his body afterwards, there was nothing like that in his system but no one bothered to report it and everyone had already read the earlier versions. People assumed he was a junkie but it's not true.' She gulped, lowering her voice and looking away again. 'Sorry . . .'

'Fiona.'

'What?'

Andrew waited until she turned to look at him. From what she'd said, she must be nineteen or twenty but could easily have been fifteen or sixteen. She was tiny, so thin that he could see the shape of her bones through her clothes. When she finally met his eyes, Fiona was blinking rapidly, trying to keep the tears at bay.

'What would you like me to do?' Andrew asked.

She picked up the small mound of notes from the radiator and thrust them in his direction. 'I don't have much but I can save some more. I want someone to believe me that it wasn't him.'

Andrew shook his head as Fiona gulped back another tear, standing and wiping her nose with her sleeve. 'I thought you were a good guy? If it's about the money . . .'

'It's not the money.'

'So what is it?'

He opened his mouth to speak, unsure how to break it to her. The police had already looked into things and, from everything he'd seen and heard of the case, it was as open and shut as it came.

Fiona stepped towards the door, re-pocketing her money. 'It's okay, thanks for the tea.'

As another blast of cold air fizzed through the door, Andrew sighed. He'd always been a soft touch.

'Fiona.'

She turned. 'What?'

'We've got something else to do this morning but if you leave me a number to contact you on, I'll see what I can do.'

Jenny shunted a pad towards the edge of the desk and Fiona took a battered mobile phone from her pocket. She began jabbing at the buttons, before copying a number onto the page.

'I can't always afford credit but you should be able to call me,' she said, adding another 'sorry'.

She peered up to look at Andrew again. He couldn't figure out if she was playing him or if she really was this fragile. He'd had people take advantage of him before, using him to do their dirty work. Was there really something going on here? Since the incident with Nicholas Carr, he'd been questioning himself repeatedly.

'I really will look into it,' Andrew said.

'Okay.'

'You'll just have to bear with me.' She reached for the door handle but Andrew continued. 'You said your father only spoke to you and some of his street friends. Do you know any of their names?'

She gazed upwards, screwing up her lips, the cold still seeping through the open door behind her. 'There was this guy named Joe – that's all I know.'

Fiona stood still for a moment, as if waiting for permission to leave. When she finally closed the door, Andrew breathed out heavily. He'd been seconds away from offering to put her in a hotel. She was so thin, so scarred, but what then? Would he end up trying to look after every waif who turned up on his doorstep? And was it just because she was female? Andrew wanted to tell himself that he'd have been equally concerned if an underfed lad had shown up asking for help but he didn't know if that was true. He always found himself questioning his own motives.

Jenny broke the silence by ruffling in her bag for life and coming up with a packet of mini rolls, waving them in the air as she tore into the purple wrapper.

'Want one?'

'It's too early for chocolate.'

She grinned, tearing an individual wrapper open with her teeth. 'Pfft. It's *never* too early for chocolate.'

'I don't know where you put it all. If I ate what you ate, I'd be a giant blob.'

Jenny tilted her head to the side as she took a bite of the roll. 'You look . . . confused.'

Andrew shunted his chair back to his desk. 'I am.'

'Why?'

'Because I don't know where I'm going to start.'

'Why didn't you tell her "no" then?'

'I don't know . . . stupidity.'

There was pause in which Jenny could have made a token effort to correct him. Instead, she turned to her monitor, half-eaten mini roll in hand. 'I can get all the news print-outs from the time if you want? We're not going to be able to see the police files without a bit of fudgery-doo-dah, so it's probably the next best thing.'

'Fudgery-doo-dah?'

'You know what I mean: greasing palms, favour for a mate – that sort of thing.'

Andrew didn't like working with second-hand information but he didn't have too many options. He checked his watch. 'I've got to go out in ten minutes.'

'I can stay and work here.'

'No, you come too. I think I'm going to need backup.'

He paused, rarely sure how to broach things with Jenny. After a moment of uncomfortable silence, she peered up from her desk and he could see the recognition in her eyes that she knew she'd missed something. Jenny had once told him that a former teacher thought she didn't show empathy for other people. She'd found that interesting rather than insulting and started to learn from observing others. Sometimes, Andrew liked to watch and wait to see what her reaction would be.

It took a second or two but then Andrew saw something akin to a penny dropping. Jenny's eyes widened ever so slightly and then narrowed again. She put the remains of the cake on her desk and started playing with her ponytail, untying it and looping her fingers through the strands. She looked as if she was remembering something painful but Andrew didn't know if that was another thing she'd learned.

'I was a student at the time of the shootings,' Jenny said. 'Everyone was scared to go out, especially after dark. There was that robbery and then those two students were shot days later. There were rumours every day that someone had been spotted close to campus with a gun.'

She hadn't said that *she* was scared.

'How long did it take to get back to normal?' Andrew asked.

'A couple of weeks? People soon move on. By the time it's getting towards the end of term, they want to go out and celebrate.'

'Did you know the kids who were shot?'

Kids to him.

Jenny shook her head. 'I didn't really hang around with anyone when I was at uni.'

Andrew's memory was patchy at best – he blamed age – but the case was recent. Sixteen months previously, Owen Copthorne and his fiancée, Wendy, had witnessed a robbery in a local jeweller's. Barely two days later, Luke Methodist shot them dead close to the university campus, a short distance from Oxford Road, before turning the gun on himself.

After a week of public mourning and outrage, police had arrested the Evans brothers – Kal, Aaron and Paulie, a trio of Scousers, well known to Liverpool authorities, with long criminal records. Fibres from Aaron Evans' shoes were found at the scene of the robbery, with one of his fingerprints discovered on the back seat of the car they'd failed to set on fire. After police found drugs and weapons hidden at Kal Evans' house, everything had come crashing down, though the stolen items were never found.

Andrew scratched at his hairline, trying to think. 'Weren't the Evans brothers sent down a few weeks ago?'

Jenny click-clacked her keyboard, nodding as she typed. 'Three weeks back. Kal and Aaron Evans each got life for armed robbery, with the prospect of parole in fourteen years, Paulie got eighteen years. He could be out in about nine.'

'Why'd he get less?'

'He wasn't holding a gun, plus the evidence wasn't as strong that he was there. They were never charged with organising the shooting of the witnesses, only the armed robbery.'

Andrew nodded along, reaching into his memory. At the time they'd been charged, it had been a big story but, as with most things, it soon went away. Police believed Luke Methodist knew Kal Evans because he bought drugs from him. It was the only link they had from robbers to killer – but there was no confession from any of the brothers.

There was speculation that Methodist owed them money and this was what they wanted as payback. Having seen what he'd done, he turned the gun on himself in shame. No one knew for sure and it wasn't as if Methodist could dispute things. It couldn't be proven in court, so the CPS did the brothers for the robbery – and Owen and Wendy's killing was officially an unconnected crime, even if everyone knew they were killed because of what they'd seen.

It was time to go, so Andrew stood again, looking around to see where he'd left his coat.

Jenny was on her feet too, leaning over to shut down her computer and then pulling her jacket on. 'Do you think Luke Methodist killed them both?'

'Of course he did.'

'Why tell Fiona you're going to look into it then?'

'I *am* going to.' He couldn't meet Jenny's gaze, stumbling over the reply. 'Crime has another side. Everyone talks about victims and criminals but we all forget there are others scarred too. Sometimes the family of the victim or the perpetrator has it as hard as anyone.'

'Right.'

Jenny accepted the explanation at face value but it was better than telling her the truth. Andrew felt sorry for Fiona and perhaps giving her a sense of closure might help him forget the girl of a similar age who'd slit her wrists when he was supposed to be watching her.

5

The haunted face of Fiona Methodist sat in Andrew's mind as he tried to forget her story, at least for an hour or so. Instead, he focused back on the woman in front of him who hadn't stopped talking in at least six minutes. He wasn't even sure she'd breathed.

Margaret Watkins was quite the woman: one for whom age was merely an inconvenience. She could've been any-where between forty and seventy – it was hard to tell. Her definitely dyed brown hair was almost a separate entity, fighting against the layers of hairspray with which it had been attacked and sprouting in all directions like a dropped cauliflower.

Some research showed that non-verbal signals made up to ninety-three per cent of all communication but Mar-garet's must've been close to one hundred – either that, or she was practising backstroke without the pool. Every time she said something, her arms flapped manically, making her husband duck for cover at the other end of the sofa.

Jenny sat patiently, taking notes, but Andrew was wondering where Fiona had gone. He suddenly realised there was silence, with Margaret's helicopter arms now by her side. She was looking at him expectantly, as was Jenny.

Andrew nodded quickly. 'Right, Mrs Watkins—'

'It's Margaret, dear.'

'Margaret . . .' Andrew glanced down at Jenny's thumb as she tapped a note on the pad in between them. Thank goodness one of them was paying attention. '. . . Can you explain exactly what an F3 Bengal cat is?'

It felt like he was reading another language but Margaret was off again, errant waft of the hand catching her husband on the side of the head as he mistimed his duck.

'You have F1, F2 and F3 Bengals, isn't that right, Geoffrey,' she said.

Geoffrey winced as if expecting another blow but nodded along in agreement. He had a neat moustache but that was the only hair anywhere near his head; the rest had presumably been batted away by his wife.

Margaret didn't stop: 'Back when they originally cross-bred the domestic cat with the Asian leopard, that litter and subsequent ones were the F1s. The F2s were the children of those F1s, and the F3s are the next generation.'

'Right . . .' Andrew blinked. 'Sorry . . . they bred cats with *leopards*?'

She stared at him as if it was a perfectly normal thing. 'Precisely.'

Andrew had no idea what she was on about. Cats with *leopards*? Was that a thing? What next? Dogs with goats? What was the world coming to?

Margaret's other arm shot off towards the canvas on the wall above the fireplace. The enlarged photograph was a picture of her surrounded by what looked like a pair of miniature leopards. The animals were a creamy orange, dotted by thick black spots.

'Those are my babies,' Margaret said. 'Elvis and Presley –

they're F3s. You should only use an F1, F2 or F3 for breeding. Mine are both studs.'

Andrew felt lost – a cat was a cat, wasn't it? He took a moment to think of a question while examining the giant photograph. The cats really did look like mini leopards. He wondered if they roared like them. Probably not.

'How do you know they're F3s?' he asked.

'Oh, Geoffrey's got the paperwork somewhere, haven't you, dear?'

Before she could take his head off, Geoffrey shot towards the cabinet on the far side of the room. If he'd had any sense, he'd have kept going through the patio doors and not looked back. The poor sod probably had a permanent concussion.

Margaret leant forward, pointing towards the photograph again. 'Everything has to be documented. You need birth certificates and proof of heritage. That's why Elvis and Presley are so valuable.'

'How much are the cats worth?'

'Oh, darling, I hate to think of it in terms of money – they're part of the family . . .' She paused, picking at an errant fingernail. '. . . But it's tens of thousands.'

Andrew chose the wrong moment to breathe in, almost swallowing his tongue and having to rely on Jenny to pat him on the back in order to not choke to death.

Tens of thousands?! For a cat! Even if she was exaggerating – which she probably was – the amount sounded ridiculous.

'Do you want some water?' Margaret began clicking her fingers in Geoffrey's direction as Andrew croaked that he was fine. Moments later and she was back in full flow: 'While we were out last week, someone came over our fence, drilled through the locks on the back door and snatched both cats. Poor Elvis and Presley must be terrified.'

Andrew had just about recovered some composure but was making sure he steered away from finance-based questions before breathing. Tens of thousands? Tens? *Of thousands?* What in the name of all that is holy was going on?

'Was anything else taken?' he managed.

'No – that's why we know the thieves came specifically for them.'

'What did the police say?'

Margaret's face sank into a grimace, as if she was being force-fed sprouts. 'Bah, useless, aren't they? They came out with their rubber gloves and dusting stuff but they couldn't find anything. When we told them it was just the cats that had gone, they lost interest. Apparently, cat theft isn't considered a crime because they can just wander off. You would've thought the drilled locks were a clue.'

'So the police are not even looking for your cats?'

'They said "it's not a priority", isn't that right, Geoffrey?' Margaret looked over her shoulder but her husband was keeping his head down, sorting through the papers in the cabinet at the back of the room, well out of harm's way. 'They're microchipped, of course,' she added. 'Well, they were.'

'Chipped?'

Margaret nodded. 'Both of them are registered with the Governing Council of the Cat Fancy—'

'The what?'

That was one Andrew couldn't let go.

'The Governing Council of the Cat Fancy. It's where you register pedigree cats. I took them down to London to have them chipped, which should mean they're traceable via GPS. Whoever stole them must have taken the chips out because, as soon as we got home, I went on the computer and checked – but there was nothing showing.'

'So whoever stole them knew what they were doing?'

'Exactly – that's what I told the police. We were trying to get them to breed with a pair of queens across the city but we'd only just introduced them to each other when this happened. We've asked around within the cat community but nobody seems to have heard anything.'

Andrew assumed she meant they'd asked *humans* within the 'cat community' – but he wouldn't have put money on it.

'How much might a litter be worth?' he asked.

'It depends on how many kittens there are and if they all survive. I've heard of some going for a hundred thousand or more.'

Andrew was careful with his breathing this time – but he still nearly lost it. Bloody hell: a hundred grand for some cats? He was definitely in the wrong business. Forget that – everyone was in the wrong business. He wondered how much money there might be in breeding goat-dogs.

Margaret muttered something under her breath, before leaping to her feet and sending her cup of tea flying from the armrest.

'Fiddlesticks,' she said, turning in a circle until she was

facing Geoffrey. 'Darling, I'm going to show them the set-up but, er . . .'

'I'll clean it up.'

Andrew and Jenny followed Margaret through the house, noting the array of faint tea-coloured stains on the carpet and skirting boards. This was clearly not an isolated incident. She led them through the kitchen until they were in the garden, where the green of the lawn was tinged with a powdery white dusting, each step making a satisfying icy crackle.

Margaret pointed up towards a tall sheet of wire mesh that extended for half a metre above the wooden fence. 'That's our freedom fence,' she said. 'It allowed Elvis and Presley to go for a walk around the garden but was too tall for them to climb. If they got too close to the edge, it would give them a gentle electric shock.'

Andrew peered up at it. Although too tall for cats, a human could easily scale the fence. With gloves, they probably wouldn't feel the shock. Andrew pointed at the pristine flowerbeds. 'Did the police check all this?'

Margaret turned to head back towards the house, nodding. 'They had a whole team come in to check for footprints and all sorts. They went away but came back and said there was nothing to find. We had to have the back door replaced, plus we got the rest of the locks redone for good measure. It's Edie I feel most sorry for.'

'Who's Edie?'

'Oh, she'll be dying to meet you.' With no other explanation, Margaret hurried inside, locking the back door and blowing into her hands. 'You're in luck – she'd usually be in school today but it's one of those inset day things.'

At least Edie was human.

Margaret led them upstairs, clunking her knee into the banister by accident, muttering 'fiddlesticks' again, and then nearly wiping out the framed photo that was hanging on the wall behind. She was seemingly desperate to prove that gravity existed.

At the top, she headed to the first door on her right, knocked twice and then pushed her way in without waiting. Andrew followed, only to step backwards at the sound of a girl's angry voice. 'Get out, Mum!'

Too late.

Margaret took Andrew's sleeve and yanked him inside, making him a part of the intrusion.

Edie Watkins was tugging a set of headphones away from her ears as she thrust her laptop to one side. She had been sitting cross-legged on her bed but leapt up, scowling towards Andrew but saving the real annoyance for her mum.

'I've told you not to come in unless I say so!'

She was fifteen or sixteen, blonde, thin, and looked nothing like either of her parents. Her walls were adorned with band posters, with a rucksack covered in purple and green badges resting against her scrunched-up pillow.

Andrew started to step backwards but Margaret wasn't letting him go. 'Come on Edie, hon, I know you're upset about Elvis and Presley but this nice man is here to see if he can find them.'

Edie's fringe covered the top of her eyes but she stared through her hair towards Andrew with barely concealed disdain. 'Whatever. Can you stay out of my room? I'm working.'

'Now, now, there's no need to take that tone.'

'I'm not *taking* a tone – I'm *doing* my homework, like you said.'

'Edie, I'm your mother and—'

'Can you just get out?'

Mother and daughter stood in a hands-on-hips impasse. Jenny hadn't even got into the room before Andrew shuffled backwards as quickly as he could, finally free from Margaret's grip.

Back on the landing, Margaret smoothed down her top, unable to stop her features folding momentarily into a frown before she caught herself. 'Usually, she wouldn't be that abrupt but, er, you can see the effect the loss has had on her. She loves those cats. They're like brothers to her.'

Andrew doubted that but Edie's mother was at least kidding herself.

In the living room, Geoffrey was at the dining table, head buried in a newspaper. The knocked-over tea had left a butterfly-shaped stain close to the sofa, which almost perfectly matched a similar one near the armchair. If Margaret kept knocking things over, she could create her own pattern. She flopped onto the sofa with a sigh and a rub of her temples, before bursting into tears. Andrew exchanged an awkward look with Jenny as they gazed at the back of the room, waiting for Geoffrey to do something.

He didn't move.

'I just miss them,' Margaret blubbed into her sleeve. 'You will get them back, won't you?'

Andrew muttered an 'erm' as she peered through her fingers, tears streaming around the selection of oversized rings. 'Money's not an issue, I just want to see them again.'

Andrew hadn't actually agreed to take the case – he'd only said he would come out to hear what Margaret had to say but could hardly turn her down now . . .

'We'll try our best, Mrs Watkins.'

'Margaret.'

'Right. Is there anything else you can tell us that might help?'

She slipped a tissue from her sleeve, blowing her nose long and hard, like a baby elephant with congestion issues. She then screwed it up, dabbing her eyes, and sliding the tissue back into her sleeve.

Lovely.

'Oh, I can do more than that,' she said. 'I know *exactly* who took them – I just can't prove it.'

'Who?'

'Harriet Coleman. That bee-eye-tee-see-haitch has always been jealous of my cats.'

It took Andrew a moment to realise the word that had been spelled out. 'Did you tell that to the police?' he asked.

Margaret flung both arms into the air, revealing her mascara-streaked face and wide, wild eyes. 'Yes! They looked at me as if *I* was the nutter. Can you believe that?'

As another clump of errant hair sprung up from behind her ear, providing what looked like a devil's horn, Andrew continued to sit on his hands. It was best he didn't answer that question.

6

Jenny leant on the passenger door of Andrew's car, gazing back towards Margaret's house. Andrew was wearing a hat, gloves, and huge coat; she had on a thin-looking jacket.

'Aren't you cold?' Andrew asked.

'I don't really get cold.'

'Why am I not surprised?'

She offered her best grin, single dimple and all. 'You're going soft – she started crying and suddenly you're agreeing to anything. If she'd have asked you to mop up her tea, you'd have done that too.'

Andrew wanted to argue but Jenny was right. 'Five figures for a cat! What's the world coming to?'

Jenny shrugged. 'I don't get pets. Why wouldn't you spend the money on yourself?'

Andrew opened his mouth to answer but reckoned they could be there all day. There was plenty Jenny didn't get. If she couldn't figure out how people worked, then animals were definitely beyond her. Plus he couldn't explain himself why someone would pay so much for a cat. A few hundred quid for a pedigree breed plus some injections was fair enough – but more money than it cost to buy a new car was baffling. Despite Jenny's assertion that he'd caved because Margaret had cried, it was situations like this that the job was all about. Sometimes, the police couldn't help and that meant people turned to him. Admittedly, he hadn't thought that would mean trying to find errant moggies.

The wind was starting to howl again but Jenny was un-affected, chewing on the inside of her mouth, presumably because her mound of snacks was back at the office.

'Shall I hang around and knock on a few doors?' she asked.

Andrew shook his head, digging into his pocket and handing her his car keys. 'I'll do it. If you head back, dig up whatever you can about the Evans robbery and Methodist's shooting. Press articles, daily court reports, the verdict, the sentencing – everything.'

'How are you going to get back?'

Andrew sighed, peering towards the ice-topped sign at the end of the street. 'Bus.'

Jenny didn't bother to hide her snigger. 'Good luck.'

The house next door to the Watkins's was covered with layers of frost-glazed ivy, the tendrils winding their way across the entire top half of the property like something from a horror movie.

Andrew stood at the bottom of the driveway, tightening the top button of his coat and tugging at the sleeves, trying to ensure the only part of him open to attack by the wind was his face. There wasn't much he could do about that. He rang the doorbell and waited, bobbing from foot to foot until the door was tugged open, revealing a dark-haired woman in huge pink fluffy slippers.

She eyed him suspiciously. 'I'm not buying anything if that's what you're after.'

Andrew shook his head, having to take a glove off to hunt for his identification. 'I'm a private investigator looking into the disappearance of next door's cats . . .'

The sigh and knowing look told him plenty. 'Her F3 studs were taken last week,' the woman said. 'They're worth a fortune, they've been trying to get them to breed with another pair across the city, blah, blah, blah . . .' She broke into a slightly embarrassed grin. 'Sorry, I know I shouldn't joke.'

'How do you know all that?'

The woman moved onto the doorstep, not quite closing the door. She waved a hand to indicate the rest of the street. '*Everyone* knows that. It's all she talks about. I got back from the supermarket yesterday, car loaded with all sorts, but she was on the driveway. The moment I was out of the car, she was off, telling me about how the police weren't interested, that there was no sign of where the cats had gone, that they'd changed the locks – everything. I'm standing out there freezing my arse off trying to think of a way to get out of the conversation – not that it's a two-way thing: you can't get a word in.'

Andrew knew that feeling.

The neighbour's face hardened slightly, her voice dropping. 'Course, it's awful to think that someone burgled next door. I've got two young lads and they're frightened that someone's going to break in here. There are a few elderly people who live on this street and it's shaken everyone up.'

'I take it you didn't see anything?'

'I wasn't even in. I'd taken the boys to football training. When we got back, there were police cars everywhere.'

Andrew nodded, knowing he was getting nowhere. The police would have already talked to people on the street – he'd be better off trying something else. He'd be even better off if he knocked at Margaret Watkins' house and told her he'd changed his mind.

'I take it you've seen the website?' the neighbour added. Andrew stared blankly at her as she snorted humourlessly. She took out her phone and tapped in an address before turning it around for him to see. On screen was a gallery of cat photographs. 'There are contact details on there too,' the woman said. 'Anyone could go on, see what both cats looked like, and then find out their address. I'm not saying they asked for their cats to be nicked, but . . .' She shrugged. 'Well, maybe they did.'

7

The wondrously alluring smell of chips, salt and vinegar greeted Andrew as he walked into the office at lunchtime. There was a spread of grease-soaked paper laid across the corner of Jenny's desk, with a smidge of mashed-up potato clinging to the centre.

'I would've got you some but didn't know when you'd be back,' Jenny said, spinning in her chair as she licked her fingers.

Andrew shivered his way out of his coat and settled for a spot by the radiator, holding his fingers as close to the heat as he could stand.

'How'd you get on?' Jenny asked.

'Not well – it looks like everyone in a three-mile radius of the Watkins's house knew they owned expensive cats. Anyone could've nicked them – that's probably why the police couldn't do much. You should see the website.'

Jenny scrunched up the chip wrapper and dropped it in the bin by her feet. 'Sounds like a right cat-astrophe.' She grinned, waiting for the laugh that didn't come. 'Fine,' she added, 'be like that. Anyway, I've got lots about the Evans brothers if you want?'

Andrew twisted so that he could face her properly. 'Go on.'

'They got away with around £700,000-worth of items

from Sampson's Jeweller's but the police only recovered a few minor things that weren't worth much. The main thing they stole was a diamond necklace and earrings that were being reset for an actress to wear to a film premiere that night. According to a "production company insider" – however reliable that is – the original setting made her look fat, so the pieces were being reworked.'

'The necklace made her look fat?'

Jenny shrugged. 'That's what it says. It was being altered at Sampson's on the day of the robbery.'

'How much were the necklace and earrings worth?'

'Quarter of a million – bit of a coincidence that the robbery happened on the day such an expensive piece happened to be there.'

Andrew wrote the number on his pad. 'Coincidences do happen.'

'I know . . .'

She was right but Andrew didn't have enough background information. It could be that Sampson frequently worked on very expensive items, meaning it wasn't a coincidence at all. The police would have most likely checked such things. He wasn't supposed to be investigating the robbery anyway, yet that and Luke Methodist's shooting were surely connected.

Jenny continued outlining what she'd discovered. 'The gun that killed Owen, Wendy and Luke Methodist was a military-issue Browning. There's nothing that says it belonged to Luke – but plenty of insinuations that he could've smuggled it home from where he was serving.'

'Any mention of how?'

'Nothing – but I found a report that said the army loses around sixty weapons a year – and that's just on home soil.'

'*Loses?*'

'That's what it says. The police didn't find anything at the site of the shootings to make them doubt that Luke shot the couple, then himself. Two witnesses were on the scene pretty quickly – but there are no names. I'll keep looking but it seems like it was a deliberate policy not to name them. At the inquest, they were Witness I and Witness G.'

She paused.

'What?' Andrew asked.

'I feel like I've read something written by one of the witnesses but I have no idea where. There's nothing with their names on, so perhaps I'm thinking of something else. Anyway, the only connection mentioned from Luke to Owen and Wendy is that Kal Evans was known to supply drugs on the street. They say Kal supplied drugs to Luke – and Kal was one of the robbers, which links him to Owen and Wendy. There's a lot of speculation but no one's got anything other than the Evans brothers wanted to get rid of the witnesses.'

'How would Kal Evans have known who Owen and Wendy were?'

'They both gave interviews to the local news channels about what they saw, plus they'd posted on the Internet about seeing a robbery. It wouldn't have taken much.'

'What about where they were shot? How did Luke Methodist know they were going to be there?'

'I suppose he didn't – but if he knew their names and where they lived, he could have followed them. It's less than a five-minute walk. Most people aren't going to pay any attention to a man in an army jacket sitting on a bench in that area.'

All unfortunately true.

Andrew was finally beginning to warm up and shrugged his coat off onto the back of his seat. He could really do with some chips. 'What about Wendy and Owen?'

'They graduated together a few months before they were killed and shared a flat not far from the university. Both had jobs but nothing to do with their degrees. Owen's brother told the paper they were thinking about moving from the area because they weren't finding the right jobs. They'd just got engaged the weekend before, which is why they were in the jeweller's – they were looking for a ring.'

Jenny stopped reading from her screen, peering up to see if Andrew was watching her. He wanted to escape her gaze but it was too late.

Sometimes she didn't know when to stop . . . 'Weren't you and Keira . . . ?'

'More or less.'

Jenny's eyes narrowed and she opened her mouth, though didn't say anything. Andrew had become engaged to his ex-wife when they'd been at the same university as Owen and Wendy and were living barely a fifteen-minute walk from where the shootings had happened. Jenny usually said whatever was on her mind but she didn't ask whether Andrew saw himself and Keira in Owen and Wendy's place. Whether that was why he'd told Fiona he'd look into things, even though he wouldn't be paid.

'What else do you know about them?' Andrew asked.

Jenny held his eye for a moment longer before turning back to her computer. 'They both had social media stuff all over the place, so I've been going through the archives of what they posted. He had a degree in English Literature; hers ended up being in physical geography – but she flitted between courses in her first year. She was doing environmental science for a while and then African Studies, or something like that. I've got some other stuff about friends and family, but—'

Andrew waved a hand to stop her.

'Too much?' Jenny asked.

'It's not that. Owen and Wendy's family and friends have been through all sorts since it happened, plus we're not supposed to be looking into them anyway – it's about Luke Methodist. We're going to have to tread carefully with who we talk to. We're going to have to take some things at face value from the reporting. It's not how I like to work but there aren't many options.'

'What are we going to do then?'

Andrew peered mournfully at the radiator. It had been a short yet satisfying relationship.

'I'm going to have to go out again,' he said. 'You can enjoy the warm, keep going through their Internet trails and then, if you get bored, see what you can dig up on Harriet Coleman.'

Jenny grinned. 'The "bee-eye-tee-see-haitch"?'

'Quite – she's obviously got some sort of feud going on with Margaret Watkins over those bloody cats, so we'll have to see if we can talk to her at some point.' He checked his watch. 'Get through what you can and then go home. I'm going to freeze to death and then I've got someone to see later.'

'Right. *Someone*.'

He knew that teasing tone. 'What are you up to tonight?' he asked.

Jenny twirled a loose strand of hair girlishly around her finger. 'Not sure. My boyfriend wants me to go to his but . . . there's this thing on BBC Four and I quite like going for a wander in this weather anyway. You never know who you're going to run into.'

'Still no name for the boyfriend then?'

'Why are you so interested?'

'It's not that I'm interested – it's that we've worked together for months and you've never mentioned his name. It's always "my boyfriend", "my friend", or something like that. You never give people names.'

Jenny let her hair go and pouted her lips. 'Hmmm . . . so you think I'm minimising my relationships by refusing to give others an identity.'

'Well I wouldn't—'

'I read a book about it once. One of those self-help things – it was a bit simplistic but I kind of knew what it was talking about. You're probably right but I could say the same to you. Instead of saying *who* you're meeting later, you say you've got to see *someone*. That's minimising the importance of it. We both know *who* you're seeing and, even though I know how important it is to you, you're trying to downplay it in case things don't work out how you hope. That way, you get to say that it was just *someone* and not the person we both know it is.'

Andrew knew it was a mistake to try to wind Jenny up. This was what always happened: somehow she turned things around and he ended up squirming.

He tried to think of something smart to say but his mind was blank, so he settled for a nod, a 'have a nice evening', and then headed out into the cold.

Andrew hurried past the Arndale Centre, surprising himself by meticulously plotting a route past the tactically placed army of chuggers. It was like playing Crossy Road.

There was the Greenpeace lot in green coats, obviously; a bunch in red jackets talking about a disease he'd never heard of; someone banging on about whales, presumably the animal, not the country. Who'd donate to save Wales?

He didn't have anything against charities and gave to a few – but it really would be nice if he could walk from one side of the city centre to the other without the zombie horde descending upon him. Given the choice, he'd take the gnashing teeth and decaying skin over the clipboards and direct debit requests. He'd certainly have more chance of getting out in one piece.

Shite.

Andrew accidentally made eye contact with someone wearing a blue jacket, breaking rule number one. It was too late to get his phone out and pretend he was on a call. She was on her way over.

'*Hola!* Do you have a few minutes free?'

The answer was no – *always* no – but she was so bloody attractive. All short blonde hair, big smile and twinkling eyes: the type of girl who'd never give him a second look in any social situation. And what was with the '*hola*'? None of them ever just said 'hello', it was always something wacky, or a dickhead with a finger puppet. On one occasion, some bloke had been juggling. Where did they find these people?

Andrew tucked his hands into his pockets, offering the weakest of weak smiles. 'I'm kind of in a rush . . .'

'Only "kind of"? It'll only take a minute. I'm Amie, with an I-E.'

Don't think of her as a person!

The voice in Andrew's head was being unhelpful.

Amie grinned wider, flashing a perfect set of teeth as she turned her clipboard around to show an image of a crying, malnourished baby.

He was really screwed now.

'This is Bethany . . .' Amie began.

It might have been two minutes, it could have been forty-five, Andrew wasn't sure. Either way, Amie ended up with his bank details and Andrew sauntered away wondering if he was a better person for donating, or if he'd just been blackmailed. It definitely felt like the latter.

It had happened again! Every time.

He continued on, weaving through the back streets of Manchester's Northern Quarter, hands in his jacket pockets, careful not to make eye contact with anyone.

When the sun was out, or even when it was a little warm, the area would be buzzing, day or night. Against the frozen backdrop of a Monday afternoon, the array of small galleries, pubs and cafes were looking a little sorry for themselves. Instead of interested tourists and hungry shoppers dropping in to see what was going on, there were a small number of locals, collars up, heads down, rushing for home, the office, or anywhere that was warm. Hearts appeared on an array of posters advertising Valentine's events, with so much red, pink and purple that it looked like all marketing budgets had been invested in a succession of cackling hen parties.

He quickened his pace as he reached Oldham Street, waiting for a bendy bus to creep around the corner, and then heading for Ancoats. Andrew checked the address he'd noted on his phone and then crossed the main road.

The Central Manchester Food Bank was either a triumph of human generosity, or an indictment of twenty-first century society. Perhaps it was both. Andrew skirted around the back of the huge church until he reached the sorry-looking hall at the rear. Slates were missing from the roof, with a skip overflowing with bricks and rotting wood plonked next to the front door.

He smiled at the group of three men standing outside who were sharing a flask and then went inside. The peeling paintwork, high ceilings and wide wooden floor of what looked like an ancient school gym offered little respite against the cold and when Andrew removed his hat he instantly wished he'd left it on. A table was set up at one end of the hall with a large vat of something steaming, next to rows of bowls and spoons; at the other, tins of various foods were stacked high, alongside a dozen loaves of bread. Packed paper bags were piled on a nearby table, each full of a day's-worth of food for a family.

Andrew was met by a smiling woman somewhere in her

twenties, with a neat bob of hair and a thick woollen jumper. 'Can I help?' she asked.

'I was wondering if you could help me find someone named Joe?'

She shook her head blankly. 'I'm not great with names at the best of times. We've got the soup kitchen here but we're also running the food bank for local families. Is he . . . ?'

'He's homeless – that's all I know.'

She shook her head. 'If you're Press, then I've got a number for someone you can call—'

'I'm not. It's, er, probably worse.'

Andrew showed his identification but, as he suspected, it didn't get him far. This was a place for privacy, where people felt embarrassed to ask for help, it wasn't for someone like him to poke around.

Out front, the trio of men were shuffling their way in the vague direction of the city centre, still sipping from the flask. Andrew hurried after them, the cold air tightening his chest and reminding him how unfit he was. He eventually caught up with them close to the main road. Cars, buses and lorries zipped past, creating a cacophony of noise as Andrew tried to assure them he wasn't a nutter – which was particularly hard to do considering he was out of breath, half-frozen, and could barely be heard. He certainly had that nutter look about him.

The trio were each wearing shabby jeans, big boots and heavy overcoats, with a lingering smell of stale alcohol that wasn't coming from Andrew. At least he didn't think it was. One of them had what looked like frozen mashed potato clumped into an overgrown beard, while another had two black eyes, and the final one was wearing a New York Mets baseball cap with a hole in the side.

When they were confident he wasn't trying to steal something, they finally started to listen, although the name 'Joe' seemed to confuse them.

'Joe or Moe?' asked Beardy.

'Joe.'

'I know a Moe,' said New York Mets man.

'I'm still looking for Joe.'

The three of them stared at each other, muttering loudly and incoherently. Andrew couldn't make out a word.

Beardy seemed to be the most aware of what was going on, although he didn't have much competition. 'We know a Joe with the shoes and a Joe with the hair. Who are you after?'

Andrew didn't want to mention Luke Methodist's name in case it caused a bad reaction, so he hedged his bets. 'I'm not sure. If you tell me where they might be, I can see for myself.'

After another mini conference, Andrew got his answer. Joe with the hair was staying somewhere close to Canal Street, because, according to the man with the pair of black eyes, 'gays like his hair'. None of them had seen Joe with the shoes any time recently.

Unsurprisingly, Canal Street ran alongside Manchester's canal, with a row of rainbow-flagged gay-friendly bars close to Piccadilly train station. Andrew had spent a few interesting nights in the area when he'd been out with friends as a student. He'd certainly seen some sights.

Dusk was beginning to darken the horizon as he hurried

from one side of the city centre to the other. The stone canal banks were dusted with frost, the freezing cobbles surely plotting treachery as he carefully worked his way along Canal Street. Aside from a few office workers and students using it as a cut-through to get to the train station, the main thoroughfare was deserted. After making his way up and down twice, Andrew moved through to the tight collection of alleys that made up the rest of 'the village'. Tall dust-speckled red-brick buildings bathed the area in shadow, with weeks-old snow packed into the verges, looping around wheelie bins and abandoned black bags.

This really was no place for anyone to be sleeping rough.

Andrew had been worried that finding Joe with the hair might be a problem – but the name was plenty enough of a clue. As Andrew rounded a skiddy corner, he spotted a man sitting close to a shopping trolley, with a tatty umbrella as a shade. He'd made a home for himself in the doorway at the back of a club, using paper bags to create makeshift bedding that looked surprisingly comfortable. Despite his situation, Joe had maintained a thick afro that was shaped into a slightly squished heart shape. It was as impressive as it was incomprehensible.

Joe was sitting in the doorway as Andrew approached, one hand on the shopping trolley, which contained a mound of carrier bags covering something Andrew couldn't see. He tugged his trousers up, eyeing Andrew suspiciously.

'Are you Joe?' Andrew asked.

The reply was gruff. 'What of it?'

'I was wondering if you knew Luke Methodist. I was told he had a friend named Joe who lived on the street.'

Joe shook his head, making the afro shake in the breeze. It must really keep him warm. 'You want Joe with the shoes.'

'Do you know where I might find him?' Andrew took out his identification card but the man didn't seem that fussed, instead eyeing Andrew up and down.

'How old are you?' Joe asked.

'Why?'

His accent was becoming more local the longer he spoke. ''Cos I'm asking.'

'Thirty-odd.'

'Hmm . . . that might work.'

'What might work?'

Joe shuffled himself into a kneeling position, rummaging around his bed, reaching underneath carrier bags that had been stuffed with packing peanuts to make pillows, and then pulling out a jam jar. He offered Andrew a smile, showing off his missing front teeth.

'You clean?'

'Of what?'

'You're not on anything, are you? Dibs, dope, crash, K?'

'I don't know what half of that is.'

'You drink much?'

'Why?'

'Smoke?'

'No.'

Joe held out the jam jar. 'I kinda need your piss.'

Andrew peered from Joe to the jar and back again. 'I'm not going to do that.'

'Why not?'

'Because I don't tend to go around weeing in pots, let alone for strangers.'

'I can tell you where Joe with the shoes is.'

Andrew glanced both ways along the alley, almost considering it for a moment. If Jenny was here, she would have almost certainly gone for it – probably while giving him a lecture about why refusing to do it showed that he was a suppressive person.

'Why do you need it?' Andrew asked.

Joe tried to pull his coat tighter but the collar caught on his hair. He stared at Andrew's shoes as he replied. 'You have to do a test if you want to get into the shelter.'

What was it with the emotional blackmail today? If it wasn't a shivering young girl, it was a bawling woman and her cats, a charity mugger, or a homeless man wanting some wee in a pot. February had sent everyone loopy.

'I really can't do that,' Andrew said.

Joe gulped, nodding acceptingly. 'Fair enough, man, I just thought that if you help me, I help you.'

'I'm not sure we share the same definitions of help.' Andrew took a step backwards. 'I could really do with knowing where the other Joe is.'

'Who'd you say you were after?'

'Joe with the shoes.'

'No, the other guy.'

'Luke Methodist.'

Joe nodded again, finally putting the jam jar down and pointing a thumb towards the canal. 'Joe got a housing 'sociation place out Ardwick.'

8

Dusk was now an aspiration, the dark bleeding across the sky, leaving a bright white moon to light the city. Andrew could have returned to the office for his car but by the time he'd collected it and negotiated the rush-hour traffic, he could've walked to Ardwick. He figured a person could only get so cold anyway and he was pretty much there.

Bloody February.

He walked past Piccadilly Station and kept going, sticking to the main road until the housing estates began to swell on either side. When he saw the spark of a cigarette, Andrew passed through a gate onto a football pitch, treading carefully across the frozen turf and heading towards a graffiti-covered, run-down play park. Sitting on the roundabout were half-a-dozen teenagers, wearing thick coats, beanie hats and trainers so white that they glowed in the moonlight. Some god-awful music was seeping from one of their phone speakers, like a drowning cat trying to escape from a sack but with more howling.

Their chatter quietened as Andrew approached, leaving him wondering if he'd miscalculated the situation. He didn't think young people were any worse than they'd been in his day – but there were six of them and one of him. Plus they had shocking taste in music, which was always a worry.

The tallest of the lads was sitting in the centre of the roundabout, smoking with one hand and sipping from a can of Stella with the other. The others looked to him for guidance as Andrew came closer and started to cough nervously.

'A'ight?' the teenager said, with a flick of his head.

Andrew nodded, trying to look more confident than he felt. 'Do you know which block is the housing association one?' Six bemused sets of eyes stared at him before the taller lad answered with a thumb-point behind him.

'I'm looking for someone named Joe who lives there,' Andrew added. 'I think he moved in recently. Does anyone know him?'

'We know everyone, mate.'

'Right, er—'

'You a fed?'

'No.'

'So why'd you want to know where he is?'

'It's a friend of a friend thing.'

The six of them exchanged unconvinced looks until the one in the centre nodded towards the almost empty crate of Stella at their feet. 'Beer's kinda expensive round here.'

Well, it was better than pissing in a pot.

Andrew dug into his wallet and plucked out a crumpled ten-pound note, holding it up into the light.

The tallest lad looked on disdainfully. 'We're not buying bloody Carling.'

'All right, ten quid now, ten quid when you find me the right bloke.'

The teenager took a long drag on his cigarette, before

sending the plume spiralling into the air as he used the tip of his trainer to nudge the lad sitting in front of him.

'Deal. Bumfluff here will do the honours.'

Bumfluff scrambled to his feet, scowling at Andrew and then at the lad who'd kicked him. There was no doubting where the nickname had come from – his chin was peppered with wispy light strands of barely there nothingness. There was scarcely enough hair to make a blanket for a bee. He adjusted his baseball cap, scragged the money from Andrew's hand and then slouched his way around the roundabout without a word, scuffing his feet along the crisped grass.

Andrew followed him towards the lengthening shadows. Beyond the hedge that looped around the play park was a three-storey cream-brick glorified outhouse that could probably be improved by losing a fight with a bulldozer. The walls were more dirt than rock, with strings of graffiti tags running along the side, plus a spray-painted allegation that someone named Sonia liked 'it' in a place that most people wouldn't.

Bumfluff kicked his way through a supposedly secure door, not bothering with the buzzers, and then waited at the bottom of a military-grey concrete slab of stairs. The whiff of cannabis hung in the air, just about masking the smell of urine. He pointed towards the next floor. 'Up there.'

'*Where* up there?' Andrew replied.

'God's sake . . .'

The soles of Bumfluff's feet couldn't have lifted more than a millimetre or two from the stairs as he skidded his way up, one step at a time, moaning under his breath. After four flights punctuated by crying babies and too-loud televisions, he stopped in front of flat eleven and held his hand out expectantly.

'That one.'

Andrew knocked on the door and waited, ignoring the accusatory stare. After another thump, the door swung inwards, catching on the chain and revealing an eye and half a cheek. A gnarled voice growled from inside: 'Who are you?'

'Are you Joe?'

'Who's asking?'

Without turning away from the door Andrew pushed a ten-pound note in Bumfluff's direction and offered his friendliest smile. 'I'm Andrew Hunter and I was hoping I could talk to you about Luke Methodist.'

The man started to close the door but Andrew was quicker, shuffling the toe of his boot into the gap and standing firm. 'It's not what you think – I'm here on behalf of Luke's daughter.'

The pressure from the door on Andrew's foot abated as the eye continued to stare at him. 'Luke's daughter?'

Andrew glanced sideways to where Bumfluff was disappearing down the stairs, before he turned back to the man and removed his foot from the door. 'Can we have this conversation in there or out here, rather than through a door?'

There was a pause and then the door shunted forward before the chain clicked off and it swung inwards.

'Are you Joe?' Andrew asked again. Better to check.

The man nodded, turning and pointing to the flat

beyond. His dressing gown hung to his knees, revealing a pair of stick-thin pigeon legs. He led Andrew into what could loosely be described as a kitchen. The cooker didn't appear to have been used in years, with a dried pool of something brown sitting between the rings on top and a grimy haze of filth covering the glass of the oven. The microwave fared little better, with something green having dribbled along the front panel at some point before setting into a spattered mask.

Joe sat at the table, which was covered in coffee-mug rings and had a saucer overflowing with ash sitting in the centre. He reached into his dressing gown pocket and plucked out a crinkled packet of cigarettes, offering it to Andrew.

'Want one?'

'No.'

'Good.'

He stretched across to the cooker, fiddling with the knobs on the front until the smell of something burning started to fill the kitchen. When the sizzling began, he pressed his cigarette to the front ring, waited for it to spark, and then turned the cooker off again.

Joe's face was even thinner than Fiona's, the skin on his cheeks sucked in between the bones, with a succession of razor nicks sprinkling his chin alongside a spread of uneven pepperpot stubble.

He nodded towards a single chipped mug on the draining board, which was propping up a lonesome plate. His voice had a sandpaper-chewing quality to it. 'I'd offer you a brew but . . .'

'It's okay. I wanted to talk to you about Luke.'

'Who are you?'

'I'm a private investigator. Luke's daughter came to me, wanting me to prove it wasn't him who shot those kids.'

Andrew hoped for a reaction but there was nothing other than a puff of smoke that disappeared towards the ceiling.

'How's she doing?' Joe croaked.

'Not well.'

Joe nodded. 'She's a good kid – came down to say hello to her dad a few times. Tried to get him away but Luke was Luke. Bloody stubborn.'

'How well did you know him?'

Another puff, another shrug. Joe's voice was getting lower the more he smoked. 'Dunno.'

'I heard you were his best friend on the street.'

'I s'pose.'

'What was he like?'

'A'ight.'

'Just all right?'

'Aye.'

Andrew paused – this was like a bad date: one-word replies, nothing in common and no sex at the end. He needed a reaction.

'Tell me about Kal Evans.'

Joe held the cigarette in his mouth, sucking deeply until he coughed slightly. The accompanying puff of smoke dribbled from his nostrils and corners of his mouth as he winced.

'He's a bad man.'

'He's also in prison – he can't do anything to anyone now.'

'Don't wanna talk 'bout him.'

'Did Luke know him?'

Joe's head shrunk into his dressing gown as he focused on the ashtray, splattering the remains of his cigarette into it. 'Luke was my friend. We'd sit and talk.'

'What about?'

'Things. He didn't like talking 'bout the army so we'd go on 'bout being kids; 'bout our kids.' He twirled his hand to indicate the room. 'It's different now I've got this.'

'No alcohol?'

Joe snorted a pained laugh. 'Right – just coffee, fags and daytime TV.'

'Sounds like being a student.'

Joe laughed properly this time, sending a spray of saliva across the table but seemingly not noticing. His eyes screwed into tiny dots, with the too-loose skin around his sockets sagging limply.

'Were you ever a student?' Andrew asked.

'Aye, they were the days.'

'So tell me about Luke.'

A sigh, shuffle and crotch-rub before, finally, eye contact. 'You need a pal on the street, someone to keep an eye out for you. We'd sleep in shifts: I'd have a couple of hours, then he would. Because of his jacket, he used to get more money and food but he'd always share.'

'His army jacket?'

'It's a symbol of respect, innit? That you've done your bit

for the country. I was just some tramp on the street – he was the ex-army guy.'

'I need you to tell me about Kal Evans.'

Joe began rifling through his pockets again, yanking out another cigarette and reaching for the cooker.

'Joe . . .'

'What?'

'Kal Evans. The police connected him to Luke Methodist because they said Luke owed drugs money. They must've got that from somewhere. Did you tell them that?'

'No.'

'So who did?'

As the smell of burning filled the kitchen again, Joe stretched his cigarette towards the cooker's hot ring. Andrew saw everything in slow motion as the chair leg scraped across the floor, ripping the cheap lino and sending Joe sprawling to the ground face-first in a flurry of swearing. Andrew was on his feet too slowly to prevent him falling but did manage to stop Joe from reaching onto the top of the scorching oven to haul himself up.

Joe continued muttering obscenities under his breath as Andrew helped him into a sitting position, lighting the cigarette for him and switching off the heat.

'Do you want me to buy you a lighter, Joe? Or some matches?'

'What?'

'You're going to burn the flat down.'

'Bah.'

'Come on – I know you care. There are babies living

downstairs – I heard them on the way up. It's not just you that lives here, there are families.'

Joe didn't move from the floor, resting his head against the filthy oven door. He reached up and tried to open the drawer under the sink. Andrew did it for him, finding five boxes of matches and at least a dozen lighters inside. He passed a lighter down to Joe, who pocketed it, slumping lower against the oven.

'Joe.'

'What?'

'Kal Evans. What did you tell the police?'

'Nuffin'.'

'You must've told them something.'

'They already knew – well, thought they did.'

'How do you mean?'

'They showed me Kal's picture and asked if I knew him. I said no but they knew I did – they knew everything.'

'What's everything?'

Puff, puff, puff. Joe was two-thirds of the way through the cigarette already. 'It's different now.'

It was like they were having two separate conversations. '*What's* different?'

Joe slammed his free hand onto the floor, not wincing, despite the fleshy clunk. 'He's a bad man.'

'You said that.'

'He'd bring around bags of . . . stuff . . . give us some for free, then others would come around to pick things up and leave us money.'

Andrew could feel his brain grinding, trying to find the answer. 'He'd give you drugs to pass on to his street dealers?'

A shrug.

'Then the dealers would bring back the profits for you to hand over to Kal?'

A bigger shrug this time but also something close to a small nod. In a weird sort of way it made sense for all sides. Kal and the dealers were never seen together and their homeless handlers got a bit on the side.

'Was Luke involved?' Andrew asked.

'No.'

'But you were?'

'The police knew me and Luke hung around together, so assumed he knew Kal.'

'Did he?'

'He didn't want anything to do with it but he'd cover for me.'

Andrew picked up the fallen chair and reached down, helping Joe up until he was sitting at the table again, slurping the final breath of the cigarette before dropping it onto the saucer. Andrew sat opposite him.

'How do you mean, cover?' Andrew asked.

'Some of Kal's lot liked to have fun.'

Andrew thought about the definition of fun. 'They'd get violent?' he asked.

'Not with Luke around. He was a bigger guy, plus he only liked to drink, none of the other stuff.'

'So he wasn't on drugs and he didn't go along with anything Kal Evans had you doing?'

'Yeah.'

'Did you tell that to the police?'

Joe began scratching at his ear, sending a flurry of dried skin flakes tumbling to the floor.

'Joe?' Andrew pushed.

'What?'

'The police.'

'They'd already made their mind up – *I* knew Kal, so Luke did too, even though Luke would be off doing other things.'

'Like what?'

'He was getting help for his . . . y'know . . .'

'Tell me,' Andrew said.

'The SPT, PST, PTD, something like that.'

'Who was helping him?'

'Dunno. He never wanted to say any more than that.'

Andrew took a breath, trying to unpick the last few minutes of conversation. 'Just to be sure, then. You're saying that Luke wasn't on drugs, didn't owe Kal Evans any money, and wouldn't have done anything for him.'

Another shrug. 'Right.'

'Would you tell that to the police now?'

Joe shook his head slowly. It took him a few seconds to reply. 'I don't talk to feds.'

9

a

'You look tired.'

Andrew blinked back into the room, suddenly remembering where he was. He'd been thinking of Owen and Wendy, Luke and Fiona Methodist, and Joe with the shoes. A bizarre tangle of barely connected people woven together in a way that he was waiting to unravel. There was definitely something there.

Around him was the scrape of cutlery, clink of glasses and general undercurrent of chatter. It was ridiculously loud considering how small the restaurant was.

'Sorry,' Andrew said, blinking again and suppressing a yawn.

'We could've cancelled if you've had a long day.'

Andrew stared at his ex-wife, the dark birthmark next to her lips, blonde bob, hints of wrinkles around her eyes that, if anything, made her more appealing than when they'd met as teenagers.

She looked as if she'd lived.

It was a date that wasn't a date. Dinner with a friend, perhaps? Anything but a date.

He managed a thin smile. 'I've spent the whole day chasing after people.'

Keira sipped her soup, returning his stare until he was forced to look away. It felt like she could read his mind.

'This is the first time we've been out for dinner in Manchester in nearly nine years,' she said softly.

'It was a bit different then.'

She nodded at the rest of the room: men in suits, women in dresses, a tapas menu, wine list and waiters with shiny shoes. The type of place where grown-ups went. 'You mean this isn't the uni refectory?'

Andrew laughed but those were the good times: cheap food in the students' union, local pubs and, shortly before they broke up, marginally posher pubs. Lots of things had changed since then.

'How's the soup?' he asked.

Pathetic: a get-out question. He'd be talking about the weather next. Anything to avoid that massive elephant in the corner that he'd left her, broken both of their hearts, and now, miraculously, they were sitting opposite each other as if it had never happened. They'd had a couple of lunches since she walked into his office three months ago and now this was the big one, or, as he'd told Jenny, this was *someone* to see.

Keira saw straight through him, flicking a strand of hair away and offering him her spoon. 'It's good – want some?'

Andrew peered down at his barely started bread that he couldn't remember the name of. 'You're all right.'

That was the end of that conversation.

Luckily, the waiter arrived to refill their wine glasses. Polite smiles, vague offerings of thanks, and they were back to their uncomfortable silence. The pair of lunches had been slightly awkward affairs, punctuated by nothing conversations about what they'd each been watching on television, the type of music they were now into, and anything else that meant they didn't have to talk about real things.

Keira finished her soup and dabbed at her mouth with the napkin, before leaning back in her chair. Andrew could feel her staring at him but remained focused on his food, sensing that something important was coming.

'So . . .' she said, pursing her lips into an O, giving herself an opportunity to stop mid-sentence. One of them had to bring it up and Andrew had always been the coward when it came to awkward conversations. 'It's been more than eight years – you must've seen someone in that time . . .'

'Not really.'

'What does that mean?'

Andrew took a bite of his starter, giving himself a moment to think. Considering he'd known this would come up at some point, he probably should've thought of an answer. Behind him, a woman broke into cackling laughter, giving him an extra few seconds. Thank goodness for tipsy women with big gobs.

'There were one or two,' he said. 'Nothing serious. I was seeing this woman, Sara, until a few months ago.'

'Why'd you break up?'

He blew out loudly. 'She was into celebrity magazines, Saturday-night TV, that sort of thing. We had nothing in common.'

'Why did you start seeing her?'

Andrew threw his hands up, trying to make it seem like he didn't know. He could hardly say that sex was great with Sara, even though he couldn't stand to actually have a conversation with her.

Keira giggled slightly. 'Eight years is a long time for "nothing serious".'

Andrew started to answer and then realised the implication. Did that mean *she'd* had something significant with someone else in that time? Or was she speaking for both of them? He should probably just ask. The obvious truth was that he'd not had a full-on relationship with anyone else because no one else was Keira. He could hardly tell her that, though.

Or maybe he should?

No, he definitely shouldn't.

Or maybe he should?

Stop it!

He felt like he was fourteen again, unsure how to talk to the opposite sex. Back then it was Jane Harris with her breasts that had developed before any of the other girls'. They'd known each other since they were five years old; their mums took them for picnics when they were kids; they'd played with Lego together and, even as young teenagers, Jane continued to speak to him in public, despite having cooler friends. Yet he couldn't bring himself to ask her out, instead ogling her chest from across the classroom, while pretending he was looking at the poster on the wall behind her.

'Me neither, if you're wondering,' Keira said, reading his mind again.

Andrew pushed his plate to one side, hoping the waiter would spot it as the woman behind spluttered into laughter once more. Didn't she realise they were trying to have a serious conversation over here? Keira caught his eye, grinning at the inconvenience, before peering over his shoulder towards the woman who was currently snorting like a rabid piglet.

'Don't look now,' Keira said, 'but the bloke she's with currently has a straw hanging from each nostril.'

'And she's laughing at that?'

Keira's blue eyes drifted back to Andrew again, smirking at him in a way her lips weren't.

'So . . . what have you been up to?' he asked.

By the time the words had escaped from Andrew's mouth, he was already wishing they hadn't. He really did say some stupid things. Weren't human beings supposed to have a sort of filter that made them think things through before the words flopped out of their mouths? He was asking her to condense more than eight years of break-up into a neat, snappy soundbite. What was the best that could happen?

Before she could reply, the waiter returned to clear the table. He'd definitely be getting a healthy tip, if only for the perfection of his timing. What a hero . . . until he left.

'I've been working for my dad,' Keira replied, making Andrew shudder at the memory of his former father-in-law. 'He retired from the bank a few months ago but is still running a charitable division for them. It's not a lot of work but he gets to decide where the money goes. Charities and other organisations can apply for grants to get their projects up and running. I'd wanted to go back to work with kids for a while but he made me apply like anyone else. I have a project that's helped create these before-school breakfast clubs around south Manchester. It makes sure they all get meals, plus allows their parents to go to work.'

Andrew was still reeling from the news that she was working for her father. The image of him was as terrifying as it had always been.

'That sounds good,' he said, autopilot kicking in again. What else could he say? 'Good stuff with the kids. Oh, but your dad's a bit of an arse'?

'Schools don't really have money for things like that,' Keira continued. 'They were looking for external funding. We've been able to get the kids painting and creating, or catching up on homework. Last summer, we even had sports. It's beginning to take off and some schools are looking at bringing it back in-house with funding from the council.'

Keira and kids . . . the two were never far away from each other. It was ultimately what had driven them apart. That and her father, or anything else which meant Andrew didn't have to blame himself.

She began to pick at her bob, relaxing into the seat and smiling. 'They're great kids. We go to the places that are most under-performing. Everyone thinks they're scum hanging around on street corners waiting to stab anyone who risks going near – but they're just young people who didn't have the chances we did. Once you give them a bit of encouragement, it's amazing what they come out with. I was working at this school in Altrincham and there's this lad there – Ethan – he's only fourteen but was expelled from his previous place and had been in trouble with the police. At first, he'd sit in the corner scowling but he's a really talented artist. It's completely natural to him. Then there's this area around Huyton where we put together the funds to build them a skate park. Last summer, we got a professional in to show them some tricks once a week. The police told us late-night call-outs from residents were down by over forty per cent between July and August. It's actually making a difference and Daddy's really supportive, he—'

Keira stopped as the woman behind Andrew launched into another mistimed burst of laughter, presumably because her partner was pulling a face, or something else of equal comedy gold.

'I'm glad you're happy,' Andrew said, meaning it.

She nodded, not quite admitting that she was. 'It's nothing to do with my history degree, of course.'

'My job's hardly anything to do with criminology.'

'How's that going?'

Andrew was saved by the waiter returning with their tapas plates. There was a pause as they both poked and prodded, trying a bit of everything, with Andrew hoping Keira had forgotten her question.

'So . . . ?' she said.

'What?'

'How's work going?'

'I'm trying to make it what I want it to be.'

'How'd you mean?'

'Being a private investigator *could* be finding out who's cheating on whom, or who the father of someone's baby is – but I don't really go for that.'

'Isn't that good money, though?'

Andrew plucked a chewy piece of chorizo from one of

the plates and munched on it, ignoring the question. He didn't need money – but could hardly tell his ex-wife that, or else she'd ask where his small fortune had come from. If there was one secret he needed to keep, that was it.

'I get by,' he said. 'Jenny's good – she takes away a lot of the smaller bits and pieces, so I get to go and talk to people.'

'She's pretty . . .'

Andrew glanced up to catch Keira's eye. 'I can't read her at all. I'm not entirely sure why she wants to work for me. She could do anything with her life but seems happy – well, content. She has a problem with people . . .'

'How do you mean?'

'I'm not sure. It's complicated.'

Keira didn't push the point but Andrew had no idea how to put it anyway.

They scraped away at their plates, listening to more booming laughter that was eventually drowned out by the general hubbub around them. The waiter returned, the table was cleared, glasses refilled, bill presented. The evening wasn't a write-off.

'My dad hates you, y'know,' Keira whispered over the top of her glass following an awkward pause.

'Okay,' he replied, unsure what to say. If only she knew the truth.

'He wouldn't approve of us being out.'

'Are you going to tell him?'

'No.' She finished her drink but continued to hold the glass in front of her face. 'We should do this again.'

'Let's find somewhere without a human hyena next time.'

Keira giggled, peering over Andrew's shoulder towards the woman. 'Deal.'

10

TUESDAY

Andrew sat staring at the house, enjoying the warmth that was blowing from his car's heaters. 'At least we've got the right place,' he said.

Jenny wiped the mist of condensation away from her window and peered through the cloudy glass. 'They've put that blue plaque up themselves, haven't they?'

Andrew squinted towards the panel above the front door. It looked like one of the traditional signs that were dotted around the country, noting where significant figures had been born or lived. They marked houses belonging to people like the Beatles, former prime ministers, artists, playwrights: people who'd changed life in Britain. This one looked as if it was made from plastic.

'I think that's the safest assumption.'

Jenny read the sign: 'Home of Michael, Tito and Jermaine: Northern Cats of the Year.'

'These people are mental.'

'You're just jealous that you don't have a Bengal.'

'I'm really not.'

'I quite like the idea of having a mini tiger around the house.'

'I can't believe there's a Cat of the Year awards ceremony,'

Andrew continued. 'What do they win? A year's supply of Whiskas?'

'Jealous.'

Andrew was still nursing a slight headache from the previous evening. He and Keira had shared a slightly clumsy hug and then gone their separate ways. He'd only opted for red wine because that's what she was having and it hadn't gone down well. The morning's coffee hadn't helped either. Still, at least she wanted to see him again. At some point, they'd have to figure out what they were actually doing. Were they back together? Is that what he wanted? What she wanted?

Bleugh . . . cats. Focus on the cats.

'Tell me about Harriet Coleman,' he said.

Jenny didn't need notes, reciting what she'd found out off the top of her head. 'Harriet was fun to look up. She's been bankrupt twice and married five times.'

'Kids?'

'Not that I could find – just her and the cats.'

'Terrific.'

Andrew opened the car door, allowing February to blast its way into the driver's seat. Bloody weather. He rubbed his hands together, trying to recatch the breath stolen by the wind.

Harriet Coleman's house was huge, something not usually associated with a person who had been bankrupted twice. It was three storeys high, with a balcony terrace running across the top that probably didn't get much use in north Manchester. A tidy, clipped lawn stretched across the front, flanking a path made of pebbles and seashells, as if the ocean had come in one day and dumped its contents in an orderly pattern.

Andrew unlatched the gate and approached the front door, ringing the bell and trying to ignore the ridiculous blue plaque above his head. Michael, Tito and Jermaine, indeed.

The door was opened by a slightly overweight woman squeezed into a peach-coloured Lycra top, with matching shorts. There was a large V of sweat in the centre of her chest, and her dark hair was wrenched back into a ponytail. Considering she'd been through five husbands, she looked surprisingly young.

'Hi, I'm Andrew Hunter and—'

'That bitch sent you, didn't she?'

'Which, er, b—'

'Oh, the Queen Bitch. Her Royal Bitchness – Maggie Watkins. Oh, don't call her "Maggie", though, else she'll have a coronary.'

'Right . . .'

Harriet held the door open wider. 'Come in then. You caught me at a good time. I've just finished doing Zumba in the living room. Michael, Tito and Jermaine love meeting new people.'

Andrew and Jenny followed her into a room at the back of the house that had certificates, trophies and ribbons lining all four walls. Harriet stood with one arm out in a 'ta-da' pose, still slightly panting. Three auburn and black cats tiptoed around the room, stopping to stare at the newcomers.

'Awww, they're all shy,' Harriet cooed.

Andrew had to admit that the cats really were intoxicating to watch. The orangey-blonde of their fine fur was speckled with black dots, like a leopard's but smaller. All three had their ears pricked high, pairs of deep green eyes focused on Andrew, making sure he didn't attempt a sudden move.

'Tito won Northern Cat of the Year last year,' Harriet said proudly, pointing towards the smallest of the trio. 'Michael was commended too. I don't know what was wrong with poor Jermaine. I think he might've had a cold that day. They were all joint first in my mind.'

Jenny nudged Andrew in the back, pushing him closer to the cats which, for all he knew, could tear him apart. They certainly had the claws for it.

Harriet dropped onto the slightly scratched flower-print sofa and held a hand out, beckoning the cats towards her. They approached slowly until there were two on her lap and another winding its way between her feet. Andrew reluctantly edged into the room, finding a spot on an armchair in the opposite corner, furthest away from the animals. He wouldn't say he was scared of them, but . . . okay, he was definitely scared of them. They looked like leopards, for crying out loud. Jenny offered a knowing grin and then sat next to him.

'I was wondering when someone else would be around,' Harriet said, nuzzling one of the cat's heads. 'First it was the police but when they went, I knew she'd send someone else.' Andrew reached for his identification but Harriet shook her head. 'Who are you? Someone from the council?'

'Private investigator.'

'That's a new one. What do you want?'

'I'm sure you know that Mrs Watkins' pair of Bengals were stolen last week—'

'And you think I had something to do with it?'

Jenny replied before Andrew could. 'Did you?'

'Have you *seen* her flea-ridden filthy things?'

Andrew answered this time. 'We've only seen pictures.'

'That nutcase has always been jealous of my little babies.' Harriet brushed the coats of the cats on her lap. 'Look at these beautiful markings. Hers look like tabbies that she snatched off the street in comparison. Have you seen her website?'

'Some of it.'

'That's not even half. She goes on all these forums, spreading rumours that other people's Bengals aren't F3s. She'll say that people have forged the paperwork.'

Andrew waited a few moments for Harriet to grow calm. 'You didn't actually answer the question.'

'Of course I didn't have anything to do with that lunatic's mangy things going missing! Why would I?'

'Do you know anyone who might have a grudge against her?'

'Only half the Internet, not to mention all of the fancier community. We're a friendly bunch, except for her. She can't accept that hers don't win the awards. She takes it as a personal insult. It's not my fault she has a face like a squashed tangerine.'

Harriet talked them through each certificate on the wall, proudly explaining how her trio had won awards at a long succession of shows over the past few years. Margaret Watkins was dismissed as 'crazy', 'demented', 'psychotic', a 'nutball', 'Mary Poopins' and 'that weirdo'. No love lost, then. If people could be arsed sending Christmas cards nowadays, she wouldn't be on Harriet's list.

She said they could poke around the house but there was no need. Andrew had only come because Margaret had been so insistent that Harriet was involved in the theft. As it was, it seemed there was a very long line of people who might have it in for her. Andrew left a card just in case Harriet thought of anything, and then he and Jenny escaped back to safety of the car.

Andrew switched the engine on and set the heaters to maximum, waiting for Jenny to settle in the passenger seat. 'I'm beginning to think I've made a big mistake,' he said.

'You're the one that told Margaret Watkins you'd find her cats.'

'She was crying!'

'So what? Do you do anything someone wants if they turn the waterworks on?'

'No.'

'Seems like it.' She laughed but was a little too close to the truth.

'I've already had enough of cats for one day,' Andrew said.

'What's next?'

'Luke Methodist.'

'That's the one you're not getting paid for.'

'If it was only about the money, I'd be doing something else – you know that. What about you?'

She didn't seem so sure. 'Maybe it was about the money

and getting a job at first. Then my parents sold their place in Italy three months ago and gave me a slice of that. They want me to go out to Corsica with them.'

It was the first Andrew had heard about it.

'Corsica? Sounds nice. Why don't you?'

'Do you want me to?'

As burning-hot air seeped from the vents, Andrew turned the heat down a few notches. 'It shouldn't be anything to do with me. You're young – you can do what you want.'

Jenny opened the pad on her lap and began reorganising the papers. 'It'd be boring out there, not doing anything. I sort of like doing this.'

A ringing endorsement.

'What do you like about it?'

The paper-shuffling halted as Jenny peered up to stare through the misty windscreen. Assuming she wasn't faking it – which Andrew didn't think she was – she actually had to think. 'Um . . . I'm not sure. I think I like you.'

'Oh . . .'

'Not like that . . . not just you. I find people fascinating. I like watching them, learning. Like when Fiona was upset yesterday. It was . . . interesting.'

It was a strange choice of words. Not many people would admit that watching a stricken, emaciated girl cry over her dead father was interesting. Heartbreaking, perhaps. Hard to watch, definitely. Andrew didn't follow it up because it was another thing he didn't particularly want to know. Jenny was easy to like if he didn't scratch too far beneath the surface.

'What was the name of the gun you said Luke shot Owen and Wendy with?' he asked.

'A Browning. Military-issue.'

'I want to ask someone about how common they are. Is it something that Luke would've brought back from his time in the army, or can anyone get hold of one?'

'I can look up a local gunsmith if you want?'

Andrew shook his head. 'Too official – we need someone from the front line.'

'Do you know a person?'

Andrew checked his mirrors and flicked on the indicator. 'It's time you met someone close to me . . .'

11

Andrew weaved his way around the small mounds of what he hoped was mud but wouldn't risk treading on just in case. The lift was sporting the same 'out of order' sign that it always did, with water pouring through all four corners of the cramped stone hallway. Across the bottom step was a crimson wash of dried blood.

'Who lives here?' Jenny asked.

'Just don't touch anything down here,' Andrew replied, as a thumping beat started to wail from a nearby flat.

After two flights of stairs, the concrete block opened onto a perilous-looking balcony, with a waist-high metal fence stretching along the length of a dozen flats. The walls had once been cream but were now drenched with dirt as more water pinged through various holes, producing an orchestra of noise that was punctuated by the shite pouring from somebody's radio downstairs.

Somebody had left the smashed remains of a stereo system outside their flat, with rain seeping into the open speaker as if it was a fancy saucer left out for animals to drink from.

The balcony provided a scintillating view of a muddy green that was surrounded by identical rows of flats that really shouldn't have been allowed to house animals, let alone people. Andrew spotted at least two dozen places where roof tiles were missing, without making a proper effort to count. The pile of tyres that had been in the centre of the grass for almost three months had finally been moved, leaving a charcoal-coloured circle of scorched ground. At the far end of the square, a child who couldn't have been more than five or six was completely naked, running along the path and squealing at the top of his voice. Behind him, a woman trailed with a pushchair, shouting at the top of *her* voice. What was it with everyone trying to be slightly louder than the previous person?

Andrew continued along the walkway, trying to avoid the dripping water as best he could. It hadn't even been raining, so he had no idea where it was coming from.

When he reached the flat at the far end, Andrew rang the bell and knocked as hard as he could. Thirty seconds passed before he heard the familiar shuffling from inside. First the bolt at the top was shunted aside, then there was a clunk from the centre. A heavy-sounding chain rattled and then the bolt at the bottom was loosened. The door stuck in the frame but opened a fraction, before being pulled open completely to reveal a pint-sized older woman wearing a dress far too big for her. It had such a mesmeric red, white and blue pattern than Andrew wondered if it had once been a magic eye puzzle. Her hair was light purple, blown into an afro-style perm that Joe with the hair would've been happy with.

Her face folded into a wide grin. 'Well, well, well. It's about time you visited your old aunt.' Her eyes widened as she spotted Jenny. 'Ooh, and a girlfriend too!'

Andrew leant forward and kissed the woman on the

cheek. 'Jen, this is my Aunt Gem. Gem, this is Jenny. She's not my girlfriend. We work together.'

Gem winked at him. 'I getcha.' She turned to Jenny, arms open. 'Well, what are you waiting for, dear? Come on in. Shoes off.'

'I'm here for Rory, Gem.'

'Oh, get away with ya. You've got twenty minutes for your aunt.'

Andrew sighed as Gem hurried into the flat with a shoe-less Jenny. He knew this was going to happen. He relocked all of the bolts and popped his own footwear off before heading through to the living room.

Even though he'd been inside many times, it was always a shock to see quite what a state the main room was in. Gem had ushered Jenny into a corner and was talking her through the collection of ceramic ducks. The entire room was filled with the type of tat that was flogged in resorts – not that Gem had ever been to the seaside. Every time somebody she knew went to Blackpool, Skegness, Scarborough, or even bloody Grimsby, they were instructed to bring her back something. It had quickly got out of hand, with her living space now a chronicle of shite. In one corner, there were stacks of postcards; another had sticks of rock that were so far out of date, they would probably break bones, not just teeth. There were magnets, snow globes, ornaments, teddy bears, ceramic teapots. If a seaside shop sold it for under a fiver, then Gem would definitely have one. Probably five. Some of the items were older than Andrew.

Andrew couldn't work out if Jenny was playing up to it

simply to annoy him, or if she was genuinely impressed. It *must* be to annoy him. No one could seriously like all of this stuff.

'Oh, that's lovely, Mrs . . .'

'Call me Gem, dear.'

Jenny pointed to a rack on a nearby wall. 'What are those?'

'Oh, that's my thimble collection, darling. Someone brought me back one from Australia. Do you know where that is . . . ?'

And on they went.

Andrew sat on the sofa, reaching down to ruffle Rory's ears. The barrel-like pug tilted his head to check he approved of the person smoothing his coat and then plonked himself back on the floor to go to sleep again.

Fifteen minutes later, Gem had exhausted herself, falling into her tattered, dog-scratched armchair and turning to Andrew as Jenny slotted in alongside him.

'You're looking thin,' Gem said.

'I'm the same as I always am.'

Jenny squidged his arm. 'I said he was looking thin too.'

'You bloody didn't.'

'Oi!' Gem scolded. 'Language!'

Jenny sniggered quietly enough that only Andrew could hear.

'Sorry,' he said.

'I can rustle something up if you want to eat. Y'know that Gavin from down the legion? His lad, Steven, runs this company that delivers meats. Gavin reckons the whole of the van is a giant freezer. Anyway, he was on his way to

Liverpool when they had an engine failure, so they were left with all this—'

'We haven't got time.'

Gem scowled at him, annoyed at being cut off mid-flow. Andrew had little choice, knowing it was going to turn into a ten-minute epic that ended with her getting a load of meat on the cheap. Most of her stories had a similar theme, with Gem apparently oblivious to the laws of handling stolen goods. He'd long since stopped trying to point out the lads who came to her door were almost certainly selling items they'd nicked.

She turned to Jenny, face cracking into a wrinkled smile. 'You're a bit out of his league, aren't you?'

'Gem!'

Jenny had collapsed into a fit of giggles, with Andrew trying to maintain something in the region of dignity.

'What?' Gem retorted. 'She is.'

'I told you, she's *not* my girlfriend – we work together.'

'Suit yourself. If you're not going to stay for a proper meal, at least let me make you some soup or something.'

'I only came to pick up Rory.'

'How about a sandwich?'

Jenny got in before Andrew could reply. 'I'll have a sandwich if there's one going.'

Gem was on her feet as sprightly as someone half her age. 'What would you like, dear? I've got ham, turkey, pickle – Branston, obviously – Marmite, tomato, lettuce, cheese – Cheddar, obviously – and I think there are some gherkins somewhere too.'

The three of them moved into the kitchen, where Gem

fussed around and Jenny played along until there was a pile of ham, cheese and pickle sandwiches.

Jenny leant against the sink munching through hers, with Gem washing up and talking over her shoulder. 'What's he like as a boss?'

'I am here, y'know,' Andrew said.

'Oh, shush. I'm asking her.'

Gem flicked a handful of bubbles in Andrew's direction before turning to Jenny.

'He's all right,' Jenny said. 'Doesn't seem to eat much, though. I think he's wasting away.'

Gem spun and pointed an admonishing finger in Andrew's direction. 'I knew it!'

'I'm not wasting away.'

'You need a good woman to feed you up.'

'That's what I keep telling him,' Jenny said.

'This is a conspiracy. I only came here to get Rory,' Andrew replied.

'You never have time for your old aunt any longer,' Gem said accusingly.

'I was here last week.'

Gem shook her head, twisting back to Jenny. 'Did he tell you that I wiped his backside when he was a baby?'

'No.'

'Gem—'

Andrew's aunt ignored his protests. 'His mother was ill and it wasn't safe for him to stay there in case he caught it. I ended up taking him for a week. Fed him, changed him, wiped his little bottom. This is how he repays me – coming round here, refusing to eat my food . . .'

Andrew couldn't remember that single week of his life, but Gem never let him forget.

Gem nodded towards Jenny. 'At least *she's* got some manners. This is what you need, Andrew Hunter. What do I keep telling you? You need to find yourself a nice girl.' She glanced between them. 'Someone in your league.'

'Thanks.'

She turned back to the worktop, reaching for the kettle. 'Who's for a nice brew?'

Jenny caught Andrew's eye, smirking like he'd rarely seen her do. It was definitely a mistake to bring her along. Rather than just his aunt to wind him up, now there were two of them.

Snap!

Gem jumped backwards as the kitchen lights switched themselves off. She was shaking her hand ferociously from side to side, the faint blueish hue from the window just enough to light the room.

'Ouch,' she said as Andrew put a hand on her back while she rubbed her hand. 'It's always doing that.'

'What is?' he asked.

'The plug sockets pop and the lights go off. I have to turn it back on at the fuse box.'

She pressed past Andrew, heading into the hall where she opened a cupboard and fumbled in the dark until there was another snap and the lights flickered on again.

'That shouldn't be happening,' Andrew said.

Gem pushed past him, returning to the kitchen and trying the kettle again. This time it clicked.

'It's been doing it for months,' she said dismissively, keeping her back to him.

'Why didn't you say something?'

'It's not a problem – I just flick it back on and everything's fine.'

'You shouldn't be getting electric shocks from turning the kettle on.'

'I'm fine.'

Andrew glanced at Jenny, urging the new golden girl to say something. If his aunt wouldn't listen to him . . .

'Andrew's right,' Jenny said. 'It looks dangerous. You should get someone to look at it.'

Gem turned around and started to fiddle with a box of teabags. 'Reg from bingo has a friend whose son is an electrician. Kevin something. He did one of those YTS courses and got his certificates. He came round yesterday and said he'd squeeze me in later in the week. He's going to do me a deal.'

'Will you let me pay for it?' Andrew said. 'I'll get someone in to do it properly – not some bloke named Kevin. You've got to have the proper qualifications nowadays. They're supposed to be on a safety register. Did he show you his card?'

'Oh, stop fussing. You know I like to keep it local.'

'*I'll* find someone local.'

'No!'

Gem glared at him, raising her voice in a way she rarely did. There was no teasing now. She continued staring for a moment or two and then turned towards the living room, voice as cheery as before. 'Rory, dear, Uncle Andrew's ready to take you out now. Rory . . .'

As she pottered away, Andrew was left sighing and shrugging in Jenny's direction. She mouthed a 'sorry' but it wasn't her fault. This was his aunt all over: she'd rather get some kid who lived on the estate to do it than have an expert look at the problem. Everything was always about a recommendation from some bloke down the legion, or from bingo. She hadn't changed in the entire time he'd known her.

Gem headed into the living room as Rory tottered out of it, stubby little legs making him bob from side to side. He was already panting from the effort of getting up. He gazed expectantly at Andrew, deep dark eyes twinkling with his tongue flopping onto the floor.

Time to go.

12

Rory sploshed his way through the puddles as Andrew tried his best to avoid them on his way down the stairs. Jenny kept pace, uncharacteristically quiet until they reached the hallway at the bottom, where Andrew stopped to zip up his coat.

'You okay?' she asked.

'She's just so . . . bloody stubborn.'

'I'm sure it'll be all right.'

'I know . . .' Rory sat next to Andrew and started to lick his own feet. 'I've tried to get her away from here so many times but she won't leave. Last year, there was a rape three doors down from her flat – some smacked-up scumbag broke in through the window and attacked a pensioner, then robbed her. When the riots happened, someone tried to set fire to the block.' He pointed to the bottom step, where Jenny was standing. 'I found a needle there three weeks ago but she won't listen. I don't know if she doesn't believe what's going on around her, or if she isolates herself away in this bubble where she convinces herself it's all fine.'

'It sounds like you've done all you can.'

'But that's not enough, is it? This place is a deathtrap as it is, without all of the scroats that live around here. When I knocked, she didn't even bother asking who it was. What's the point of having all those bolts if you open up the moment someone bangs on the door?'

Jenny bit her bottom lip and offered a weak smile. He didn't expect her to understand.

'Which side of the family is she on?'

'She's my mum's sister. She's lived here as long as I can remember – probably since it was built. It would've been a nice area then and that's how she remembers it. I didn't grow up around here but I've been coming to visit since I was a kid. I remember playing football on the green when it wasn't covered in dog shit, needles and burnt tyres.'

Rory was chewing on his own foot, utterly carefree.

Jenny nodded at him. 'Where'd he come from?'

Andrew puffed out a long breath. 'Gem called me one morning a few years ago. She was crying like I'd never heard before. When I got here, she was sitting on that step covered in blood and tears. Some local shits had used Rory for a kickaround. His eye was hanging out of its socket, fur torn to pieces, and there was blood everywhere. She had no idea who he belonged to but had found him on the way to the Spar. We got him over to the vet and they spent a week patching him back together.'

Rory peered up, showing off the flattened side of his head on which he was permanently scarred.

'After that, Gem took him in. It was okay at first but she can't walk too far any longer. I come over a couple of times a week to get told off for not eating, and then take Rory for a walk.'

'Is that what we're doing?'

'We have someone to meet, so I thought I'd do two things at once.'

Andrew bent down to play with Rory's ears as the pug glanced between him and Jenny, looking for sympathy which, admittedly, he probably deserved.

'This is why you hate cats, isn't it?' Jenny said.

'I don't hate cats.'

'You're a dog person.'

'If you say so.' Andrew stood again, ready to set off, but Jenny didn't move. 'What?' he asked.

'I don't know. It's just sort of . . . sad.'

'What is?'

'Rory and your aunt . . . it's really nice but . . . I don't know. I don't have an aunt. Both my parents are only children, so am I. It's just the three of us and they live abroad.' She stared at Rory, then Andrew, before pushing past. 'Come on then, where are we going?'

Andrew followed her into the chill and then led the way across the estate, cutting through a set of double arches, looping around a paved concourse that was riddled with overgrown grass and graffiti, before reaching a row of small bungalows that were in a decent shape considering the area. He knocked on one of the doors, waiting until it was opened by a tall man wearing heavy Doc Martens, jeans and a thick padded coat. He had thin, blond hair, with squished ears from years of playing rugby, and a solid jaw that could – and had – taken a few knocks over the years.

He slammed the door behind him, before beaming and patting Andrew on the back. 'Good to see ya, Andy lad.'

'This is Jenny,' Andrew said, nodding sideways. 'She works with me. Jen, this is Craig. He's an old mate.'

They shook hands and then Craig strode ahead, seemingly unable to prevent his long legs from walking at anyone's pace other than his own. He stopped at the end of the path to wait and then held his arms out. 'Which way?'

'You pick,' Andrew replied. 'It's not as if there are sweeping fjords around the corner for us to look at.'

'True.'

Craig nursed a definite limp but tried to slow his pace enough for the dog to keep up. 'How is Rory?' he asked.

The pudgy little dog trotted along, tongue lolling, oblivious to the chatter about him.

'Same as ever.'

'And your aunt?'

'Ditto. She still won't move.'

'Aye, it's no place for someone that age. Any age, really.' Craig turned to Jenny, lips curling into the man-about-town grin that Andrew had seen in the past. He offered a raised-eyebrows, don't-even-try-it gaze in his friend's direction but Craig ignored him.

'So, what's Andy told you about me?' Craig asked her.

'Nothing.'

'Nothing?! All these years of friendship and that's what you get – he doesn't even tell a pretty girl that I exist.'

Bleugh. His height and natural good looks meant that schtick might have worked with some girls but not Jenny. She shrugged and continued walking. 'He introduces me to the *important* people.'

Craig burst out laughing, nudging Andrew in the arm

and leading them through a set of chicane barriers into a tight ginnel that was doubling as a wind tunnel. A group of kids were kicking a football against the wall but they stopped as Craig walked past, offering an array of 'all right's – which was surely as respectful as it could get.

'We were at university together,' Andrew said as they reached the far end.

'I only got through one year,' Craig explained. 'Then I went off to join the army and Andy found the love of his life.'

Andrew squirmed. It was true but didn't sound as good out loud.

'Now we're both back where we started,' Craig added, nudging Andrew in the arm again. 'How are things with Keira?'

'Awkward.'

A pair of teenagers coming in the opposite direction offered nods and something close to a smile in Craig's direction as they passed. Craig led Andrew and Jenny past a rank of shops with an overflowing bin spilling crisp packets and chocolate bar wrappers onto the pavement. He stopped and picked the rubbish up, shoving everything down deep into the bin and then wiping his hands on a nearby bush.

After passing through another alley into a small park, Craig slowed his pace once more, wincing as his knee clicked noisily. He reached for a bench and eased himself down, fighting the pain and grinning at Jenny. 'How can I help?' he asked.

Andrew sat next to him, with Rory burying his head in

the bush behind and straining at his lead. 'What do you know about Browning pistols and the army?' Andrew asked.

'They've been standard issue for years but they're gradually being phased out and replaced by Glocks. It was supposed to happen quite quickly but most of the lads I know still get a Browning as their sidearm.'

'How are you assigned a gun?'

Craig began rubbing his knee, clearly trying not to show how much it hurt with Jenny nearby. 'Everything's counted in and out, whether you're here or abroad.'

'So none can go missing?'

'I wouldn't say that.'

'We found a report that said the army lose around sixty guns a year.'

Craig snorted, sitting up straighter. 'Sixty? And the rest. Who did they ask?'

'How many?'

Craig shook his head. 'It doesn't work like that – the numbers aren't really important. If you get caught bringing a gun home from abroad, or if you've somehow got one out from a base, then you're in big trouble.'

'It still happens, though?'

'Sort of. Say you're actually out in somewhere like Iraq or Afghanistan, there are guns everywhere. Some of them have been given out by us to bolster the local security forces, other times you might confiscate one for whatever reason. It's only you and maybe a mate who knows you've got it. Maybe you hand it in when you get back to base, maybe you don't. I would, but I know plenty of boys who like to keep mementoes.'

'How would you get it home?'

Craig turned to face him. 'Do you really need to know?'

'I suppose not.'

'There are ways. Mementoes is probably the wrong word. There's another thing too. Out in places like Afghanistan, it can be dangerous, even on routine patrols. One minute you're driving along, the next, someone's taking pot shots at you – or a roadside bomb goes off. Say your vehicle takes a hit. You get to safety, perhaps return fire, but one of your guys has been killed. No one back at camp's running around asking what happened to his weapon. If it lands by your feet and you pocket it, that's it. It could be the last thing you have of the other person's.'

Jenny shuffled on the bench, most likely thinking the same as Andrew: according to the reports, Luke *had* experienced a roadside bomb. Andrew tugged Rory away from the bush, bending over and unclipping his collar. Instead of running away to explore, the pug lay on Andrew's foot and closed his eyes.

'So it wouldn't be too hard for a soldier to get a military-issue gun back from wherever they were stationed?' Andrew asked.

Craig blew a small raspberry through his lips. 'I wouldn't put it like that. I couldn't just contact someone I know in the forces and say, "Get me a gun" – plus, you're missing the obvious.'

'What?'

'This all affects the black market. Say you did get a gun home, what are you going to do with it? Most army lads don't go out shooting – they don't even want to look at a gun until they have to. Even if they did, it'd be unregistered. If you get caught with it, you're going to prison.'

'I don't get it.'

Craig tapped Andrew on the shoulder with a smile. 'And you're the one with the degree. How do you think most of these guns find their way onto the streets? Some of them are smuggled in on shipping containers from South America or Africa, others sneak across from Northern Ireland via people who can't accept the Troubles are over. That's big-time, though. Gangs are smuggling them in and perhaps selling a few things on.' He nodded backwards towards the estate from which they'd come. 'The small-time stuff – the scroats who think they're big men, the kids who don't know what they're doing – they're all Brownings. If you wanted a gun, give me forty-eight hours and I could get you one. It'd definitely be a Browning.'

'I don't want a gun.'

Craig ignored him. '*Those* guns are the ones that are sold by people like me – if that's what I was into. Say I'd somehow got a gun home, I don't want it sitting in my bedroom waiting to be found. There are always buyers out there, so give me a hundred quid and we'll forget about it. That gun then gets sold up or down the chain over and over. Before you know it, some teenager's waving it around side-on as if he's on the streets of Detroit.'

Andrew finally thought he got it: 'So you're saying that if professional criminal gangs have guns, then they could be any make – but Brownings are what are used by someone who's desperate? A kid, or someone with a score to settle . . . ?'

'Exactly. It's never a hundred per cent but yes.'

'How easy is it to buy a gun?'

Craig shrugged. 'It depends. For you? No chance. What are you going to do – walk into a pub and ask the bloke in the corner? It's a bit different when you live round here and you know people.'

'All the kids around here respect you.'

'Right – not because I'm army, just because I've done a few things locally. They know who I am. If I was to take the right kid aside – or wrong kid, depending how you look at it – he'd know who to talk to. It's not easy but it's not hard either.' He pointed back towards the estate again. 'I guarantee there'll be a Browning somewhere out there, sitting under some kid's bed in a shoebox, or under a mattress.'

Andrew thought of his aunt, sitting peacefully in her deathtrap of a home, surrounded by a mountain of tat, not even knowing the danger on her doorstep.

In the moment of silence, Craig glanced between Andrew and Jenny, forcing a smile. 'Anything else?'

'Do you know anyone with PTSD?' Andrew asked.

'Are you kidding? Everyone who comes home knows somebody.'

'Where would you go if you were looking for help?'

Craig puffed out a long breath that said more than words. 'There are a few mental health places but you know what it's like with funding nowadays, plus you have to admit you've got a problem.'

'Everything's confidential, then?'

'Obviously. If you're worried about someone, I can ask around.'

Andrew shook his head. 'Right, who's up for a trip to the chippy?'

13

Jenny was, of course, up for a trip to the chippy. Rory didn't mind either, even if he had to wait outside. After dropping the pug off with his sulking aunt, Andrew and Jenny headed back towards the city centre.

As if the ice wasn't bad enough, a horror-movie cloud had descended, clinging to the low buildings and enveloping the entire area in its freezing tendrils. Visibility was appalling, with long rows of red car lamps bleeding into the mid-afternoon haze. Andrew was driving with the clutch pedal, the accelerator not needed as they crawled towards the office.

Jenny finished sorting through her notes and then dropped the file onto the back seat, before saying what they'd both been thinking. 'Luke's gun could have come from anywhere, then? He might have smuggled it back but it's just as likely he bought it off a mate. It might have been resold over and over. The fact he's a soldier doesn't actually matter.'

'Sounds like it.'

'In all of the reports about the shooting, none of them said it was *his* gun – there was simply an assumption that he'd brought it back from the battlefield. Perhaps a correct assumption . . .'

'It's still guesswork. He could have brought it back, he

could have bought it, or it might've been given to him. It doesn't sound like anyone knows for sure. They wouldn't have needed to do a deep investigation because it was so obvious he shot them. Easier to say he was a rogue officer that smuggled a gun home. No messy paper trails up the chain of command.'

Andrew indicated to head onto what he thought might be a cut-through, only to be met by another long row of blinking red taillights. 'I found Luke's friend, Joe. He said Luke didn't know Kal Evans. There was a vague connection through Joe himself but Luke didn't do drugs and was a big enough guy to look after himself.'

'What does that mean?'

'I don't know . . . probably nothing, but it's a different picture of Luke to what's been painted.' Andrew paused, realising what he was saying. 'It doesn't mean he's innocent.'

Jenny remained quiet but she must have recognised that Andrew was trying to convince himself more than her. For whatever reason, he wanted to believe Fiona's story, to think that the killing of a young couple wasn't so senseless.

Travel through the university district was so slow that it would've been quicker – although colder – to walk. After fifteen minutes of barely moving, Andrew pulled onto a side street and parked.

'Want to do something stupid?' he asked.

'Always.'

'Just play along.'

Andrew pulled his coat tight and walked around the car, crossing Oxford Road with Jenny next to him. He weaved into and out of the cut-throughs, heading towards the centre before he saw what he was looking for.

According to the scratched black and gold sign above the door, Sampson's Jeweller's had been established thirty years previously. It was situated on a corner, with two windows showcasing its wares and heavy-looking shutters hanging above. An A-framed metal sign was sitting on the street close to the front door, creaking back and forth, telling passers-by that Sampson paid for gold by the gram. In the window were banners offering credit, along with others proclaiming the shop to be a 'diamond specialist' and 'Manchester's finest'. Quite who had decided that was unclear.

The jewellery in the window was more or less the same as would be found anywhere: rings and necklaces that looked decent but didn't cost too much. The really expensive stuff would be inside.

Jenny pressed in next to Andrew, peering along the lines of jewellery. 'You're not going to ask me to marry you, are you?'

'Craig probably would.'

'He's not my type.'

Andrew was getting cold feet – in more ways than one – but it was too late. Jenny wrapped her arm around his and dragged him towards the entrance. 'Come on then.'

He glanced up as the bell above the door jangled its greeting, welcoming them in from the cold. As he closed the door, Jenny continued yanking on Andrew's arm, pulling him towards the closest cabinet.

'Look at these, hon!'

Really?

Andrew rolled his eyes – this had been his idea, after all. He crossed to the display, where Jenny was pointing at the ring with the biggest stud. It was pointy, not as sparkly as Andrew might have expected, and cost a bloody fortune. If she ever did get engaged, this would definitely be the ring she made the poor sod buy.

A man was working at a bench behind the counter across from the front door. At the sound of the bell and their voices, he turned, wiping his hands on his stripy red and white apron and forcing a smile.

'Afternoon . . . is there something I can help you with?'

He unhooked his glasses, letting them dangle to his chest from a chain around his neck. He was almost bald, with the little hair he did have brushed back over his ears. There was no reason to but Andrew took an instant dislike to him. He looked like a rat.

Jenny was too far ingrained in the role to care, reaching out to take Andrew's hand. 'My boyfriend, sorry, *fiancé*, proposed to me last night. It was *so* romantic. I live on the banks of the canal and he arranged for a barge to sail past. He'd hired this folk band to stand on deck and play me a song that he'd written. I'm called Jenny and the song was named "Marry me, Jenny" – he's so clever like that. I came out onto my balcony and he was playing the triangle and mouthing the words. There were balloons, confetti, these pretty bows, all sorts. There were loads of people watching and they all cheered when I said yes.'

She sighed with happiness at the made-up memory. There was a terrifying glimmer of a moment in which

Andrew thought she was going to turn to him and ask him for an encore.

The shop-owner's eyes flickered towards Andrew with that 'what-a-prick' look. Even though it hadn't happened, Andrew hated himself a little bit.

'That's beautiful,' the man said, cracking into a clearly false smile. 'Welcome to Sampson's. I'm Leyton and this is my shop. Feel free to browse and ask anything you want. If you're after a diamond, then they're my speciality. I've got contacts in Botswana and they mine things directly. There are no middlemen, so you won't find a better price anywhere around here.'

Jenny rested her head on Andrew's shoulder. 'I *told* you this was the right place to come.' She nudged him with her elbow. 'He usually works in London but he's on a week off. We're going to Monaco tomorrow. He was saying we could get something out there but it's always nice to put a bit back into the local community, isn't it?'

Sampson's eyes nearly popped out of his head as the possibility of a huge sale washed through him. Jenny was perfectly dismissive, sashaying across Andrew and flirting her way towards the next case.

'Hon, isn't this the place that was robbed a couple of years back?'

The shop-owner's face sunk back to normal as if he thought he'd won the lottery and then realised he was a number out. Andrew caught his eye as Sampson offered a faint smile. 'We were in the news . . .' Sampson replied.

Jenny didn't look up from the case. 'Wasn't there an expensive necklace taken? It was going to be worn at a film premiere by that actress: whatshername? I remember reading about it in one of my magazines.'

Sampson shuffled around until he was next to his workbench, in front of the case Jenny was inspecting. 'There were a few things taken. It was an incredibly scary time. Luckily, everything's back to normal now.' He glanced over their shoulders, as if expecting more raiders to burst in.

Jenny drummed her fingers gently on the cabinet, again pointing to the most expensive item. 'What do you think, hon?'

Andrew peered at a ring that looked much like the others. 'If that's what you like.'

He *really* hoped she didn't tell Sampson to box it up. It was the type of thing he figured she'd do for a laugh.

'Hmm . . . I'm not sure.' She side-stepped to the next counter, tugging on her ponytail. 'How did they know it was here?'

Nobody replied for a moment until Sampson realised she was talking to him. 'Sorry?'

'The robbers. How did they know the necklace for the movie premiere was here?'

The shop owner shuffled nervously but Jenny hadn't glanced away from the cabinet. She was scarily good at lying. Andrew had seen her in action before but not quite like this.

'I don't know,' Sampson said, stumbling over the words. 'I do repairs and resets for production companies fairly regularly, so it could have happened at any time.'

'How much was the necklace worth?'

'Er . . .'

Jenny finally gazed up, hitting him with her light-up-a-room smile, dimple on show, hair-twiddling aplenty.

'They said it was about £250,000.'

'Wow.' She twisted back, reaching for Andrew's hand again. 'Would you buy me a necklace for that much if I asked you to?'

'Um . . .'

She was back peering at the rings. 'I suppose it was just bad timing then . . . ?'

Sampson was stumbling over his words worse than Andrew. 'The police said they looked into it. I think they interviewed some of the production assistants – that sort of thing. I don't really know.'

'How long did it take you to get back up and running? It must've been a nightmare with the insurance and every-thing. We were broken into last year and it took ages to sort out.'

'It wasn't too bad – they didn't steal everything, it was more about getting the shop into a decent state again. The men who did it were sent to prison a few weeks ago, so it's nice to move on.'

Sampson tapped gently on the case, ensuring that was the end of the conversation.

'You can't let them grind you down, can you?' Andrew added. It was something his dad used to say.

Sampson nodded, shuffling back towards his workbench until Jenny caught him in her gaze once more.

'There are some nice things here,' she said, 'but I think I'm looking for something a bit . . . bigger. You said you get your own diamonds in . . . ?'

The shop owner glanced from Jenny to Andrew and back again.

'Money's not really an issue,' she said, looking particularly pouty.

He glanced over his shoulder towards a door next to the workbench. 'I do have something in the back . . .'

In a flash, he skipped across the shop, locked the front door, and flipped the sign around to read 'closed'. He delved into his pockets and unlocked the internal door, leading Andrew and Jenny inside. The room was small, with a long table built into the wall on one side and rows of drawers and cabinets on the other. At the far end was a safe, almost hidden by a filing cabinet. There were no windows, only a bright white strip bulb overhead.

As Sampson headed for the safe, Jenny peered around Andrew towards the table. He followed her gaze towards neat rows of small tools: tweezers, what looked like a dentist's scraper, silicon, plus chain links for a watch and a few other odds and ends.

'How about this?' Sampson said.

The ring he was offering Jenny looked like a child's toy because it was so large. The prism-shaped diamond gleamed in the light, a row of tiny red jewels surrounding the main crystal. He licked his lips as Jenny took it, first twisting it around in her hand and then slipping it onto her little finger.

'Wow.'

'I set the stones myself.'

'How much?'

Sampson leant forward and whispered the amount in

Jenny's ear. She nodded along, adding a low whistle for effect before handing it back and waving Andrew towards her. As he bent his knees, she pushed onto tiptoes and spoke softly into his ear: 'This is fun.'

Andrew stepped back, smiling. 'It's up to you.'

'When are you expecting your bonus?'

'Any day now.'

She nodded, twisting back to Sampson and offering a little curtsey. 'We'll come back after we've been to Monaco in that case.'

The shop owner's face fell as he crouched, returning the ring to the safe. Jenny was looking past Andrew towards the worktop again but he couldn't figure out what had caught her attention. When the safe was locked, Sampson hauled himself up and ushered them back towards the main area of the shop.

Jenny hurried towards the front door, unlocking it herself and calling 'thank you' over her shoulder. She grabbed Andrew's hand and pulled him across the road until they were well out of earshot.

'What?' he asked as they slowed to a walk.

'I need to go back to the office to check a few things . . . but I might have something.'

14

Andrew pottered around the office making tea as Jenny typed on her computer. She stopped to make notes on a pad and then carried on with what she was doing. He knew she was taking things seriously when she had her glasses on and hadn't opened any of the biscuit packets from her bottom drawer.

After wasting as much time as he could, Andrew sat in his chair, fiddling with his phone to see if Keira had texted him. He hadn't sent her a message because he didn't want to seem too keen but he hadn't received anything either. It really was like being a teenager again.

'Did you see what was on the workbench in the back room of the jeweller?' Jenny asked.

'Tools.'

'What else?'

'I don't know – I wasn't really looking. I was more worried that you were going to agree to buy that ring. How much did he say it was worth?'

Jenny grinned. 'A lot. We should do that more often.'

'We really shouldn't. What did you see?'

'Cufflinks.'

She said it as if it was a major revelation but Andrew stared on blankly. 'Cufflinks?'

'Didn't you see them? He was setting some sort of jewel into them.'

'Okay . . .'

'They were in the shape of letters – a "B" and a "T". Either he's a big fan of British Telecom, he's interested in tuberculosis, or they were for someone with the initials BT or TB.'

'I still don't get it.'

Jenny reached into her bottom drawer, pulled out the mini rolls and unwrapped one. 'Have you heard of Thomas Braithwaite?'

Andrew scratched his head, trying to pluck the information from wherever it was lost, before shaking his head. 'I know the name.'

'He owns Braithwaite's – it's a chain of factories, largely across the north. My old flatmate applied for a job there, so I looked him up. Been keeping an eye out ever since, I suppose. They originated in Liverpool but there's a factory in Leeds, a couple in the north east, one as far south as Stoke, and another down the road in Stockport. There's also an import-export side to the business and he's worth a fair few quid.'

'Liverpool?'

She smiled. 'You're getting ahead. Anyway, he got off a bribery charge last year. There was a lot of reporting that he tried to buy planning permission to put up a new factory not far from Liverpool city centre. There were recorded phone calls, a money trail through the banks – all sorts, but it collapsed before it got to court. The councillor who was implicated denied all knowledge and was re-elected a few weeks ago. As far as I can tell, Braithwaite's kept his head down since then.'

Jenny handed Andrew a print-out from a local newspaper and then talked him through it. 'Braithwaite's not mentioned in that report but it relates to him. Two years ago, customs impounded a shipping container at Liverpool docks that had arrived from Colombia. They held it for three months, pulling it apart and checking everything on the manifesto. That's not necessarily uncommon – but it was bound for one of Braithwaite's factories. Braithwaite filed court papers demanding the release, alongside making threats of lawsuits for compensation. Presumably the police didn't find anything because it was never reported again, but the authorities have obviously got a thing for him.'

'So his business might not be entirely what it seems?'

'Perhaps. It probably *is* manufacturing, plus importing and exporting – it depends what he's bringing into the country and sending out of it again. This is where he lives.' Jenny passed across a sheet of paper with a print-out from Google Maps. 'It's huge – big walls and gates, like a prison. That's a lot of security for someone who runs factories.'

'Maybe he likes his privacy?'

'Or maybe there's more to him than it appears.'

Andrew scanned through the pages of news reports and focused on the map again, still not really getting it. 'All right,' he said. 'Let's assume Thomas Braithwaite has a bit more going on than it might first appear. That doesn't mean those cufflinks were anything to do with him – lots of people have the initials BT or TB.'

Jenny grinned. She handed over a final sheet of paper, a

print-out of something Andrew had read very recently. It was why the name Braithwaite seemed familiar.

Aaron Evans, 25, Kal Evans, 22, and Paulie Evans, 29, all from Merseyside, are being questioned in connection with the incident at Sampson's Jeweller's, in which £700,000-worth of rings, necklaces and bracelets were stolen.

CCTV footage showed three masked figures entering the shop shortly before midday, with two brandishing sawn-off shotguns.

The case took a sinister turn with the tragic shootings of Owen Copthorne and fiancée Wendy Boyes, both witnesses to the robbery, forty-eight hours later. Police have so far been reluctant to link the cases.

Greater Manchester police spent yesterday working with Merseyside colleagues. They raided the homes of the three men and were seen carrying computer equipment out of a property in the Wavertree area of the city. They also visited a factory belonging to Braithwaite Industries in the Toxteth area of Liverpool, where at least two of the brothers were recently employed. A spokesman for the company insisted none of the trio still works at the site.

The goods have yet to be recovered, with police appealing for witnesses.

15

WEDNESDAY

The weather had taken a marginal turn for the worse: freezing fog replaced by murky grey skies and drizzle. Technically, it was a degree or two warmer, but by the time the spine-chilling rain had dribbled through people's clothes, it didn't feel like it.

Andrew left his car engine idling, the windscreen wipers squeaking back and forth in a losing battle against the elements. Jenny had spent the journey in the passenger seat sorting through her notes. It took her a few moments to realise the vehicle had stopped. She flicked her glasses off and plopped the cardboard file on the back seat.

'Are we here?' she asked.

'That's why the car's not moving.'

'Did you make contact with—?'

'Yes but I'm going to have to wait until tomorrow, so that means today is—'

'Cat day. You're just annoyed because you're a dog person who's scared of cats.'

'I'm not scared of cats.'

'Pfft. Why are we here?'

'I got a call from someone named Pam Harris last night,' Andrew explained. 'She owns the Bengal queen cats that

Margaret Watkins' studs were supposed to be mating with. She said she had something to show us.'

'It's not her cats, is it?'

'I bloody hope not.'

'Because you're—'

'I'm not scared of cats!'

Pam welcomed them into the house with caramel-coloured cups of tea and shortcake biscuits already waiting in the living room. Jenny was delighted.

Pam was a small, thin woman with a tight curled bob of dark hair who worked as a freelance accountant from home. She said her husband was on business abroad but Skyped twice a day so that he could have a 'conversation' with the cats. Andrew assumed it was largely one-way.

With the husband marked down as the nutter in the family, Pam appeared far more normal than either Margaret or Harriet. The walls of the house were either plain, or adorned with family photographs, with no certificates, trophies or gigantic cat canvases in sight. What set the place apart was the prison-like security. There were CCTV cameras fixed to the front and back of the house, with beaming white motion-sensor lights and high mesh fences surrounding the rear garden.

'They're all my husband's,' Pam explained with a slight roll of her eyes.

Definitely the normal one.

When she finished showing them around the downstairs gulag, she took them upstairs, waiting at the top, hands on hips. 'It's my son you really need to talk to,' she said, knocking on one of the doors and waiting patiently until she received a 'come in' from the other side.

Damian Harris was sitting at a desk using a laptop and desktop computer at the same time. As his hands shot frenetically from side to side, he glanced over his shoulder towards Andrew and Jenny, offering a subdued murmur that was either a 'hi' or a burp. He was seventeen or eighteen, with shoulder-length dark hair and round-rimmed John Lennon glasses. Andrew knew whose style the young man was emulating because the walls were covered with Beatles posters and prints of album sleeves.

'I'll leave you to it,' Pam said, edging out of the room and closing the door behind her. Damian didn't look away from his computers.

Jenny turned to Andrew, who offered a shrug. 'Damian?' he said.

'Uh-huh.'

'I'm Andrew and this is Jenny. Your mum tells us you have something that might be helpful. Something to do with cats . . .'

'Yeah . . . er, hang on.'

He bashed away at the laptop, on which he was playing some sort of fantasy role-play game, before turning his attention to the second monitor, where rows of text were streaming upwards.

Andrew shuffled awkwardly, not knowing what to do. The room smelled of deodorant, with fraying socks littering the corners and a Lego Millennium Falcon hanging from the ceiling. Andrew shared a smirk with Jenny, although he was a little jealous.

Damian spoke without turning from the screen. 'Do you know what IRC is?'

The letters prickled at the back of Andrew's mind – he'd definitely heard of whatever it was, but without Google in front of him, he was lost.

'Internet Relay Chat,' Jenny replied.

Damian glanced over his shoulder towards her, giving her the quick toe-to-head scan, followed by a nod of approval that presumably doubled as a mating call. 'Right,' he said, focusing back on his laptop. 'What do you know about it?'

'Not much. They're chat rooms that run on their own servers and are separate from the web itself.'

'Have you ever used one?'

'No.'

Damian nodded towards the monitor with the scrolling text. 'That's an IRC room for the latest Doomslayers game.' His attention returned to the laptop. 'In the game itself, there are moderators who keep an eye on what everyone says or does. IRC is completely separate, plus, because it's not on the web, it's largely unregulated. Players go on to trade items for real-world money.' He paused, mouth gaping. 'Hang on.'

On the laptop screen, what looked like a giant green lizard clad in heavy metal armour was walking on its hind legs, carrying a battleaxe. Damian grunted, weaving his head one way then the other as the lizard buried the weapon in the head of what could only be described as a child-sized squirrel. Blood sprayed the screen as he bashed the keyboard and then clicked the tracker pad ferociously. Bats swooped down from the dark parts of the screen, making Damian duck in real life as the pixelated lizard hacked at the skies with the axe.

'Oof-oof-oof. Take that.'

Damian bobbed in his seat as the bats splatted to the floor one by one. When the hack-a-thon was finally over, he guided his character towards the edge of the screen, waiting in shadow.

'Sorry, I'm on a mission,' he said, not turning around. 'I can't pause, else I'll lose the credit.'

'Right,' Andrew replied.

Kids today. Still, better than going out with an actual battleaxe.

'Do you play MMORPGs?' Damian asked.

It sounded like a sexually transmitted disease: I copped off with Sharon out the back of Lidl and she gave me MMORPG.

'What?' Andrew asked.

'Massively Multiplayer Online Role-Playing Games.' Damian risked another glance at Jenny. 'You?'

'Not really.'

'You should. I can teach you.'

'I'll bear that in mind.'

Back to the laptop. The lizard was edging his/her/its way through some caves. 'I'm on a quest to find the haunted sea horn,' Damian said. 'When I get that, the game-makers offer two options – I can either wear it for twenty-five per cent magic protection, or I can sell it at one of the marketplaces for in-game money.'

'Okay . . .' Andrew replied.

'Except that I'm already at level sixty-eight, with ninety per cent magic protection and more in-game money than I can spend.'

Damian paused, as if that was enough information.

For Jenny, it seemingly was: 'So that's why you use IRC?'

'Right. The makers only offer those two options to keep people within their world – but I can work outside of that and sell the horn for actual pounds. Someone on a lower level might want the magic protection or the in-game money. They PayPal me the actual cash, I wait until it drops in my bank account, tell them where I am on the map, and . . . hang on.' Bash, bash, bash on the keyboard. 'Then I give them the horn.'

Jenny giggled.

Andrew gave her a disapproving glance and then continued watching the laptop screen. The lizard had emerged into some sort of forest and was edging around the trees, axe at the ready.

'How much could you sell the, er, horn for?' Andrew asked.

'Fifty quid, perhaps? It depends on if I put it up for auction, or sell for a set price. It's why we're all on IRC. Technically, it's in the game's terms and conditions that you're not supposed to sell things. If you put something on eBay, or a regular web forum, they'll shut it down. On IRC, no one knows we're there. The server is run from someone's private computer, so the games company have to find that person to shut it down. With all the proxies, they'd never be able to do that but, even if they somehow did, people would start a new one two minutes later. It's not illegal.'

'How much do you sell in a week?'

'This is my job. I make maybe six hundred if I take the weekends off, more if I don't.'

'Six hundred pounds?'

'Yeah.'

'Actual, real-life, UK pounds that you can spend in shops?'

'Yep.'

What with the hundred-grand cat litters and six-hundred-quid-a-week computer game players, Andrew wondered where he'd gone wrong in life. First cats and now this. What else was he missing out on? He was lost for words, as if he'd been smacked in the chest.

Meanwhile, the lizard was winning a fight with an over-sized pelican.

Six hundred quid!

Damian thrashed at the keyboard, offering his own 'ooh-ooh-ooh' sound effects, to which Andrew would've felt far more superior if it wasn't for the fact that they were probably worth fifty pence per 'ooh'.

Six hundred quid!

It was Jenny's amused gaze that finally reminded Andrew what he was supposed to be doing.

'That's very impressive,' he said, 'but what does that have to do with cats?'

'One minute.'

After more mouse-hammering, lizard-slashing and pelican destruction, Damian spun to face the main monitor, clicking through a few screens, before returning his attention to the laptop and talking without looking up.

He pointed at the main computer. 'That other IRC room is dedicated to Doomslayer – but there are different ones. Look.'

Andrew and Jenny gazed at the monitor. The window was labelled 'UK Pets FS', with rows of users along the left-hand column. On the right were long lines of what looked like computer nonsense.

'FS means "for sale",' Damian said. 'That's a list of people selling various animals. The same principle applies.'

Andrew got it: if a person had a standard dog/cat/budgie to sell, he or she would do it on a classifieds website, or somewhere open where the maximum number of people would see it. If a person had something unusual or, more likely, illegal or stolen, he or she would need another way. Exactly like the Doomslayer room.

Andrew stared at the monitor again, scanning through what he first thought was code.

@Franz123 - 0409: Ylw prrt. £150. NE. DM only.

In context, it made sense. Andrew turned to Damian, who was still facing his laptop screen. 'So, at nine minutes past four this morning, a user named Franz123 offered a yellow parrot for sale. He lives in the north east, wants a hundred and fifty quid and you've got to message him for the details?'

'Exactly. Move up to half two yesterday.'

Jenny scrolled up.

@Devilsedge1 – 1429: Bangle. NW. Msg.

'I figure they can't spell,' Damian said.

Jenny was copying details from the page onto a notepad.

'I can set us up with this in the office and send him a message.'

'No need,' Damian replied, flapping towards a Post-it note that was underneath the keyboard. 'I sent him a message last night asking for details. I thought there might be a photo or a price – or even confirmation it actually *is* a cat – but all I got was a mobile number.'

Andrew made sure he could read the writing and then pocketed it.

'Pow-pow-pow-pow!' Damian leapt from his chair, thumping the space bar with his left hand as he steered the mouse with his right. His lizard was taking chunks from a yeti-like figure that was fighting back with some fearsome-looking claws. 'Shiiiiiiiiiiiite . . . come onnnnn. Yes! Boom. Take that.'

The yeti fell, bloody and defeated.

'Well done,' Andrew said, unsure if that was correct etiquette. Jenny glanced at him as if he was her granddad. 'Thanks for the help,' Andrew added.

Damian, still focused on the laptop, mumbled something under his breath that Andrew didn't catch. It sounded friendly enough.

'Can I ask you something?' Andrew said.

'Un-huh.'

'What's it like with the cats?'

'Huh?'

'It looks like your dad is pretty keen on them, if not your mum too. They haven't got the awards on display all over but your garden's like a fortress. It must take up time and money.'

'I s'pose.'

'What's that like for you?'

'Dunno. I don't worry about it – I earn my own money. Last year, Dad brought home two pairs of custom-made cat boots from Copenhagen to stop them getting their feet dirty when they're in the garden. If that's what he likes, then fair enough. Seems a bit stupid to me.'

Okay – the games-playing, lizard-controlling, six-hundred-quid-a-week entrepreneur was the sensible one in the family.

Andrew thanked Damian again, said goodbye to Pam, and then returned to the car. As he waited for the windscreen to defrost, he huddled within his coat as Jenny fiddled with her seatbelt.

'Maybe I should take up game-playing?' she said.

'Wouldn't you get bored?'

'I dunno. Thirty-odd grand a year, weekends off, working from home. Sounds all right.' She nodded towards his pocket. 'Are you going to give that number to the police?'

Andrew took out the Post-it note and fixed it to the dashboard between them. 'What do you think?'

'I get why he didn't call the police – he doesn't want them looking into all his chat room activity too closely – but it's a lead in a potential criminal case, isn't it?'

'Not yet,' Andrew replied.

Jenny took out her phone. 'Shall I call? They'll probably think they can try it on more if I'm a woman.'

'Put it on speaker, and just . . .'

'What?'

'You know.'

Jenny smiled sweetly, as if she'd never contemplated doing or saying anything reckless.

The tinny-sounding ringtone spilled from the phone three times before a man's voice answered.

'A'ight. Who dis?'

'Hi. I got your number from the chat room. I think you've got a cat for sale.'

'You fed?'

'No, I'm just a normal woman.'

'Tomorrow.'

'Er, okay . . . ?'

'Cash only, girlie.'

'How much?'

'Big one. You bring Jack, I bring bangle.'

'What does the cat look like?'

'Huh?'

'Can you send me a photo?'

'No, no, no, no. Jack for bangle. Tomorrow.'

'Where?'

'Text.'

Jenny started to reply but her phone screen went black as the call dropped. Andrew felt as if he'd been listening in to two people speaking another language.

'Jack?' he asked.

'It's simple – if we take the money, he'll bring the cat. He's going to message us somewhere to meet tomorrow. I think he's one of those white kids that thinks he's a gangster. Either that or he's got severe brain damage. I guess we'll find out. I was going to ask him if he had two cats, but it sounds like just the one. Still, if he's got one it might lead us to the other.'

Moments later, the text tone sounded on Jenny's phone. Whether they wanted to or not, the next day they were going to see a man about a cat. One who might or might not have taken a few blows to the head.

16

THURSDAY

It was the silence that Andrew found disconcerting. A nice bit of peace and quiet would usually be wonderful. Sitting next to the window in his flat, feet up, brew in hand, watching the world pass by. Lovely. It was much better than watching the television.

Here, it just felt wrong.

Andrew expected prisons to be noisy, with inmates banging on bars, fights over the pool tables and whatever else he'd seen in movies. He was sitting in the large visiting room, where loved ones would wait for their partners to come down from the cells and have a catch-up under the watchful eye of the guards. He'd had to ask a few people for contacts and, ultimately, favours. Then he'd had to explain what he was after to too many people and be searched – luckily with his clothes on. He'd also had to drive to Preston, which was an indignity in itself.

The room had long rows of grey and red tables bolted to the floor, with matching chairs. Steep, barred windows gave intoxicating views of more walls, with lines of vending machines at the back. Pinned up all around were posters with words like 'respect' and 'think' in large capital letters.

It was a bit late for that.

From the silence, rain suddenly started to fall, slapping at the windows, creating a cathedral of thunderous noise.

He'd spent the rest of Wednesday doing odds and ends around the office, with Jenny phoning around vets, trying to find out how easy it would be to remove a tracking chip from a cat. The answer was, apparently, quite easy – with the biggest danger that the cat would scratch to pieces the person trying to cut him or her up. If it was drugged or subdued, all that would be needed was a scalpel. Someone had removed the chips from the stolen cats but Jenny found instructions on the Internet for how to insert and remove pet trackers. That ruled out Andrew's idea that a vet would have had to have been involved at some point.

As for Thomas Braithwaite, they'd dug and dug, finding out as much as they could about him. Sooner or later, Andrew was going to have to decide what he wanted to do. That was where the trail for the truth about Luke Methodist had led them – but he had to think of his own safety. If Braithwaite was a simple factory owner, there was no problem. If he was more than that, Andrew would have to tread lightly.

Andrew started drumming his fingers on the table. He'd been brought to the prison's visiting room almost ten minutes previously and left by himself. As the rain's tempo increased from pneumatic downpour to outright monsoon, he wished for the silence of a few moments ago. Noah could've definitely come from the north of England. He was probably a Prestonian.

Barely audible over the storm, there was a thump and footsteps from behind. Andrew turned to see a wedge of a man striding towards him. A pair of prison guards followed him into the room but stopped to rest against the wall, one of them offering Andrew the merest of nods. Paulie Evans was wearing jeans and a plain white T-shirt, his short black hair greased backwards, like he'd stepped out of a 1950s movie. His chest was puffed out, shoulders wide as he strutted closer, sitting opposite Andrew and splaying his hands on the table to reveal a web of tattoos that weaved from each of his wrists up to his elbows.

'Whatcha want, pal?' he asked, broad Scouse accent cutting across the rain.

'I wanted to talk about your brother,' Andrew said.

'Which one?'

'Kal.'

'What about him?'

'I'm a private investigator and—'

Paulie eyed him up and down, jaw working ferociously on a piece of gum. 'I ain't talking to no bizzie.'

'I'm nothing to do with the police.'

'So whatcha here for?'

'Luke Methodist.' Andrew left a pause but there was no reaction other than more chewing, so he continued. 'I'm looking into what happened with the shooting of Owen Copthorne and Wendy Boyes. Lots of assumptions have been made, mainly about your brother and, to an extent, you.'

Paulie shrugged. 'What about it?'

'Are you happy with that – everyone assuming you arranged for a pair of kids to be shot dead to stop them being witnesses?'

134

'What's it matter? I'm in here anyway.'

'You'll be out in nine or ten years.'

'So why would I say anything else that'd get me in trouble?' He sneered the words, flicking his chin up to challenge Andrew's stupidity. He shunted his chair back, ready to leave. 'That all?'

'If you did arrange the shooting, I understand why you'd keep quiet. It'd be more years inside, perhaps even a full-life sentence. But, if you didn't, why not say so at the time? Everyone outside assumes you or one of your brothers got Luke Methodist to do it but if you'd said that wasn't true, you'd have persuaded a few people – perhaps even members of the jury who sent you down. They were asked to deliberate on the robbery charges and nothing else, but every one of them would have known the names Wendy Boyes and Owen Copthorne.'

Paulie shuffled in his seat, checking over his shoulder and lowering his voice. 'Why do you care?'

'I just do.'

'Who are you working for?'

'No one you'd know.'

'So why should I talk to you?'

Andrew didn't reply for a few moments, letting the drumbeat of the rain hammer through the almost-empty room.

'Because it can't do any harm,' he whispered. 'Tell me you didn't have them shot and I'll believe you. Shrug and walk away and that's fine. It doesn't matter what I think but there are people out there who deserve to know what happened. You've got two boys yourself. If something happened to Duke or Nathan, wouldn't you want to know who did it and why?'

Paulie's brow rippled. He started flexing his arm muscles, stare fixed on Andrew. 'You come here and bring my kids into it?'

'I just mentioned their names – two clicks on the Internet and anyone can find that out. I'm making the point that Wendy and Owen were somebody's children, too.'

Paulie started cracking his knuckles, glancing over his shoulder towards the guards again and then facing Andrew once more. 'I was told not to talk about it.'

'Who by?'

'The solicitor dude told us all to say "no comment". Bizzies checked our phones, houses, computers, the lot, but there was nothing there. He said they already had enough to try us for one thing and that we'd only make things worse. Everyone assumed we got Methodist to do it anyway.'

It took Andrew a few moments but then he realised that the solicitor had played the stupidity defence. The brothers had been senseless enough to get caught for the robbery – the failure to set a car on fire, the fingerprints, Scouse accents, and everything else. The solicitor assumed they'd arranged the shooting too but suspected the police had no evidence for that. Rather than risk one of them saying something incriminating, he'd instructed them to say nothing when questioned. They'd gone down for the robbery they'd almost certainly committed, but not even been charged with arranging the shooting. Losing a case when defending armed robbers was one thing; having clients sent to prison for a full-life term didn't look great whichever way it was spun.

It was a solicitor's last trick when he or she wound up with a bunch of morons to represent: the stupidity defence.

That explained a few things. 'If it wasn't for your solicitor, what would you have told the police when they asked about the shooting?' Andrew asked.

Paulie shrugged, chewing the inside of his mouth. He looked bored. 'Don't matter now, does it?'

'It would to some people.'

He shook his head and started to stand. 'I wanna go back.'

'Hey!'

Andrew's stage whisper was louder than he meant. He peered around Paulie towards the guards who hadn't moved. Slowly, the prisoner eased himself back into the chair.

'Look, pal,' Paulie said. 'I might not be an angel but I know who's fair game and who ain't. If I *had* burgled that shop – and I'm not saying I did – those kids would've been right there. Why wait to do the job on them?'

'Because you didn't realise the police were onto you then. They went on the news telling everyone they'd heard three Scousers, and suddenly it dawned that people were looking at you.'

Paulie shrugged once more. 'Whatever. You figure it out for yourself. It's not like I'm getting out of here anyway. We done?'

'Just one more thing – I want to ask about Kal.'

'So why are you talking to me? Talk to him.'

'I know that Kal used to use people who lived on the streets as middlemen for his . . .' Andrew dropped his voice to a whisper, '. . . *merchandise.*'

'You'd have to ask him.'

'That's how the police connected Luke to him and, in the end, you. Luke Methodist was homeless and hung around with a guy named Joe, who did odds and ends for your brother.'

'So what?'

'It seems a bit flimsy to me. Joe went along with things because he was using at the time – plus he's a little guy. Luke was an ex-squaddie – not many would pick fights with him, even if they thought they'd win. He'd certainly get a few blows in on anyone who went for him. Had you come across him before all of this?'

'Luke Methodist? Never heard of him.'

'What about Kal? Did he know Luke?'

'Ask him.'

'I'm asking you.'

'Why?'

'You know why – he's your little brother and you worked together. I read the court report of his day on the stand and he's all over the place. It says he spent most of the time glancing towards you and Aaron in the dock. There's no way he'd have arranged any of this without you knowing – so if you didn't know Luke, then chances are Kal didn't know him directly either.'

'You deaf? I told you I didn't know him.'

Andrew scraped his chair back slightly: blood successfully

extracted from stone, though he wanted to push the point. Time for some ego-massaging.

'What about Kal? It strikes me that you're the smart one of the bunch. Would he have acted on anything without you knowing?'

Paulie shook his head and snorted. 'Dude, neither of my brothers do anything without my say-so.'

17

As soon as Andrew left Preston, the rain abated to a slow drizzle and, eventually, a misty sort of nothingness as he reached the outskirts of Manchester. He picked up Jenny from the office and then headed back up the M61 towards Wigan. It really was a tour de Lancashire, with a stop-off at Gregg's to appease Jenny's hunger for good measure. Steak bake sorted, they followed the instructions from her text message to the back of a burnt-out pub on the edge of Wigan town centre. The car park was strewn with crumbling bricks, shattered pieces of wood and a pair of overflowing skips. The ground floor of the pub was boarded up, with flame-licked black streaks around the windows and doors. Upstairs, a flower-print purple and white curtain flapped through a smashed window. Someone had graffitied the f-word over a sign that had once read 'The Frog and Toad'. Whoever had the spray paint had given the toad a comedy-villain twirly moustache and giant penis, which would surely make hopping across lily pads impossible. Well, unless it was used as some sort of propeller.

It was the sort of place a person might go camping if he or she had a thing about war zones.

Andrew parked behind one of the skips where only the front of the car could be seen from the road. Just in case anything unexpected happened, he had a clear run across the pavement onto the main road. They were fifteen minutes early, which might give Jenny enough time to clear the flaked pastry from her lap.

'Classy place,' Jenny said, delving into the backpack between her feet and pulling out a grease-soaked paper bag. She licked her lips as she moved on to a cream doughnut. 'Want a bite?'

Andrew shook his head. 'We're here to potentially buy a stolen cat. They're hardly going to meet us in the town centre.'

'Do you reckon they went into the bank with this as a business plan? "We've got an idea: we're going to steal pets, advertise in private chat rooms, and then meet buyers in dodgy pub car parks. All we need are start-up costs – two grand for a van and thirty quid a month to pay the phone bill".'

Andrew laughed as Jenny wolfed down the cake and then opened the door to brush away the crumbs.

'Do you believe Paulie Evans?' she said.

Andrew sucked on his bottom lip. He'd spent the car journey running through the conversation from the prison in his mind. 'Probably. Kal was the youngest, so they sent him onto the street to do their dirty work with the drugs. They'd have had to keep their heads down because they're Scouse lads and wouldn't have wanted to upset whoever runs the drugs around Manchester. They were small-time. I can't believe Kal suddenly decided to organise killing two people by himself. I don't think Paulie knew anything about it, which means it probably didn't happen the way everyone's saying. It feels wrong anyway. They're scroats, scallies, selling drugs on the street. How do they go from that to robbing a jeweller's and having two kids killed?'

'You don't think they were the robbers?'

'No, I *do* think it was them. The police wouldn't have messed up that badly. But think of all the ways the brothers screwed up – they didn't manage to burn out their getaway car, one of them left a fingerprint and, in the end, they got caught. Their solicitor thought they were too stupid to be allowed to talk to the police. If that's all true, how did they arrange for two kids to be shot, yet not have anything come back to them? Even if they did, why Luke Methodist? They must've known more suitable people in Liverpool who could've done the job.'

'Wouldn't the police have thought of that?'

Andrew was drumming on the steering wheel once more. A bad habit. 'Almost certainly but they're coming at it from a different angle. All the evidence is there that Luke Methodist shot Wendy and Owen, they just don't know why. He's not around to tell them, so we end up with something plausible relating to the Evans brothers. It starts to come apart when you pick at it but no one wants to pick.'

'What does that leave us?'

'Fiona wants us to say that it wasn't her dad but we'll likely never be able to do that. The best we might be able to do is give her a "why".'

Jenny picked up her phone and checked for new messages as the agreed time came and went.

'Shall I call?' she asked.

'Not yet. There's a green car that's driven past twice in the past five minutes. They're probably checking us out.'

'Do you think we should've told someone we were coming?'

'Like who?'

'I don't know – the bloke selling the dodgy cat could have a gun. Probably a Browning.'

Andrew didn't look sideways but Jenny's remark sounded decidedly smirky.

'Nice of you to mention it now,' he replied.

'I figured you'd already thought of it.'

'I have but what can we do? We're here to look at a cat, not start a fight. It's not like I'm going to turn up packing heat.'

'*Packing heat?* How old are you?'

'Old enough to watch American movies. Anyway, there are two of us.'

'There might be two of them. Or three. Basically, your thinking is that everything's fine because if they're a bunch of nutters who go mental, they're at least going to have to murder the pair of us, rather than just you?'

It really didn't sound so good when she put it like that.

'We're in Wigan – it's hardly the gun capital of Europe.'

At least he was trying to convince himself.

As Andrew finished speaking, a banged-up green Citroen flung itself into the car park, catapulting over the kerb and nearly hitting a concrete post, before swerving sideways and spinning one hundred and eighty degrees. The rear bumper was held on with duct tape, with the exhaust howling like a tractor that had failed its MOT.

Nice and incognito.

Jenny was out of the car and on her way before Andrew

could stop her. By the time he'd opened his door, heaved himself out, and pulled his trousers up, she was almost by the green car.

A man stepped out of the other vehicle wearing a purple basketball vest, baggy grey three-quarter-length shorts and Converse trainers.

In. Bloody. February.

Jenny was right: he probably was a nutter. He was white, with cornrows and, apparently, no mirror.

A second man bundled his way out of the passenger seat, wearing a puffed-up coat so huge that he looked like a giant grey bubble. He was wearing a baseball cap with sunglasses.

In. Bloody. February.

Cornrows eyed Jenny up and down. 'You a'ight, baby?'

She wasn't fazed: 'Have you got the cat?'

'Jack first.'

Andrew wondered if the translation app on his phone would be of any use. Not only was Cornrows talking nonsense, he was doing it in an accent that had a sort of Australian-American twang, albeit with a Lancashire inflec-tion. It sounded like he'd had a stroke.

Jenny turned to Andrew, who still had his hands in his pockets, thinking that it might look a tiny bit intimidating. No one had to know that the only thing in his pockets was a half-eaten packet of Polos.

'We want to see the cat first,' Andrew said.

Cornrows shook his head. 'No way, bro.'

Baseball Cap had walked around the car, all five foot four of him. With the coat, he was almost as wide as he was tall. Andrew took half a step backwards to try to peer through the rear window of the green vehicle but the glare was too intense.

Andrew attempted to catch Jenny's eye, but she was trying to hide her disdain for the walking marshmallow. He reached into his back pocket and took out a handful of notes, holding them out towards Cornrows, but then re-pocketing them as the man leant in to take the money.

'That's two hundred and fifty,' Andrew said. 'The rest's in the car. Now show us the cat.'

Cornrows and Baseball Cap nodded at each other, before slouching around to the boot. After arguing over who had the keys, they popped it open, revealing a cardboard box with scissor-stabbed holes in the top.

'There you go, Bo.'

Andrew presumed he was the 'Bo', although it wasn't entirely clear. He stepped towards the boot but Cornrows blocked his way, with an arm across the chest.

'Time for the cabbage.'

'Cabbage?'

'The jack.'

'We've still not seen the cat.'

Cornrows looked at his mate. 'You open it.'

'I ain't opening it, that thing's crazy.'

Baseball Cap tried to roll up the sleeve of his coat but it was as if he was wrestling with bubble wrap. In the end, he unzipped it, pulling out his arm to show a long line of painful-looking scratches close to his elbow.

Cornrows turned back to Andrew. 'I ain't opening it neither. It's well messy, bruv.'

He stepped aside, motioning Andrew towards the box and potentially demonic cat within.

Andrew looked from Cornrows to the box and back again. 'Er . . .'

Jenny shoved him aside. 'Fine, I'll do it – it's only a cat.'

Cornrows looked impressed, flicking his wrist so violently that it might have dislocated. 'You is crazy, baby.'

Jenny stood over the box, one hand on either side. Cornrows and Baseball Cap each took a step backwards, nervously glancing from Andrew to Jenny to the box.

In one quick movement, like ripping off a plaster, Jenny pulled the top of the box off.

Nothing happened.

Andrew took half a step forward, standing on tiptoes to peer inside.

Hisssssssss.

'You scared her,' Jenny said accusingly, turning to scowl.

Andrew took two steps back. Whatever was in the box did not sound friendly.

Cornrows was edging backwards too. 'Yo, I told you, bro.'

Jenny reached carefully into the box, slowly emerging with an orange and black cat and cradling it in her arms. It might have been a trick of the light but, from where Andrew was standing, it looked like the animal was glaring at him, its green eyes of death threatening to slice him into shreds if he risked going any nearer.

Andrew didn't dare move, thinking it would be more productive to try to remember the details. He glanced down at the car's number plate and ran the digits through his head, repeating them until he thought he might be able to recite it back. Memorising the owners wouldn't be too much of a problem.

Jenny was stroking the cat's back, whispering quietly to it as Cornrows and Baseball Cap edged forward. Andrew couldn't work out if it was one of Margaret Watkins' stolen creatures. It sort of looked like them but he was too far away to be sure about the distinctive markings.

'How much?' Andrew asked.

'Toldya – big one,' Cornrows replied.

'A grand's way too much,' Jenny said, not looking up.

'We had a deal, girlie. That's a bony-fido bangle.'

Jenny set the cat on the floor, where it scowled up at Andrew, daring him to go closer. 'It's not a Bengal,' she said. 'It's just a normal cat – some sort of tabby. The markings are all wrong.'

Cornrows peered down at the cat and then turned and bashed Baseball Cap in the shoulder with the back of his hand. 'Yo, I *told* you, man. It don't look like no tiger. You got the wrong one.'

Baseball Cap was busy trying to get his jacket off again. 'Look at the scratches! Only a tiger can do that.'

'It's not a Bengal,' Jenny repeated.

Cornrows whacked his friend again. 'I told you it was the house next door.'

'You said the orange cat – that's what I got.'

'The wrong one!'

Jenny removed the box from the boot and set it down next to the cat. 'How much do you want for her?'

Cornrows straightened himself up, smoothing down his

vest and trying to retain some degree of dignity, not that he'd had much to start with. He hoiked his boxer shorts up so they were covering his arse and then checked his oversized watch.

'Ton,' he said.

'I'm not paying a hundred quid for a tabby you nicked.'

Cornrows stepped towards the cat, arms outstretched.

Hissssssssss.

At least it wasn't just Andrew the demon wanted to attack.

Cornrows skipped backwards again, eyes narrowing.

Jenny stood, pressing onto the tips of her toes and facing him. 'How about you let me take the poor little thing to a cat sanctuary somewhere?'

'No way, bitch.'

She stepped forward, making him take another stride back. 'Either that, or I could just call the police to give them your number plate and phone number.'

Jenny reached for her pocket but Cornrows was ahead of her, snatching her wrist with one hand, and scrambling in his shorts with the other. Andrew moved forward but Baseball Cap elbowed him away, catching him under the ribs.

Andrew gasped to catch his breath but, as the clouds shifted slightly, a glimmer of sunshine flittered through, reflecting into his eyes from the lock knife in Cornrows' hand.

18

The blade was slightly curved, the handle thin and metallic. Cornrows grinned as he waved it towards Jenny, showing off a single golden tooth that Andrew had missed before. Suddenly the ridiculous appearance and gangster talk didn't seem so funny.

Andrew straightened himself, slightly winded from the elbow to the chest. He held both arms out, palms up, being as unthreatening as he could. They were close to the corner of the pub, hidden from the main road, but visible to any pedestrians who might be nearby. His eyes flickered towards the empty pavement, willing someone to walk past.

Cornrows flashed the blade between Jenny and Andrew, still holding on to her wrist. 'You disrespectin' us?'

Andrew took a small step forward, still wary of the cat, but focusing on the knife. 'Hey, there's no need for that. We can all walk away from this.'

Considering how quickly his heart was thumping, his voice sounded surprisingly steady.

Cornrows rotated the knife in his hand, showing off the glittering studs embedded within the handle. The blade was thin and pointy at the end, bowing down to a thick join where the bolt had locked in place. As he waved it towards Andrew, Jenny took the moment to snatch her wrist away from his other hand. Andrew expected her to step backwards, out of harm's way, but instead she pressed herself onto tiptoes again, angling forward until she had Cornrows' attention.

'Whatcha gonna do, gangsta boys?'

Her tone spat disdain, top lip snaking into a smiling, aggressive snarl. Cornrows twisted from Andrew to Jenny, unsure where to look.

'Jen . . .'

Andrew was ignored by everyone.

Jenny wasn't flinching. 'You gonna slice us up here in broad daylight?'

Cornrows was beginning to panic, his hand with the knife shaking as he swapped a glance with Baseball Cap, who had taken a step closer to the car.

'You gonna leave us in a pool of blood and drive off?'

Jenny stepped forward, making Cornrows move back further. Her eyes were locked onto his, dimple on show, cocky smile fixed.

She nodded past him towards the main road. 'There are number plate recognition cameras whichever way you go on that road, meaning you'll have already been recorded coming here. You were stupid enough to pass by the car park twice, so you're probably on there more than once. When the police find our bodies and start looking for suspects, that's the first thing they'll check.'

Another step forward.

Jenny tilted towards the link road. 'Try going that way and there's a giant Tesco with cameras on the forecourt of the petrol station, so you'll be spotted too.'

The knife was now at Cornrows' side, his arm hanging limply.

'And that's if you drive away. You could abandon the car and run for it – but then you've got housing estates on three sides and the town centre on the other. You're wearing a bright purple vest and shorts, while your mate looks like a giant beach ball. Do you think there's a chance that at least one person might remember you?'

Cornrows had backed away so far that he was almost at the driver's door. Baseball Cap was on the other side with the passenger's door already open.

If anything, Jenny's voice found a new level with which to taunt. It was like she was bullying a smaller kid for his dinner money in a playground corner. 'You want to cause all of that trouble for the sake of a cat that's not even worth anything? A cat that's not even yours?'

Cornrows made his decision, flicking the blade back into the handle and lunging for the car door. Baseball Cap did the same on the other side and, with a ferocious growl of the engine, they were racing towards the main road, leaving Andrew coughing in a cloud of exhaust fumes.

Jenny shrugged, watching them go and then crouching to pick up the cat, which started to lick at her hands.

She spun on her heels. 'Are you going to bring the box?' she asked as she took a step back to the car, as if she'd just returned from a relaxing stroll in the park.

Andrew felt frozen. 'Jen.'

'What?'

'What was that?'

'I dunno. I figured we could find an animal sanctuary

somewhere. She's obviously been nicked, so perhaps the owner's looking for her.'

Andrew didn't move. 'Not the cat. I mean with them. He had a knife.'

She shrugged again, apparently not seeing the risk. 'They're idiots.'

'But idiots can still be dangerous. Usually that idiocy makes them *more* dangerous. The guy in the jacket could've had a gun, like you said. Or the one with the knife could've used it.'

'Nah.'

'That's not an answer – you didn't know if he was going to use it.'

'He didn't.'

'But he could have!'

'Pfft.'

Jenny was walking too quickly for Andrew to have a proper conversation with her. He trailed behind, heart still thundering. Back at the car, he packed the box into the boot, with Jenny giving the back seat over to the cat. As Andrew climbed into the driver's seat, he glanced nervously over his shoulder, meeting its beady green eyes and deciding the creature could have its space. He certainly wasn't going to try to move it on. Jenny was leaning against the passenger's side window, humming something upbeat.

Andrew sat, breathing in the car's slightly stale air. His fingers twitched on the ignition key but he didn't turn it.

'How did you know about the cameras?' he asked.

'What cameras?'

'The number-plate ones.'

Another terrifying shrug. 'I guessed – they're everywhere nowadays. Someone's on the *Guardian* website every day banging on about surveillance. It seemed like a fair assumption. It's not as if they were going to know any differently.'

'But why do all of that for a cat? I thought you didn't get pets?'

Jenny shook her head with an infuriating dismissiveness, apparently unaware that there had ever been any danger. She glanced to the back seat, where the cat was stomping in a circle, making a nest for itself, or whatever it was that cats lived in. 'I dunno – she didn't seem happy in that box and it wasn't as if they were going to look after her. It felt like the right thing to do.'

Andrew wasn't convinced that fronting up to someone with a knife was ever the right thing to do. He was firmly in the run for it school of thinking. He wasn't sure he'd ever heard Jenny expressing such concern for another creature, so perhaps this was a step forward. She was so hard to read. As he watched her, she reached into her backpack and pulled out a can of fizzy Vimto, popping the ring pull and taking a slurp.

Not a care in the world.

As he ran over what she'd actually said, Andrew realised that she hadn't actually shown any concern – she'd said it *felt* like the right thing to do. Not that she thought it was, or that she was bothered herself. She did what she thought she probably should. Perhaps more worryingly, she had again shown no concern for her own welfare.

A chill licked his spine and Andrew shuddered.

'Were you scared?' he asked.

'Um . . .' Jenny leant back in her seat, can pressed to her lips. '. . . I'm not sure.' A pause. 'Probably not.'

'I was.'

She turned to face him, eyebrows arching. She seemed confused. 'You didn't show it.'

Andrew twisted the key, making the engine growl to life. What else was there to say? One day they'd have to have a conversation about Jenny doing stupid things . . . just not today. He was too much of a wimp – and he wasn't sure what scared him more. It *should* be men with knives. It *was* men with knives. But sometimes, every once in a while, there was a glint in Jenny's eye that made him think he didn't know her at all.

Eventually, he turned back to the windscreen, his heart rate slowing to something normal. 'I suppose we'd better find an animal shelter.'

Getting rid of the hissing, spitting ginger ball of fur wasn't as easy as Andrew had hoped – though he hadn't lost any fingers, nor been scratched to pieces, in the process of off-loading it at an RSPCA place just north of Manchester city centre. It was the fifth spot they'd tried, with all the others saying they were full. That was one afternoon he wouldn't be getting back any time soon.

Considering the antagonising effect Jenny could have on people, it was an irony that she was the only person the cat didn't want to attack. The green-eyed demon gave one final death stare at Andrew, before disappearing into the animal care area of the shelter. He pitied the poor kid who ended up with *that* as a pet. Whoever it was would have to sleep with one eye open.

Andrew was on his way back to the car when his phone started to ring. He checked the screen and then held it out towards Jenny. 'Do you want to answer it?'

'Who is it?'

'Gem. She's going to go on at me about not eating properly. If you answer and tell her I'm busy, she'll forget why she called.'

'I think she's lovely. If I answer, I'll tell her you're avoiding her calls.'

'Fine.'

Andrew answered with an optimistic-sounding 'hello'.

Gem's tone was frazzled, out of breath. 'Andrew?'

'What's wrong?'

She stammered, sniffing and coughing. Crying. 'I don't know . . . please come.'

19

Andrew blazed through the decidedly red-looking traffic light, ignoring the beeps of annoyance from behind and bumping over a road hump, sending the back of the vehicle catapulting into the air.

'Andy . . .'

Jenny never called him that, only Andrew. It was his name, after all. Why did people always want to shorten things? They were both two syllables, how much time were people saving? Salespeople wanted to do it all the time: 'Can I call you Andy?' No, you sodding well can't. Can I call you 'dickhead'?

'What?' he replied.

'You're driving like an idiot.'

'You didn't hear her on the phone.'

'If you get pulled over by the police, or smash into a wall, you're not going to be any use then, are you?'

Andrew ignored her, pressing harder on the accelerator and shooting inside a red Peugeot that was taking too long to turn right.

'Andy.'

'Shut up, Jenny.'

Her tone remained utterly calm. 'Don't talk to me like that.'

'I'm the boss, okay? You work for me. If I want to tell you to shut up, I can.'

'That doesn't mean you're not driving like a prick.'

'You can get out.'

The traffic lights ahead had been on green for too long. Andrew was nudging fifty but leant harder on the pedal, taking them close to sixty and flying across the junction.

'Did you see that pedestrian about to step out?' Jenny said.

'I had the green light – they should be waiting.'

'You know that's not what it's like around here. People cross where they want.'

'Their fault then.'

'So if you hit them at sixty in a thirty, it's their fault because they didn't wait for the light?'

Andrew didn't reply, easing off as the cars ahead stalled into a queue of red brake lights. What was it with the bloody traffic in this city? Every day, jams stretched from one side to the other, yet nobody ever did anything. He checked his rear-view mirror and then slammed on the brakes, skidding right but turning left.

'There's a school on this street,' Jenny said, remaining annoyingly calm.

'I know! Just shut up.'

'You should be slowing—'

'Shut up!'

Cars were parked on both sides of the road, leaving a gap in the centre wide enough for only one vehicle. Andrew sped towards it, noticing too late that there was already a car coming towards him.

Beeeeeeeep!

He hammered the horn, flapping his hand in an effort to make the other driver reverse. It was a young woman, Jenny's age, in a little black Micra. The other driver slammed on her brakes, eyes wide in surprise and fear as Andrew continued towards her. After a moment of hesitating, she put it in reverse and shot backwards without looking. Andrew slowed but kept driving forwards until he was past her. He indicated and then turned right, across the front of a horn-honking white van.

'Twat,' Andrew muttered under his breath.

'Are you talking about yourself?'

Andrew stamped on the brake, bringing the car to a skidding halt in the centre of the lane.

'Out,' he said, turning to Jenny.

'I'm not moving.'

'You work for me and I'm telling you to get out.'

She stared back at him, defiant but not angry. 'What are you going to do? Drag me out? Try it.'

He glared at her for a few moments, until turning back to the road and setting off again. He took the next corner at a speed that was almost sensible, before accelerating towards the main road – hoping to be in front of the queuing traffic.

'You didn't hear her voice,' he whispered.

'No, but I can hear yours. You're scared, which is fine. She's your aunt and you want to look after her – but there's a sensible way to do things and this isn't it. If you want to look after her, you've got to look after yourself.'

'Says you! You were tied to a tree in the woods with a knife in front of you and didn't flinch. Just now, you egged on some wannabe gangster kid who had a blade. You're not scared of anything.'

There was a short, pregnant pause and then: 'I'm not you.'

Andrew almost stamped on the brake. Jenny's simple sentence sent another chill whispering along his back. She was only saying what was true – of course she wasn't him – but the haunted way in which she spoke made it sound as if they weren't even from the same species.

Andrew just about held it together, slowing as he reached the junction with the main road, quickly checking right and then slewing around the bend.

'It's a thirty,' Jenny said.

Although he didn't reply, Andrew dropped his speed so that he was only doing forty. They didn't have far to go and the journey continued in silence until Andrew reached his aunt's estate. He parked next to a chassis propped up by piles of bricks, and threw himself out of the car, ignoring the jolts in his back and setting off with something close to a sprint. By his standards, anyway.

Andrew took the concrete stairs two at a time, almost toppling over the barrier at the top as he slid onto the balcony. Gem's house looked fine from the outside: no smoke damage, no fire, no broken windows. Those had been his first fears.

He tried the front door handle, expecting it to be open.

Bang, bang, bang.

Andrew rapped on the door and squinted through the glass next to it. All he could see through the net curtain was darkness and the vague outlines of his aunt's tat in the windowsill.

'Come on, come on,' he muttered.

He spun with surprise as something brushed his arm: Jenny. She smiled gently at him. No dimple.

A squeaky sad-sounding voice came from the inside as the bolts were slowly unlocked. 'All right, all right . . .'

Moments later, the door creaked open. Gem was wearing an apron with brown handprints on the front. Rory was mooching around her feet, staring doe-eyed up at Andrew, wondering what all the fuss was about. Behind her, everything was dark.

'Oh, Andrew,' she said with a relieved sigh, before turning to Jenny. 'It's nice to see you again, dear.'

'What's wrong?' Andrew asked, failing to keep his voice level.

'I didn't mean to worry you.'

'You didn't.'

She turned towards the flat. 'I'd just put a Yorkshire pud in the oven and everything cut out.' She held her hand up, showing a vicious-looking red whip mark across the webbing between her right thumb and index finger.

Andrew held her wrist gently, rotating it. 'How did you do that?'

'I plugged in the kettle and there was this snapping sound, like a giant Coco Pop.'

'Wasn't someone supposed to be coming to fix things?'

'He was round yesterday – lovely young man. He complimented my teapots.'

'If he did a proper job, you wouldn't be getting burn

marks from an electrical socket. We need to get you to casualty.'

Gem snatched her hand back. 'It's fine – don't fuss. It looks worse than it is. I only called because I can't get the lights back on. I tried the fuse box but it wouldn't stay on.'

Rory toddled onto the balcony, sniffing Andrew's feet and then moving towards Jenny. She crouched and played with his ears, which made him roll onto his back.

'Oooh, he likes you,' Gem said. 'He doesn't do that for anyone, not even Uncle Andrew.'

Jenny stroked the pug's belly, looking up at Andrew. 'I'll wait here.'

Andrew moved past his aunt into the flat. Aside from the light seeping through the open door, the hall was an ocean of darkness, long, grim shadows puncturing the corners and combining in the middle. He used his phone to offer a pathetically dim light as he headed into the cupboard containing the fuse box.

Gem had called him because she didn't know who else to contact – but he didn't know what he was doing either. Andrew stopped to sniff the air, wondering if there might be gas. Was that right? He'd seen it on television but had no idea. There should be some sort of post-graduate course in all this stuff – an MA or MSc in adulthood. It'd show people how to change a fuse, plumb in a washing machine, alter a light fitting – the sort of stuff that dads knew how to do. Andrew didn't have a clue about any of it. Forget studying the history of European art, how do you bleed a radiator?

There were half-a-dozen switches, with five of them in the 'on' position but the one marked 'master' was off.

Andrew waited with his thumb hovering over it. Could it electrocute him? Did plastic carry electricity? He dabbed it with his thumb quickly, once, twice, three times. No shock. Surely a good thing? Andrew eased the switch back into the 'on' position, only for it to immediately snap off again.

Anything other than flicking a switch was definitely beyond his limited skills. From the evidence, it didn't look as if the bloke Gem had got in to check everything over knew much more than he did.

Andrew moved into the kitchen, where Gem had laid the table for one. It was a sad sight to see the single knife and fork, sitting next to an open can of orangeade – the cheap kind sold by the local Londis for 10p.

What was wrong with him? He almost hadn't answered his aunt's call and here she was, preparing to eat lunch by herself. To really pour salt into the wound, Rory's empty bowl sat on the floor next to her seat.

Andrew returned to the front door, where Jenny was sitting cross-legged against the railing, stroking Rory's belly. Gem was in full flow: '. . . so I called "house" and the entire room groaned. Janet couldn't believe it – she's been going for thirty-odd years and has never won the Christmas pot. Even Reg had a bit of a strop on. I gave him a little wink to rub it in, then took my card up to the front. When they confirmed I had the numbers, all hell broke loose . . .'

She turned back, noticing Andrew. 'Hello, love. Did you fix it?'

Andrew shook his head. 'You and Rory can come and stay at my flat tonight. There's loads of room.'

'I don't want to be a burden, lovey. Plus you live in that giant tower thing. My knees can't take all of those stairs . . .'

'There are lifts. It's Rory I might have to smuggle in – we're not supposed to have pets but I'll figure it out.'

'No, no, I like being here. I didn't want to call – you know what it's like to phone a mobile. It's like ten pounds a minute or something stupid. It was poor Rory. He likes his food warmed up but the cooker wasn't working. He's a sensitive little soul and I couldn't bear the thought of him not eating. I tried getting him a different flavour of his food last month but he had two sniffs and walked away. He was so upset that he didn't sit with me to watch *The One Show*. You know what he's like.'

'The cooker works at mine and I've got some steaks in the fridge. Rory can eat like a king for a night – you too.'

At the sound of his name, Rory rolled back onto his front, tongue flopping onto the floor. Steaks, you say?

'Oh, darling, I couldn't do—'

'You're coming. This isn't a discussion. Go inside and pack a bag. I'll find someone who can come out and rewire the place properly. You can stay with me for as long as it takes – longer if you want.'

Gem opened her mouth to protest but closed it again as she realised Andrew wasn't messing around. 'All right, dear, but I have a very particular routine. Rory likes to eat at half past five when I have my tea. Then we'll watch the local news, then *The One Show*. Then it's *Emmerdale*, *Corrie*, *East-Enders*. Rory's normally asleep by then, but—'

'The telly's yours, Gem. Actually the flat's yours.'

She smiled. 'You're such a sweetie – I've always known it,

even when I was wiping your bottom. I knew then you'd grow up to be something special.'

Gem squished Andrew's cheek and then headed into the flat, carrying his phone to provide some light. Rory sniffed Andrew's feet, tilted his head apologetically towards Jenny, and then tottered after Gem, making it clear where his allegiance lay.

Andrew took a breath and turned to lean on the balcony, facing the mucky green where the mixture of rain and overnight temperature drops had created a mini skating rink in the centre. Someone had left an upturned shopping trolley on top. Jenny was at his side, their elbows touching. 'You're right,' he said. 'I'm a prick.'

'Yes you are.'

'I'm sor—'

'Just stop,' Jenny snapped. 'I don't need apologies. At least you got us here without crashing. Your aunt's fine, Rory's okay – it'll all work out.'

There was a lump in Andrew's throat and he angled his face away from Jenny in case she tried to look at him. 'I'm worried about you.'

'*You're* worried about *me*?'

He stepped back to the front door and closed it slightly, then returned to the railing, lowering his voice. 'Why aren't you scared of things, Jen? It's the normal way to be.'

'Depends on how you define normal.'

'Being scared is normal.'

She shook her head. 'I'm just me.'

'But you shouldn't be marching into battles for me and picking fights with people wielding knives.'

'Is that because you're a bloke and you think you should be looking after me?'

Andrew stuttered and stumbled over a reply. 'No . . . I don't know . . . I just . . . I worry that you're going to do something really stupid one day because you don't even realise you're in danger.'

'Pfft.'

'And stop doing that. That doesn't make it okay.'

Jenny turned back to face the flat. 'I don't want to talk about it. I know who I am.' She sounded firm and decisive. End of conversation.

Andrew wanted to argue but what could he say? He was already in the wrong for driving like an idiot and telling her to get out. They'd both done stupid things in the past hour.

A thud behind Andrew made him turn. Gem had dropped a large bag for life on the ground behind him and was heading back into the flat. 'That's Rory's stuff.'

The bag was full of blankets, dog food tins and soft toys – including an Elmo so well chewed, the poor sod was missing an eye. Andrew picked Elmo up, only to get a handful of canine saliva. Lovely. Gem reappeared moments later with two more bags for life.

Andrew peeped into the top of the first one. 'There are blankets at my flat.'

'I like to be warm at night.'

'I can put the heating on – and I have blankets! I have a spare duvet too.'

'I don't want you to fuss.'

Andrew didn't want to argue any longer. Gem handed

him the dog lead and then they all headed to the car, over-flowing bags in hand.

If nothing else, it was going to be an interesting night.

It probably wouldn't have been approved by the RSPCA but Rory was smuggled past the security guards in Andrew's building at the bottom of a bag for life, where he sat peacefully. Picking up the roly-poly so-and-so was another problem entirely. Andrew wobbled his way into the reception area smiling too much, although it was largely to stop himself from keeling over from the weight of the dog. The security guards gave Andrew a nod and he headed directly to the lifts. Jenny and Gem carried the other bags between them but, as soon as the lift doors closed, Andrew put the Rory-occupied bag down and started wringing his arms.

'You're going to hurt his feelings,' Gem said.

'Rory's?'

'I told you – he's a sensitive soul. He's already in a place he doesn't know, packed in a bag, and now you're throwing your arms around as if he's too heavy.'

Andrew peered down at the bright round eyes staring up from the canvas bag, wanting to say that he *was* too heavy but God forbid he upset the dog.

The lift pinged and Andrew took a breath before picking up the bag again, avoiding Jenny's smirk. She and Gem headed along the corridor as Andrew groaned his way after them, swaying as if he had piles.

As soon as he unlocked the door to his flat, Gem stepped inside, dropping the bag at her feet and heading to the window in the same way everyone did. Beetham Tower was the tallest building in the north of England and Andrew owned a flat near the top.

'Oh, Andrew . . .' she whispered.

He'd tried to persuade his aunt to come over for a meal on many occasions but she was so hesitant to leave her estate that this was the only time he'd ever managed it.

The days were technically getting longer but it was still dark before five o'clock. Below, long lines of red and white lights stretched into the distance: commuters desperately trying to get home on a Thursday evening. Lights glimmered along the length of the canal, dotting its ancient passage through the city, with tower blocks, housing estates, factories, offices and all manner of mismatched buildings dumped higgledy-piggledy as far as the eye could see. If any planning had actually gone into the area, then it was impossible to detect.

Gem crept towards the glass, arm outstretched as if to make sure it was there. 'This is wonderful, sweetie.'

Andrew plucked Rory from the bag and placed him on the floor. His claws instantly started to slide on the varnished wood as he half-waddled, half-skidded across to the living room area and started sniffing at the glass coffee table, before plopping down on the rug and licking himself.

Jenny caught Andrew's eye, dimple definitely back on show. 'Don't act as if you've never done that after a long day,' she said with a giggle.

Andrew smiled and mouthed a 'thank you' as she headed for the door, calling 'goodbye' to Gem over her shoulder.

Gem finally stepped away from the window, taking in

the rest of the ridiculously modern flat. Andrew felt embarrassed by it as she ran her hands across the spotless stainless steel appliances and the painting on his wall that was probably worth more than her flat. He had all this and she was stuck in a deathtrap. Why hadn't he done more to try to get her away? Not simply try to talk her round, but *tell* her she was moving.

'This is lovely,' she cooed, sitting next to Andrew on the sofa.

'There's more to life than living in a small corner of Manchester.'

It came out harsher than he meant it and she slapped him on the leg, slightly harder than playfully. 'Don't be such a snob, Andrew Hunter. That's not how you were raised.'

'Sorry,' he replied, suitably chastened.

Neither of them spoke for a moment, before he added: 'I'm going to get someone to go into your flat tomorrow.' He pointed towards the far end of the room. 'My bedroom's through there. You can sleep there with Rory. I'll take the sofa.'

For a moment, he thought his aunt was going to argue but she rested her head on his shoulder and hugged his arm tightly.

'Thank you.'

20

FRIDAY

Andrew held the mobile six inches from his ear, wincing as he wondered if he'd perforated an eardrum. 'Gem, you don't have to shout – a mobile's like any other phone.'

'Pardon?'

'I said a mobile phone's like . . . forget it. I wanted to make sure you and Rory were okay.'

'We're fine, dear, you go off and enjoy yourself.'

He almost started to tell her that he was working but that would only mean another five minutes on the phone. He'd already spent enough time explaining that it didn't cost him much to call the phone in his flat. She was convinced people needed to remortgage to use a mobile.

Andrew pocketed the device and stared across the road to the towering iron gates beyond. They were at least three metres high, welded to a thick wall that stretched far into the distance in both directions. Cameras were dotted along it at regular intervals, each pointing towards the pavement.

The person inside definitely didn't want anyone going over the top.

Andrew double-checked that he had the correct address – it would be pretty embarrassing if he didn't – then locked his car and crossed the road. Through the gates, he could see a paved driveway winding towards a house that was like a scaled-down stately home. There were three floors, each with seven windows – and that was just the front. Leafy evergreens lined the edge of the drive, swaying gently in the chill breeze. Manchester was cold – but it was a degree or two cooler where he was now, north of Liverpool. There were no cars propped up on bricks around here, no needles left in stairwells. Instead, each property was separated by high walls and huge bushes. This was an area for privacy.

There was a mechanical fizz and Andrew looked up to see both of the CCTV cameras above the gates swivelling to bore down at him. He pressed the button attached to the wall.

Buzzzzzzzzzzzzz.

Andrew felt watched. He peered up to each of the cameras and then took a step backwards so the monitor screen built into the wall could see him too.

He waited. And waited.

Andrew had barely slept on the sofa, constantly twisting in an effort to get comfortable. When Rory started snoring at half-three in the morning, his nasal growls rumbling through the flat like an earthquake, Andrew gave up and made himself breakfast.

He couldn't work out if Jenny was a bad influence on him, or if he was on her. It stuck in his mind that they probably weren't good for each other.

Buzzzzzzzzzzzzz.

Andrew continued to wait, checking his watch, pacing up and down along the length of the gates as the cameras followed him. Sooner or later, someone would pay attention.

Buzzzzzzzzzzzzz.

He needed Jenny here to start climbing, or do something equally stupid.

Buzzzzzzzzzzzzz.

Andrew was about to press the button again, when a gravelly man's voice rattled through the speaker. 'Will ye piss off wi' that.'

'Can I talk to Mr Braithwaite?'

There was a short pause, then: 'Who is it?'

'My name's Andrew Hunter and I'm a private investigator and—'

'Piss off.'

'I'd like to do that but I really need to talk to him.'

Static filled the speaker for a few moments before the man's voice sounded again. He was either Scottish or Irish but it was hard to tell for sure. 'Do you want me to come out there and make you get lost?'

'I want to talk to him about Luke Methodist.'

The line went silent again, leaving Andrew to wonder whether the Celtic warrior was going to come down and kick his arse.

'Wait there.'

Andrew did as he was told, continuing to pace the length of the gates in an effort to stay warm. If Jenny could stand up to someone with a knife, then he could act like the big man when there was a giant set of gates to separate him from the angry-sounding man.

He checked his watch. One minute passed. Two. Five. Andrew gazed through the railings towards the house but there was no sign of movement. The cameras were still unmoving, watching. He'd told them his name, so Braith-waite could be looking him up right now. His website was basic but it contained his office phone number and address. Anyone could find that, but a man of Braithwaite's stature could check the other stuff too: perhaps his *actual* address? Credit rating? Maybe even his ex-wife's name?

Seven minutes. Eight. Nine.

Eventually, a figure appeared at the far end of the drive. At first, he didn't look too big, but as he came closer to the gate, Andrew began to feel nervous. The man was over six foot and built like a rugby player: big chest, shoulders . . . thighs.

Why was he looking at the other man's thighs?

Regardless, the other man could definitely kick the crap out of Andrew should he wish.

He was dressed smartly in a suit and shiny shoes, and continued along the drive until he was at the gates.

'Hi,' Andrew said.

Thunder Thighs didn't reply, glancing disdainfully at Andrew, before removing a small black box from his pocket and pressing a button that made the gates hum open. Andrew stepped through and started to follow the other man along the driveway towards the house.

'What's your name?' he asked, not receiving a reply.

Despite the time of year and the rough weather, the gardens were perfectly manicured, with a tidy lawn and rows of tightly clipped bushes, waiting for spring. A Bentley and a red sports car were parked in front of the house, hidden from the road by a fountain.

Instead of heading for the front door, the man led

Andrew towards the side of the house, skirting around the edge of a double garage and passing underneath an archway carved into the hedge.

The back garden was even more spectacular than the front, with a stable block built into the far corner next to a circular course of jumps. In front was another expanse of jade lawn, with evenly mown light and dark lines stretching from wall to wall.

Attached to the back of the house was a conservatory that was bigger than Gem's flat. They were almost at the glass door when the rain started to fall, drumming from the surroundings as if signalling Andrew's death march.

Thunder Thighs opened the unlocked door and squeezed inside, not holding it open as Andrew almost caught its full force in his face.

Sitting at a small black metal table was Thomas Braithwaite, easily recognisable from the photos Andrew had seen of him. His black hair was beginning to grey but it gave him a distinguished look, instead of making him seem old. He had a neat beard and moustache and a trim physique, but it was his eyes that set him apart. Andrew froze the moment Braithwaite's water-blue gaze settled on him. They stared through him, as if examining Andrew's very soul.

Braithwaite glanced sideways. 'Thank you, Iwan.'

The accent had a hint of Scouse but it was lighter, as if he'd taught himself not to stretch the vowels so much.

He turned back to Andrew. 'Mr Hunter, you should have called ahead.' He motioned towards the empty seat across from him. 'I'm having a late breakfast. I'm told it's known as brunch nowadays but that sounds like the type of thing only a fool would say. What say you?'

'I don't really eat in the mornings.'

'Breakfast's the most important meal!' He pointed towards a triangle of toast. 'Are you sure I can't tempt you?'

'I'm all right.'

Braithwaite looked back up at Iwan, who was hovering close to the door. 'You can leave us.'

Iwan glanced sideways at Andrew. 'You sure?'

There was no reply, merely another steely stare, which Iwan acknowledged with an apologetic nod, before heading into the main house. The rain continued to beat on the glass, with Braithwaite seeming to sense how uneasy it made Andrew. He sipped at a small cup of steaming espresso, allowing the tension to build, before returning it to its saucer.

'Where's your office, Mr Hunter?'

'You can call me Andrew.'

'I realise that, Mr Hunter.'

'Manchester.'

Braithwaite nodded knowingly. 'You're a long way from home.'

'Not really.'

'Perhaps it's only thirty or forty miles on a map – but distance can be relative when you're walking into something unknown.' Braithwaite paused for another sip of coffee. 'You look tired.'

From nowhere, Andrew found himself yawning – a full-on, limb-stretching, jaw-dislocating, back-cricking stretch and gasp.

'Sorry,' he said.

'Something keeping you awake at night?'

'Not really. Some cowboy redid the wiring at my aunt's flat and nearly caused a fire. She's staying at mine and . . .' Andrew stopped, wondering why it had popped out. He'd not meant to start giving things away about his life. Braithwaite had a way of talking that was unnervingly disarming.

He purred his reply: 'You can't trust anyone these days.'

As he stretched for his coffee once more, Andrew noticed the glint from the 'T' cufflink hanging from his tight-fitting shirt. The other side surely had the 'B' inserted. Andrew didn't know if they were the ones Jenny had seen.

Braithwaite finished the drink with a slurp and delicately placed the cup down again. 'Not many people come to visit me here, Mr Hunter. You may have heard, but I'm effectively retired. People like Iwan do things for me.'

'I'm looking into the deaths of Owen Copthorne, Wendy Boyes and Luke Methodist.'

Braithwaite licked his lips, smiling slightly. 'Don't we have police for that sort of thing? If you're looking for a proper job, I'm sure I can find something for you to do.'

'Everyone assumes Owen and Wendy were killed by Luke on behalf of the Evans brothers because they wanted to get rid of witnesses after the jewellery robbery.'

'I'd read something to that effect.'

'The Evans brothers used to work for you and there are whispers that you were linked to the robbery too . . .'

Andrew let it hang as Braithwaite smiled thinly. He stared out towards the empty garden, leaving them in silence for all but the steady drumming of the rain. Andrew didn't know how long passed. It might have been a few seconds but it felt a lot longer.

Braithwaite eventually replied without looking at Andrew. 'You can't expect me to be responsible for everything my current or former employees might choose to do. I offer livelihoods to thousands of people.'

'I've heard all sorts of rumours since I started asking questions. People talking about the type of business you might be running alongside the importing. I'm not interested in any of that, I'm bothered about people.'

There was a scratching sound from behind, with Andrew turning to see an orange cat slinking along the gap from the conservatory to the house. He did a double-take, cricking his neck to check the black stripes and spots. It looked like a mini leopard. He had to force himself to blink away from it.

Braithwaite leant forward and took the final triangle of toast from the table, biting off the corner and chewing with his mouth closed.

'Rumours are dangerous things to listen to, Mr Hunter.'

'I completely agree – which is why I'm sure you wouldn't want anyone to listen to the whispers that you could possibly be associated with the deaths of an innocent young couple. Two kids in love with their entire lives ahead of them.'

Braithwaite paused before speaking, choosing his words carefully. 'What are you saying?'

'I don't think the Evans brothers got Luke Methodist to shoot anyone. I don't think the eldest one even knew him – so if it's nothing to do with them, then it's nothing to do with you.'

'Why should I care what you think?'

'Because it isn't just me. All those little insinuations and assumptions will go away if I can find out what really happened. All your friends in the police who keep coming after you might think differently.'

A grin cracked across Braithwaite's face. 'You're a great philanthropist looking to do me a favour?'

'Actually, it's nothing to do with you. There are other people I want to find the truth out for. You just happen to be a part of it.'

Braithwaite finished the slice of toast and wiped his hands over the plate, before dabbing his lips with a thick embroidered napkin.

'Oh, Mr Hunter, you've put yourself on such thin ice. Why would you do that?'

He dropped his hand down as the cat approached, slinking between the legs of his chair and nuzzling his fingers. At the back of the conservatory, a second cat was padding around, staring up at the rain-soaked windows. Andrew didn't want to appear too interested but they definitely looked like Bengals with their distinctive mix of dark spots and stripes against the gingery-orange fur. Andrew took a risk, holding his own hand down until the second cat sloped across the floor looking for food. It drifted past his hand as he ran his thumb across the back of its neck, feeling the chip underneath.

Could they be Margaret Watkins'? They could've had the old chips removed and new ones inserted and it wasn't beyond the realms of possibility, even if it would be an enormous coincidence.

Braithwaite watched the cat sniff at Andrew's fingers before heading off to the far side of the conservatory.

'Are you a cat person, Mr Hunter?'

'Not really.'

'Fascinating creatures: such independent thinkers.'

Andrew left the silence hanging, though it didn't have the same gravitas as when Braithwaite did it.

'Do you have a daughter?' Andrew eventually asked, already knowing the answer. Even if he didn't, the stables would have given him a clue: not many teenage boys were interested in horses.

Braithwaite's eyes narrowed. 'I think you should leave.'

'Luke Methodist has a daughter. She has to live with everyone saying her father's a murderer. He probably is – but all I'm trying to do is find the truth for her.'

Silence except for the rain. Andrew watched Braithwaite, who was staring out of the window, stroking his beard. He looked furious, knuckles white with tension.

'It's all about reputations,' Andrew added. 'And not just that of Luke's daughter.'

From nowhere, Iwan appeared in the doorway between conservatory and house. He stood tall, bobbing on the backs of his heels. Andrew had no idea if there was some sort of secret button, or if he'd been listening in, but his timing was dangerously impeccable.

Braithwaite spun in his seat, smiling gently at Iwan, before offering a small nod in Andrew's direction. Before Andrew could move, the giant of a man had taken two steps forward, cracking his knuckles and breaking into a grin.

21

Andrew tried to stand but the seat slipped on the tiled floor, making him stumble forward. He caught himself on the edge of the table but Iwan was barely a metre from him, the pops from his knuckles echoing over the rain.

'Iwan,' Braithwaite said calmly.

The brute stopped where he was. 'Sir?'

'Grow up.'

Iwan stepped back, confused. He stared from Andrew to his boss. 'Sorry, Sir.'

Braithwaite rolled his eyes. 'I want you to tell Mr Hunter all about Mr Brasso. Okay?'

There was a momentary pause. 'Yes, Sir.'

'Is that a problem?'

'No.'

Braithwaite turned to Andrew, lips pressed together. 'You're either incredibly brave or really, really stupid to involve yourself in something you needn't. I very much hope you know what you're doing. There's an order to things, checks and balances; if that begins to fall down, then what are we left with?'

Andrew couldn't tell if he wanted an answer and didn't really know what he was talking about. Braithwaite held him in his gaze for a few moments, before nodding towards Iwan again.

'That'll be all.'

No smile, no goodbye; simply a solemn trudge through the rain along the driveway, half a step behind Iwan. Thunder Thighs didn't seem bothered by the weather, not even ducking his head as he sauntered across the paved area, slowing the further they went. Andrew wondered if the other man was egging him into overtaking but he didn't anyway, staying in line and marching to the beat.

Iwan used the device in his pocket to open and close the gates and then crossed the road, coming to a halt next to Andrew's car. 'It's not going to drive itself.'

Andrew dripped his way into the driver's seat, feeling the suspension drop and the car groan in protest as Iwan climbed into the passenger's side. It felt like the vehicle was tilting to the left.

'What are you waiting for?' Iwan growled.

'I don't know where you want me to go.'

'Just drive.'

Andrew did as he was told, crawling away from the house, wondering what was going on. He checked his mirrors, wondering if he was being followed, though his only accompaniment was the mid-morning rain.

'You drive like an old woman,' Iwan said.

'I still don't know where you want me to go.'

'Stop being a girl.'

Andrew headed towards the motorway and the route back to Manchester, assuming he'd be told if he was going the wrong way. Iwan said nothing, spending around thirty per cent of his time scratching his crotch and the other seventy tutting at Andrew's driving. The car was feeling increasingly hard to manoeuvre, with Iwan's bulk weighing it down. Andrew tried to come up with things to say – 'So when did you start being big?', 'What's it like being a right-hand man?', 'Where do you get clothes to fit?' – but he didn't think they would be appreciated.

He was about to cross the M60 ring road on the way back into Manchester when Iwan finally piped up: 'Next left here.'

'Left?'

'Opposite of right. Are you thick?'

'I understand the concept of left, it's just that we've had such wall-to-wall chatter that I didn't quite catch what you said.'

'Funny.'

Andrew took the turn, sloping down a ramp towards a set of traffic lights. 'Where now?'

'Wherever.'

'Are you the voice of my sat nav? I get similarly clear instructions from that.'

'You should do stand-up – I'd bottle you off.'

Andrew turned right at the junction, glancing towards Iwan for a reaction he didn't get. 'So . . . is that an Irish accent you have? Or Scottish . . . ?'

'Piss off.'

'I'm terrible at things like that. I had a Brummie mate at university and spent a year thinking he was from Newcastle.'

No reply. Andrew was going for Scottish but with Irish parents. Or Irish with Scottish parents. Or Northern Irish! What did that accent sound like? Sort of Irish, but as if the speaker had swallowed a cheese grater. Where a simple 'hello' came with an undertone suggesting that someone might find himself being kicked down a flight of stairs if he wasn't careful.

'Northern Irish?' Andrew added.

'Prick.'

'I've been called that a lot recently.'

'You must know some very observant people.'

'Maybe *you* should do stand-up? I wouldn't dare bottle you off, if that helps.'

'Prick. Right here.'

'Right?'

Finally a proper reaction. Iwan twisted in his seat to face Andrew. 'Opposite of left.'

Andrew pressed on the brake a little too harshly, sending his passenger shooting forward until the seatbelt slammed him back into the seat with a clunk. Iwan grimaced as Andrew took the turn, deliberately slowly. He could sense Iwan stewing, seething even. Braithwaite had told him to help Andrew out, so he wouldn't risk anything stupid. If he wasn't going to talk to him properly, then winding him up might yank down the veil and give Andrew a glimpse of what was actually going on.

'How's business?' Andrew asked.

'Next left.'

Andrew reached forward and switched the radio on. 'My sides are aching from all the witty banter,' he said, fiddling with the buttons until it settled on the local station.

'. . . *that was taking you all the way back to 1987 with "Love In The First Degree" by Bananarama. The follow-up track, "Love In The Second Degree", didn't do quite so well . . .*'

The DJ laughed at his own joke, which was just as well as no one else was going to.

'. . . *Coming up after the news and travel, Debbie Gibson is "Lost In Your Eyes"; watch out, ladies, because we have Genesis' "Invisible Touch"; Rick Astley's "Never Gonna Give You Up"; and Falco will be "Rocking", er, "Me Amadeus"* . . .'

Iwan reached forward and used his giant thumb to punch the radio off, which elevated him in Andrew's opinion.

'Pull over,' Iwan ordered.

Andrew did as he was told, wondering if Falco had pushed things a little too far. Either that, or Genesis. Who could possibly be offended by Rick Astley?

The rain had stopped, leaving the tarmac glistening in the murky grey, ready to freeze overnight. There was only one lane heading in each direction but the road was wide, with evenly spaced skeletal trees scattered along either side and a smattering of houses.

Iwan leant back in his seat, facing forward. 'Do you know what Brasso is?'

'That stuff you use to polish trophies and jewellery?'

'Aren't you the clever one?'

'I try.'

'In certain professions, having things cleaned for you is a very useful thing.' He waited for a reply, before adding: 'Do you understand?'

Andrew knew exactly what he meant but wasn't ready to let on. Sometimes, it was better to underplay your hand, make the other person spell things out.

'Like with a launderette?' he said.

Iwan didn't laugh, didn't even snigger. Andrew waited for him to say something else but he didn't move at all and barely even breathed. Slowly, the windows were steaming up.

'I get it,' Andrew replied eventually.

'Sure?'

'If I *found* a sack full of money, perhaps one that tumbled from the back of a lorry, I might need someone who can help me get the cash into a bank account where I can use it without arousing suspicion.'

'Watch a lot of TV, do you?'

Andrew didn't reply.

Iwan nodded towards the house across the road from the car. Andrew had to wipe away the mist with his sleeve until he could pick out the tall hedges standing in front of the property beyond. It wasn't as large as Braithwaite's but was impressive in a different way: six or seven bedrooms, two storeys, a large front garden and a sloping glass structure on the side that was reflecting the shimmering blue of an indoor pool.

'What do you think?' Iwan asked.

'I've seen worse places to live.'

'Not too bad for someone who owns a simple jewellery store.'

'Leyton Sampson?'

'Mr Brasso.'

Cogs whirred. Andrew had already assumed a connection to Sampson, which was why he'd driven to see Braithwaite in the first place.

'If Sampson serves a purpose in certain circles,' Andrew

said, 'if he cleans up those sacks of money that fall off lorries for people, why would you tell me this?'

'Not my decision.'

'But you must have an idea.'

'Mr Braithwaite doesn't like it when people go off and do their own thing. He doesn't like the rumours regarding the deaths of those kids and the links to people who used to work for him. He's very affected by things like that. He made a few inquiries about what might have happened but answers haven't been easy to come by. If Mr Sampson – Mr Brasso – has other interests away from those we know of, Mr Braithwaite would be very interested in finding out what they are.'

Iwan turned to face Andrew, features as expressionless as an Easter Island statue.

It was only then that Andrew realised what he'd done. Jenny facing down a man with a knife was reckless – but he had been just as careless.

Somehow, he had talked himself into taking on a job for Thomas Braithwaite.

22

Frustratingly, Jenny didn't understand the situation.

'I don't see where the problem is,' she said, her voice crackling through the speaker in Andrew's car.

Andrew had just dropped Iwan back at Braithwaite's house outside Liverpool. He checked his rear-view mirror and pulled away, speaking to her through the hands-free system. 'You're the one who pointed out that Braithwaite probably isn't what he seems,' he said.

'So?'

'So that means I'm working for a potential gangster. I shouldn't have come.'

'But we're not doing anything we weren't doing before – and you're not working *for* him.'

'I am!' Andrew realised he was shouting, so lowered his voice. 'Braithwaite implied that Leyton Sampson does a bit of work on the side, tidying up stolen items so they can be resold. Sampson told us he does his own repairs and resets on-site. Presumably those in the know give him pieces they've nicked and he clears engravings, melts down the metal, removes jewels – that sort of thing. He takes stolen goods and turns them back into money.'

'Do you think he arranged the robbery of his own store?'

Andrew puffed out a breath, checking his rear-view mirror again. It was empty. 'I don't know and Braithwaite didn't say. I genuinely don't think Braithwaite knew about Owen and Wendy being killed, though. He's hard to read but he seemed annoyed by it, as if he knew a line had been crossed.'

'Did he tell you about Sampson because he thinks it was something to do with him?'

'I suppose but it feels like I'm missing something. Where does everyone fit in? How does Sampson know the Evans brothers? Or Luke Methodist? Why them? And why kill Owen and Wendy? It's like a jigsaw where we have the pieces but they're not joining together. And now I'm going to have some factory-owner-importer-exporter-possible-mobster on my case about it.'

'We'll be fine.'

Andrew took the turn towards the motorway, following the exact route he had earlier in the day. Without Iwan weighing the vehicle down, the car was actually responding to the accelerator. 'There's one other thing,' Andrew said. 'Braithwaite had a pair of Bengals.'

'Bengals? Like the ones stolen from Margaret Watkins?'

'I don't know, they were just cats. One of them had a chip under its fur but that could have been redone. I was hardly going to ask him if he'd nicked a pair of Bengals recently.'

'I'd have asked him.'

'Which is exactly why I didn't bring you. I don't know why I didn't tell her we were too busy to find the darn things. Don't the fire brigade look for cats?'

'Do they?'

'I don't know – but it's ridiculous that we're doing it.'

Jenny had that I-told-you-so tone to her voice. 'You're going to have to learn how to say "no" to crying women then. If it's any consolation, I've had to turn two people away this morning. Both came in wanting their partners followed because they reckon they're having affairs. I said we didn't do that kind of thing and they just looked at me.' She stopped to munch on something crunchy. 'You off down south now?'

'Yep – back tomorrow. Don't hang around the office if there's nothing on. Go home and . . . do whatever it is you do.'

'I'm still checking odds and ends for now. I'll text you if I find anything interesting.'

'All right – thanks. See you Monday.'

'See ya.'

The line went plip and then the radio kicked back in with a serious-sounding female newsreader.

'. . . with the minister insisting that the teenager was only in his office for work experience. Now the weather: the cold spell is set to continue, with icy north easterly winds blowing across from the arctic. Temperatures could reach as low as minus five, with the added chill factor taking that down to minus ten or eleven. Better wrap up warm, or, better yet, stay indoors for the weekend. Geoff . . .'

Andrew flitted through the stations before turning the radio off. If it wasn't cheesy DJs, it was bad news or appalling music. He checked his watch. Despite his morning exploits taking far longer than he'd intended, he was still going to be on time for his appointment.

One motorway became another, before he skirted onto

the frost-dusted country roads. Overgrown hedges jutted onto the carriageway, scratching at the car's side as Andrew kept tight to the edge, with traffic zipping past in the opposite direction along the narrow, winding road.

It was mid-afternoon when he reached the outskirts of the village. This was what some people would call 'real' England: picturesque stone bridges, babbling streams, a tiny post office that doubled as a general store, pretty cottages with thatched roofs, snow shovelled to the side of the streets, and acres of fields, green in the summer but blanketed with a sprinkling of perfect white. The only surprise was that the village wasn't overrun by postcard photographers.

Andrew parked on a side street and began layering up: jumper, coat, gloves, hat and whatever else was in his boot. He was thirty miles south of Manchester, but away from the city and high in the hills, it was another climate.

Young children in grey and red school uniforms skipped along the pavements oblivious to the cold, throwing snow at one another, and sending the sound of giggles spilling through the otherwise empty streets. They'd soon learn. Snow was great for the young – snowmen, snowball fights, days off school, shovelling elderly people's paths for a fiver; it was all good while it lasted. The day a person knew they were a grown-up was when looking out of the window to see a wintery covering the word 'shite' popped into their mind, instead of 'wa-hey!'

Andrew crunched around the post office over the bridge and headed for the only cafe in the village. One combined post office and shop, one cafe, two pubs, obviously – it was

England, after all. Even in the middle of winter, the beer was probably still warm, too.

The sign outside the cafe promised an array of cakes and Andrew wasn't disappointed as he opened the door and walked into a gust of sweet-smelling sugary goodness.

Keira was already waiting for him, fingers cupped around a mug of cappuccino, still wearing her scarf. Flecks of sugar were stuck to her lips: proof, as if it were needed, your honour, of sneaky cake consumption. Her hair was in its usual bob but had started to grow out, with wispy blonde strands snaking towards her shoulders. She scratched at the birthmark by her lip and cracked into a smile.

'Am I late?' Andrew asked, turning to check the clock over the door.

'I'm early.'

He nodded towards the counter. 'What's good?'

'The Bakewell slices.'

'Is that why you've still got half of it around your lips?'

Keira blushed, wiping the crumbs away. 'I was saving it for later.'

Andrew ordered and then sat opposite her at the rickety table, dropping his mass of warm outer clothing on the floor next to him. The coffee machine whooshed and popped as they made small talk about his journey and the weather. Always the weather.

When the waitress arrived with his drink, cake and bill, Keira insisted on paying. 'It was me who invited you down,' she said. When the waitress had gone, she added: 'You look tired.'

'I've spent all day chasing around.'

'Want to talk about it?'

Andrew thought about it but shook his head. 'It's just work stuff.'

She gazed at him for a little too long, sensing something was wrong. He tried to put Braithwaite out of his mind, not to mention Iwan the brute.

The door tinkled behind, with a mother directing two young children and a pushchair inside. She settled them with colouring books in the corner, wrestled the pushchair closed without losing a finger, and headed for the counter, beaming.

Keira leant back in her seat, catching the other woman's eye. 'What are their names?' she asked.

This was the type of thing people could get away with in a small community. Ask about someone's kids in a city and the police would be carting you off before you could say, 'I'm not a paedo.'

'Mia and Ben,' the woman replied. She was rosy-cheeked and out of breath, trying to grapple a purse from her jacket pocket. In the corner, the children were passing crayons to each other.

'I bet they're loving the snow,' Keira said.

'You can say that again. I went out to help them build a snowman earlier but I was freezing and exhausted in no time. They could've stayed out all day if I hadn't made them go inside. Mia's school is shut because of the roads and Ben doesn't start until September. They grow up so quickly.'

'They should sleep well tonight.'

The woman snorted slightly. 'I'll believe that when I see it.'

Keira's gaze drifted to the corner again, smile fixed. Andrew wanted to say something but he still knew her too well, even if they'd only seen each other a handful of times in the past eight and a bit years. If they'd not been ready to start thinking about having children of their own, their house of cards wouldn't have come collapsing down. That's what he could tell himself anyway.

When the mother had returned to her children, Keira focused back on Andrew. 'Sorry.'

'It's fine.'

'I did have an ulterior motive for getting you down here on a Friday.'

'I figured.'

She giggled. 'Am I that obvious?'

'Go on.'

'You remember I told you about working for my father . . .' Andrew's face must have twitched with annoyance because her features hardened. '. . . I know you didn't get on, but the division he runs does a lot of good. If it wasn't for him—'

'I know.'

Keira nodded and they each had a drink to ease the momentary tension. 'I'm organising something this summer,' she continued. 'It's a careers fete, a sort of cross between the type of careers day they do in schools and a summer fete. We're going to have stalls, places for people to eat, perhaps some rides – that sort of thing. I've been getting together a list of people from various industries to talk to young people.'

'So you're going to con them with the promise of stalls and food, then try to get them thinking about their futures?'

'Exactly! I was hoping you might be able to help. I figure you know people, plus you're good at organising. You ran that club at uni – what was it?'

Ick. Andrew had forgotten about that, successfully wiping the memory as if it had never happened.

'I can't remember,' he said feebly.

Keira was spinning a finger in the air. 'That game thing. There were you and those other lads. You had to do all the room bookings and make sure everyone knew what was going on.'

Andrew puffed out a breath, shaking his head. 'Did I?'

'I think it was called the board and card-gaming society?'

How had he ever been married? Ever had sex?

Andrew nodded, trying to appear unconvinced. 'I don't really remember. It sort of rings a bell. Are you sure *I* organised it?'

Keira grinned. 'Don't you remember? You had all those boxes of cards under your bed. They had warlocks and dragons on. You used to book that room above the Unicorn and Golden Bell on a Thursday night, then you'd play games until the early hours . . .'

It dawned on Andrew that he had been as geeky as Damian Harris, but in a different technological age. He could have quite happily gone through the rest of his life never remembering that.

'You were really good at sorting things out,' Keira added.

'I don't know that many people in Manchester any longer. I could do with someone who knows the local area well enough to recommend a few potential speakers. We can only really cover expenses and perhaps a small fee.'

Talk about a bloody guilt trip. He'd dumped her all those years ago and, as punishment, he had somehow walked into doing something he didn't really want to do. Twice in one day!

Andrew nodded, trying to fake a smidgeon of enthusiasm. 'It sounds really good. I'm sure we can work something out.'

'You don't have to do it if you've got lots on.'

Yes! An out – an acknowledgement that helping wasn't compulsory.

But, no, Andrew's body was betraying him. Instead of making up something about having a busy summer ahead, he found himself shaking his head, with words coming out of his mouth that hadn't passed through his brain. What was going on?

'Oh, it's no problem,' Andrew's lips said. 'I'd be glad to help out.'

Glad? Where had that come from?

'I've got all the information on email. I'll forward it to you.'

Keira took out her phone and started tapping away. For Andrew, the only glimmer of hope was that he might go down with glandular fever when the planning phase kicked in. If he was *really* lucky, Thomas Braithwaite might dismember him. It would probably hurt – but would at least give him an excuse to not take part.

As his phone buzzed with the forwarded email, it dawned

on Andrew that it was this exact type of negativity for which he'd cursed himself when he'd wanted to avoid Gem's SOS call. Jenny would be peering over her glasses at him, reading his mind.

'Whatcha thinking about?' Keira asked.

'Huh?'

'You seemed lost for a moment.'

'Oh, er, nothing . . .'

'I do have a second favour to ask you . . .'

Yes! Another favour. Brilliant. Be positive! Bring on the new Andrew Hunter.

'You remember that camping trip we went on . . . ?'

Oh, God, no.

Andrew was panicking. He'd have loved to spend a weekend with his ex-wife. At any point in the last eight years, he'd have craved some time alone to explain what he'd done, if not why he'd done it. But camping?

'Do you mean that festival?' he replied, trying not to sound nervous.

'Right. You were really good at that outdoorsy stuff.'

Andrew burst out laughing. 'Are we remembering the same thing?'

Keira bit her bottom lip. 'Okay, you were rubbish – we both were – but I'm a bit stuck. I'm organising this outdoor living demonstration tomorrow—'

'In this weather?'

'It's complicated. It's an outdoor demonstration but we're hosting most of it *indoors*.'

'Right . . .'

'It's things like how to collect condensation to use as drinking water . . .'

'I have no idea how to do that.'

'Me neither but we've got groups of young people attending. There's someone else showing them how to start a fire from twigs—'

'Indoors?'

Keira shook her head. 'That bit's outdoors.'

'So it's an outdoors demonstration that's indoors, but with some bits outdoors.'

'Right. We've got a survivalist, someone else talking about trails, this plant expert to talk about what's edible, that sort of thing.'

Andrew was confused. 'What do you think I can do? Show the kids where to buy a big coat?'

Keira giggled. 'I've got something you can do.'

'Brewing up?'

'You can do that too if you want.' She reached forward, tugging on his sleeve, fingers brushing his, making eye contact. 'It'd mean a lot if you can help. I know it's short notice . . .'

How could he refuse now?

Andrew had no idea what it was she thought he was capable of. Of all the words people might use to describe him, 'outdoorsman' would be somewhere near the bottom of the list, close to 'optimist', 'action hero' and 'astronaut'.

He started to reply and then saw the truth. She *wanted* to spend time with him. They'd been making excuses for why meeting up wasn't a 'date' and this was another. They could spend an entire Saturday together and not have to call it anything other than one friend helping out another.

Andrew linked his fingers through hers and squeezed gently. 'It's not as if I've got anything else on tomorrow,' he said. 'Let's do it.'

23

THIRTEEN YEARS AGO

Andrew was delicately treading the boundary between being awake and asleep. The gentle in-out breathing next to him was almost certainly Keira's; the dragon he'd been fighting was probably imagined. Only probably, though. His calling could come at any time, just look at St George – and he had an entire flag named after him in the end.

He rolled over slightly, trying to rid his right arm of the pins and needles, without nudging Keira awake. His face was freezing but the rest of him was deliciously toasty. If any zen philosopher wanted to hear the sound of one hand clapping, then Andrew was giving him or her a demonstration, patting his fingers into his palm in an unsuccessful attempt to get some feeling into them.

Bloody hell, it was cold.

What was he thinking? The problem with the world was definitely pretty girls. If any of his male friends had asked if he wanted to spend four days in a field in order to see some bands he wasn't fussed about, he would have definitely said no. Keira batted her eyelids, put on that girlish voice of hers, and he crumbled in under a minute. 'Yes, of course I want to go.' Mud? No problem. A hundred and fifty quid I don't have? Don't worry – I'll find it. Sleeping in a tent? Of course – it's not as if we have a perfectly nice flat to stay in. He really should have built up some resistance to her by now.

Andrew opened his eyes properly and propped himself up on an elbow to watch her sleep, which *definitely* wasn't weird. Her nose twitched each time she breathed in, eyelids fluttering as she dreamed. The morning light was fighting through the heavy dark green canvas, but even in that dimness, she looked incredible.

And she liked him!

The cramped space suddenly became darker as something passed across the early morning sun, the shadow joined almost instantly by the tinkle of rain on tent. Wonderful – they were going to spend the day dodging showers. Even if they managed to do that, the ground would be a swamp by the evening – and they had two more days of this after today. The rain sploshed noisily before easing off and then starting again . . . which didn't sound like rain at all. Andrew stared at the left side of the tent where the sun-blocking cloud looked distinctly human-shaped.

Hang on a minute . . .

Andrew scrambled out of his sleeping bag like a drunken caterpillar with vertigo, trying to wriggle from its cocoon. He shivered his way into the area at the back of the tent where they'd dumped all of their stuff and undid the main zip, exposing his pasty bare chest and tatty pyjama bottoms to the field beyond. There was a kaleidoscope of coloured tents stretching as far as he could see, with smoke rising in the distance and the smell of barbecuing sausages drifting on the gentle breeze. The sky was blue, the sun was shining and it wasn't raining. Instead a lad with ruffled curly black hair was standing a metre away from Andrew, eyes closed, off his head, having a piss.

On their tent.

The young man was naked except for a pair of boxer shorts, which were currently around his ankles. His feet were covered in muddy sludge, with 'BeNDeR' written on his forehead in fluorescent orange ink and 'I love cock' sprawled across his chest. He'd certainly had a rougher night than Andrew, with friends who were clearly comedy geniuses, and had been sent off into the wild to find the toilets.

It was a difficult one to judge. On the one hand, Andrew *did* want to stop him from emptying his bladder over the place where they slept, he just didn't want to risk splash-back by getting any closer. It didn't appear as if the teenager was going to finish any time soon.

'Er, mate . . .' Andrew muttered.

Mr Piss's eyes fluttered open, as if he'd sleepwalked his way here and had just woken up. 'Whuuugh?'

'Can you stop weeing on our tent?'

The lad glanced down at his lower half, apparently realising for the first time what he was doing. 'Oh . . .'

He didn't stop.

'Sometime soon would be nice.'

'Er . . . yeah.' He started to crouch, trying to pull up his boxers, simultaneously giving Andrew a perfect view of his hairy arse and all the while continuing to urinate. He must have a bladder like a watermelon.

Eventually, Mr Piss's evacuation became a dribble. He mumbled something that might have been an apology, yanked his pants up, turned, and stumbled away, only to trip over a nearby guy rope and fall face-first into the muck. Because he wasn't covered in enough filth, he rolled onto his back, struggling to haul himself up, like an upside-down tortoise. It took almost a minute before he found his feet again, by which time he was splattered head to toe in mud. He turned in a circle, scratching his head, before pointing towards the nearby burger van and faltering in its general direction.

This was day two!

The early morning sun tickled Andrew's bare skin but he was still cold. Someone was playing a guitar in the distance, and a radio blared nearby. He checked his watch – quarter past-six – and wondered if guitar man had just woken up, or if he'd been pissing everyone off through the night. Any requests from the audience? Yes – shut the hell up.

Everywhere Andrew looked there was something going on: a line of dishevelled-looking girls padding their way towards the showers, towels and wash bags in hand; a drunken lad following them, hoisting a toilet roll in the air as he shouted 'I'm going for a shit!' A few tents over, a young man was slumped in a fold-up canvas chair, can of John Smith's in his lap, as a foil barbecue tray steamed on the dew-soaked grass in front of him.

Since Andrew and Keira had gone to bed in the early hours, tents had popped up on almost every patch of clear land – huge domes wedged into impossibly small spaces, with even tinier pop-up shelters next to them.

A seething heap of people living in squalor on top of one another, all because a band they'd barely heard of was going to belt out a song they wouldn't like from a stage they'd never get anywhere near.

Andrew felt a shuffling behind him and then Keira appeared, yawning and stretching. Her hair was all over the place, but, with the spaghetti strap of her teddy bear pyjama top hanging limply around her upper arm to expose a tantalising amount of tanned flesh, Andrew was still left open-mouthed.

She rubbed her eyes, managing half a smile, before rearranging her clothes.

Spoil sport.

'What time is it?' she asked through a yawn.

'Six fifteen.'

'Ugh. How long have you been up?'

'Not long.'

Andrew put on his hoody and unfolded their camp chairs, setting them outside, away from the puddle of urine. Keira joined him, still yawning, as she placed their camp stove on the ground, trying to find a flat patch of land.

'It looks like a refugee camp out here,' she said.

'Only we've paid a hundred and fifty quid for the privilege.'

She smiled and yawned again, taking in the rest of the enveloping scene around them. All across the campsite, the masses were beginning to wake, disturbed by the simmering noise and increasing light. The queue for the showers was already a dozen people long, with three times the number of people waiting for the toilets, each with a bog roll in hand. The wind changed slightly, wafting a light grey cloud over the top of the trees and sending the smell of burgers across to them. Andrew's stomach grumbled.

Keira was pouring water into the camping kettle they'd bought from Oxfam for three quid the previous weekend. 'Brew?' she asked.

'I think I need some food.'

She shrugged and set the kettle boiling. With the pitiful heat of the stove, it'd probably be around fifteen minutes before the water was anything like hot enough. She dropped two teabags into mugs and left them on the ground.

They relaxed in their seats, starting an impromptu yawning competition, before giggling themselves stupid.

'Are you going to cook?' she asked.

Andrew nodded at the tiny stove. 'I can barely manage beans on toast at home with a proper oven, let alone on that thing.'

'I thought you were an outdoors guru?'

'When did I ever say that?'

Keira snuggled into his arm, resting her head on his shoulder. 'That must be my other boyfriend, then.'

'Har-de-har.'

The lad with the John Smith's in his lap jumped awake as his sausages started to burn, sending dark smoke clouding into his face, and the whiff of charcoal drifting across the nearby tents. He jabbed at the tin-foil barbecue with a stick, rolling his breakfast onto a paper plate before noticing he was being watched.

He nodded at Andrew and Keira, grinning, before holding up his can of bitter. 'Want one?'

'Bit early for me,' Keira replied.

Andrew waved a sympathetic hand as the other lad tried to eat with his fingers, dropping a sausage into his lap with a clamour of oohing and aahing.

From nowhere, the grey cloud started to deposit a gentle patter of rain. There was blue sky in all four directions, the weather so localised that it seemed like it was only their field being dumped on. Andrew and Keira shuffled into the open flap of their tent, sitting on the matting inside as the tempo increased.

'Whatcha thinking about?' Keira asked, still holding onto Andrew's arm, head on his shoulder.

'I dunno . . . nothing really.'

'It must be something.'

'I suppose . . . I was just thinking that I'm happy. Everything here is ridiculous – it's filthy, there are people everywhere, it's noisy, I've hardly slept, the food's awful, it's going to rain on and off all day, but I don't really mind. It's nice.'

Keira didn't reply for a moment but he could feel her breathing. When she answered, her voice was soft, almost inaudible over the rain.

'Do you think we should get married?' she said.

'Sorry?'

'Not right now. I've got to do that rearranged exam in two weeks. After that.'

'Straight away?'

'More or less.'

'Where are we going to go?'

'I don't know. Gretna? Vegas? Somewhere easy. I can get us flights if we go abroad.'

'What about—?'

'I won't tell them. My mum will understand and my dad will get used to it eventually. Your parents will be fine. If we do it any other way, we'll spend ages trying to get mine on board and then haggling over the stupid things. Even if my dad is all right with it, which he won't be, he'd want to take over because he'd insist on paying.'

'I . . .'

Andrew didn't know what to say but Keira cut in anyway. 'It was only an idea.' She giggled, releasing his arm. 'I've just realised that this was the worst proposal in the history of proposals.'

'Is that what it was?'

'I suppose. I woke up and it was on my mind.'

Andrew put an arm around her as Keira nibbled on his ear, breath fluttering across his lobe. 'Well, in answer to your question, yes, I do think we should get married,' he said.

'I think you should ask me properly,' Keira replied.

'*Here?*'

'Why not?'

Well, there was the puddle of piss, but . . .

Without thinking, Andrew shuffled himself down, one foot on the canvas of the tent, his knee in the mud, rain sprinkling down his back. He took Keira's hand but she instantly burst out laughing.

'What?' he said.

'I don't know . . . it's just . . . okay, go on.'

Keira's short blonde hair was tucked behind her ear on one side, with a clump poking out at a sharp angle on the other. Her pyjama-top strap had slipped again and there was a smudge of dirt on her cheek that must have been there all night. She was biting her bottom lip, trying to stop herself from giggling, which only made Andrew want to laugh too.

Okay, deep breath, not a big deal, it's only the rest of your life. Go!

'Will you marry me?'

Andrew got the words out in one go, which was just as well because his heart suddenly lurched into action as it realised what he'd done.

'Of course I will.'

Keira hunched forward and pecked him on the lips. There was no ring, no joyous explosion of worlds colliding. Instead, in a muddy field, surrounded by half-asleep strangers clutching toilet rolls and cans of John Smith's, barely a metre from a puddle of urine, they got engaged. Andrew felt the spark surging across him as they kissed, knowing they were going to spend the rest of their lives together – and nothing was going to change that.

24

SATURDAY

Andrew jolted awake, heart thumping. Doof-doof-doof. Wake up!

He'd been back in that muddy field, Keira's hand in his, their lips brushing. They were going to spend the rest of their lives together . . . and then they hadn't.

Rain was licking the window, tip-tapping as it had on the canvas all those years ago. Andrew tried to blink himself awake but there was still the rainbow of tents in front of him, the smell of burgers, the sizzle he felt when he and Keira touched. None of it was in the room, replaced by untucked heavy sheets, grubby skirting boards, the stain above the mirror.

Where was he?

He remembered Braithwaite, Iwan, driving . . . and then Keira had asked him to do something and he'd said yes. The part of him that had hardened since they'd separated had been in the back of his mind, grumbling and spreading negativity as it always did, but he couldn't say no to her.

He was in a bed and breakfast room above the pub in her village.

Alone.

It wasn't unusual for him to wake up by himself but

Andrew felt the loneliness and sense of loss more than usual. He and Keira had spent the previous afternoon together and now she wanted a whole day with him.

Sort of.

He rolled over, reaching for his phone to check his messages and emails. There was the usual barrage of spam: how many blue pills did he want? Did he want a Rolex for a fiver? Had he been recently injured in an accident that wasn't his fault? Tips for 'the one and only way to satisfy her'. Delete, delete, delete, delete, until he reached Keira's email. She'd gone back to being Keira Chapman, instead of Hunter, and the last name jabbed away at his chest.

Andrew called his own flat, waiting for four rings until it plipped through to his answer machine, and then trying again. And again. And again. At the seventh attempt, it was picked up with a nervous-sounding 'hello'.

'Gem, it's me.'

'Who's me?'

'Andrew.'

'Oh, sweetie, I told you last night I'd be fine by myself. You go and have fun.'

'I wanted to make sure you and Rory were all right.'

'Of course. Your little friend popped over last night and—'

'Who?'

'That pretty one you were with.'

It took Andrew a moment to realise who she meant. 'Jenny visited?'

'Oh, we had a right little chinwag. She's *lovely*, Andrew.

If she wasn't so out of your league, I'd be saying you should—'

'What did you talk about?'

'This and that. She helped me take Rory out for a walk. I keep telling Reg at bingo that young people aren't all bad. He thinks they're all hooligans.'

'Did she just drop round?'

'She even brought me a small sherry. I don't know how she knew it was my drink but we had a fantastic evening. Even Rory stayed up. Honestly, Andrew, I don't know where you found her but she's a little star. Make sure you hang onto her.'

Andrew wasn't sure what to say. He was going to ask Craig to visit his flat that day to help take Rory for a walk but there was no need now. He'd told Jenny he was staying in Cheshire for the night and would be on email, but hadn't asked her to visit Gem. It felt strange, his worlds colliding, almost like an invasion. What had they spent all evening talking about? Him? And why hadn't Jenny told him she wanted to keep Gem company?

Gem was oblivious to the awkwardness. 'I'm going home at lunchtime,' she said. 'The man called last night to say he'd finished doing whatever it was he was doing with my electrics. I hope he's not moved anything around – I had everything exactly as I liked it. Still, if he had to move things, he had to move things. Jenny's popping over to help. I don't know why I brought so much stuff, I've not taken half of it out of the bag. Rory's been enjoying your steaks. Anyway, Susan from bingo reckons her daughter gets ten per cent off at Argos and I was looking at a new kettle anyway. Are you coming round for lunch tomorrow?'

She'd packed so many different topics into what was close to a single sentence that it took Andrew a few moments to realise he'd been asked something.

'Um . . . yes . . .'

'Jenny said she'll help me clear out the freezer. Some of it will have spoiled but Reg's grandson works at Iceland and can get me a deal. Then there's the little ginger kid from over the way that's always knocking. He can get all sorts – beef joints, liver, sausages. I had some lamb shanks from him the other week . . .'

Gem continued talking but Andrew couldn't get past the fact that Jenny was apparently spending the day with his aunt. What was going on? It would be nice for Gem to have some company and help but he'd never known Jenny show that much interest in anyone.

'. . . anyway, dear, you go and enjoy yourself. I'll see you tomorrow. I'll put something special on.'

Andrew said goodbye and thought about calling Jenny. He would have done if it wasn't for the fact his aunt had been chattering for over half an hour. Realising he was going to be late, Andrew quickly changed into the clothes he'd been wearing the day before and hurried downstairs to his car, excited to be spending a day with his ex-wife.

As Andrew expected, Keira's activity day had been organised with military precision. The hall was a few miles from the village where she lived, with an army of volunteers helping to direct people where to park, register children, brew up, and fulfil any number of other roles. Stands were dotted around the perimeter of the hall, with tables and chairs set up for the various events. A large marquee had been erected, with a handful of pop-up pagodas spaced around the car park ready for the outdoor demonstrations.

Keira was in the centre of the hall, bundled up in a warm jumper, tight jeans and boots, fingers cupped around a steaming mug.

She didn't notice Andrew at first, turning in a circle to make sure everything was in place. When her eyes settled on him, they sparkled and she beamed in the way they used to. She glanced at her watch.

'I'm not late,' Andrew said.

'Nearly.'

'I got trapped on the phone with Gem.'

'Your aunt? How is she?'

'Still in that flat.' Andrew didn't want to talk about it. 'You've done an incredible job here.'

'We're still missing a few things. I've been on the phone all morning but there was a crash on the M6 and one of our couriers is stuck in traffic. Mrs Harris was supposed to be here to sort out lunches but she's gone down with rabies, or something, so—'

'*Rabies?*'

Keira grinned. 'I'm joking. She's ill anyway.'

'It looks like you've got enough people here. How did you persuade so many to give up their time?'

She shrugged. 'Bribery and blackmail, mostly.'

Andrew knew the truth: she could get most people to do what she wanted if she asked.

Keira linked her arm through his and led him towards the back of the hall, where a group of people Andrew didn't recognise were pouring orange squash into a giant vat. She introduced him as her 'old friend from Manchester', which wasn't untrue, though it did miss out the 'former husband' part. For a while, it was like a glorified coffee morning, until she led him around the various stalls. The array of people she'd roped in was astonishing. Someone had flown in from Sweden to explain survival techniques; a man had come up from London to talk about how to spot edible food in a forest; a couple from Cornwall were giving an orienteering demonstration.

None of it was particularly Andrew's thing, nor Keira's from what he knew of her, but that only made it more impressive that she'd put together something for those who were interested. Parents were stopping on the road to drop off their children, with a general hubbub building as the hall and marquee filled with people. Keira probably had things to do but she stuck with Andrew, introducing him to the other adults, while finding a smile and a 'thank you' for everyone.

'Who are the kids?' Andrew asked, as a group of young-sters climbed out of a mud-spattered once-white minibus and headed towards the free biscuit and squash table.

'They're from various communities around the north west. Some have had problems with their parents and been left effectively homeless, others are known through poverty charities. We've tried not to be too exclusive, so there are some high-achievers here as well. We contacted schools and charities across the region and let them nominate young people they thought might benefit. It's not just about the activities, we're splitting everyone up to make them all work together. There'll be youngsters with straight As who are in all the top sets at school working alongside kids who've not been to school in a while. It's the second time we've done this. We do different themes – late last year was creativity: art, writing, that sort of thing. We're doing a sportier version in the spring when the weather gets better.'

'And this is all funded by your dad?'

'Not him personally, the charitable division he manages. They give away millions every year.' She squeezed his arm. 'Come on, let's not talk about my father. I've not shown you what you're doing yet.'

Andrew was hoping she'd forgotten – he would have been perfectly happy trailing around after her all day.

She took him past the fire-starting station, waved hello to the man who could perform the miracle of turning condensation into drinking water, and kept going until they were underneath one of the small awnings at the edge of the car park. There were a dozen stools arranged around a ready-made campfire next to a row of barbecue tools.

'You want me to cook?' Andrew asked disbelievingly.

'It's not that hard.'

'Don't you remember when we went camping last time? I must be the only person in the history of food who's burned baked beans.'

'This is the final outdoor station,' Keira said. 'We've got people explaining where to find food and what's safe to eat, plus someone telling them about how to gather the correct type of wood for a fire and how to light it. This is the fun bit – tell them about bacteria in lake water and why you have to boil it, that sort of thing. We've got a couple of cool boxes full of burgers and sausages, so all you need to do then is chat about whatever you fancy and show them how to cook slowly enough to get rid of the pink on the inside and avoid burning the food. Simple – you get to be the hero who cooks for all the kids.'

She linked her fingers into his and Andrew felt the tingling flashback to that campsite from thirteen years ago. It really was an easy task and he wasn't as bad a cook as he liked to pretend. He turned to face her, gazing into her eyes and, for a moment, Andrew thought they were going to kiss properly for the first time in what felt like a lifetime. There was a moment of hesitation and then Keira pushed herself onto tiptoes and pecked him on the forehead.

'You'll be great,' she said. 'I've got to go and check on a few things but if you need a hand then shout up. I'll be around.'

She didn't lie.

Andrew found himself enjoying the morning far more than he'd thought possible. The children were full of enthusiasm, asking questions and often answering each other's. Every time Andrew glanced up, Keira was there in the background, half watching him, half keeping an eye on everything else.

Time flew by and, after a couple of hours, everyone was ready for a break, with kids and adults massing into the hall in an attempt to warm up again. Andrew wanted to talk to Keira but the Swedish guy was chewing her ear off, being all blond and smiley.

The arsehole.

Andrew hovered nearby, wondering if the man would stop wittering anytime soon, but he was laughing away about something or other, probably IKEA or Volvos, and Keira was playing along.

With nothing better to do, Andrew drifted into the marquee outside, getting himself some tea and then finding a corner where he could be by himself. He was watching Keira effortlessly play the room when he jumped as someone tapped him on the shoulder. Andrew spun around, stepping backwards in alarm at the sight of the figure.

Iwan's lips were pressed into something close to a smile. He nodded towards the car park. 'A word.'

25

Andrew was so shocked to see Braithwaite's right-hand man that he followed him without question until they were standing close to a row of stinking wheelie bins on the edge of the car park.

'Who's the blonde?' Iwan asked, nodding towards the marquee. Keira had escaped from the Swede and was chatting to a group of children.

'What?'

'The tart you keep staring at. Have you got a bird on the go, or are you just a creepy stalker?'

'She's, er—'

'Don't matter to me, like. Some of my best friends are creepy stalkers.'

Andrew turned away from Keira, back to Iwan. 'What are you doing here?'

'Mr Braithwaite's concerned.'

'What are you on about?'

'He woke up this morning feeling a little unhappy with how things are going, worrying about the potential consequences.'

'How did you know where I was?'

'Are you listening to me?'

Iwan's lips were arched into a tight smile. He'd been wearing a suit the previous day but was now in loose-fitting jeans and a jumper, with a pair of brown loafers. Like a slimy politician on Sunday television, giving an interview at home and trying to pretend he was an actual human being.

'How did you know where I was?' Andrew repeated.

'I told you – Mr Braithwaite's concerned.'

'I don't care. How did you know I was here?'

'Telepathy. Now, Mr Braithwaite wants to know what's going on with our jeweller friend.'

'Are you following me?'

'Your name is Andrew Hunter, no middle name. You're thirty-five years old and drive a blue Toyota. You own an apartment in Beetham Tower, Manchester – very nice – and work as a private investigator. You're divorced with no children. Your parents are—'

Andrew pressed his forearm into Iwan's chest, instantly regretting it as the bigger man pushed him back, danger in his eyes.

'You want to go?' he dared him.

Andrew straightened his top, glancing towards the marquee. Keira had left the group of children and was out of view. He turned back to Iwan. 'You know who I am, so what?'

'You walked into the lion's den yesterday, sunshine. Mr Braithwaite was kind enough to welcome you and even pass on certain pieces of information. As I told you, he's now concerned about your progress.'

'Do you expect me to call you every time I do something?' Andrew said. 'Even if I was going to do that, you never gave me a phone number.'

'If Mr Braithwaite wants something, he'll come to you.'

'So what does he want? What do *you* want?'

'As I said, he's concerned. He'd like to know what you've discovered about our mutual jeweller friend.'

'I've not found out anything – I've been busy. I have a life away from work.'

Iwan tilted his head, screwing his mouth into something that was a cross between a smile and a grimace. 'That's what Mr Braithwaite feared. He feels he's trusted you and brought you into his inner circle. He expects results.'

Andrew took a step towards the hall but Iwan grabbed his wrist, pulling him back to the bins.

'We're not done.'

It hurt, but Andrew twisted his wrist free. 'I'm not standing for this. I'm not having anything to do with Sampson today, I'm working here with children – and I don't appreciate being followed.'

'Why involve yourself then?'

Andrew didn't have an answer. For himself, it was all about finding the truth for Fiona Methodist and getting justice for the young couple that had had so much in common with him and Keira. Yet, while he hadn't expected Iwan to turn up with his demands, he had known there was going to be a consequence to visiting Braithwaite.

A flicker of movement caught his attention, and his eyes glanced around Iwan to where Keira was drifting across the car park.

'Aye, aye,' Iwan muttered under his breath.

Keira was smiling nervously between them. 'Hello.'

Iwan stuck out a paw before Andrew could say anything. 'Pleased to meet you, er . . .'

'Keira. I'm organising the event, and you are . . . ?'

'Iwan – one of Andrew's friends from Manchester. It's an absolute pleasure to meet you, Keira.' His tone was softer, definite hints of Irish in his accent. 'I was just saying what a fabulous event this is, without realising it was you who'd arranged it. It's so terrific that people are giving back to their communities. It's a tough place out there for kids nowadays.'

Keira glanced at Andrew, slightly confused, before turning back to Iwan.

'Oh, don't mind me,' Iwan added. 'Andrew was looking for a little company and I'm only passing through. I'll be off shortly.'

'Right, um . . .' She turned to Andrew. 'We start again in just over ten minutes.'

'No worries, I'm just saying goodbye.'

She nodded before walking back to the marquee, hands in her pockets, not looking back.

'Keira . . .' Iwan said, rolling the syllables around his mouth. 'I know that name. *Keira* . . .'

'Just go,' Andrew replied.

Iwan clicked his fingers, making a ridiculously loud crack. 'The ex-wife. Well, well, well, isn't that a turn-up?'

'Get lost.'

'Are you hoping to get everything back on track with her? Is that why you're wasting your time with this bunch of losers?' He blew out loudly. 'Actually I don't blame you – I'd do anything for a go on *that*.'

He nodded towards the marquee but Andrew dropped a shoulder, angling forward and cracking the taller man in the chest with his knuckles. He drew back his left fist, rage seething through him, but Iwan had barely moved, reaching out and *squeezing* his wrist.

He squinted down, grinning as broadly as Andrew had seen him. *'Really?'*

Andrew gripped the fingers of both hands into fists, desperate to fight back, wanting to use his anger. It took a moment but his head won. There was only going to be one outcome if he started anything and it wasn't going to be pretty for him. The wrath slipped, his fingers loosening, before Iwan released him.

'Good boy.'

Iwan reached forward and patted him on the head. Andrew pulled away, batting the hand off as his tormentor laughed.

'Mr Braithwaite would appreciate knowing what's happening *before* it happens.'

'I don't know how to contact him.'

'And I told you that we'll be in contact. Mr Sampson serves an important function in the community but that doesn't mean he's untouchable. If he has been up to anything behind Mr Braithwaite's back, then it would be considered a courtesy if we were to find out before you tell anyone else.'

'Fine.'

'And he would also appreciate some progress.'

'I'm off for the weekend – I have things to do.'

'Good for you. I'll be in touch.'

Andrew watched as Iwan swaggered towards the road. The big man waved over his shoulder and then climbed into a shiny black diesel-chugging vehicle and roared away. Andrew continued watching until the car disappeared around the corner and then walked back to the marquee, where Keira was waiting a little inside the door.

She nodded towards the road. 'Who was that?'

'Just . . . something to do with work. I didn't know he was coming.'

'You've gone white.'

It took Keira to say it for Andrew to recognise that his heart was racing. He held his hands behind his back to stop her noticing they were shaking. She stared at him for a couple of seconds too long before nodding towards the main hall.

'You've been great this morning. All the kids love you. These sessions are part of a pilot scheme and we've had a few people from the council milling around . . .'

'I didn't realise.'

'I didn't want to make you nervous but they've gone now, smiles all over their faces.' She was beaming with excitement. 'They were talking about helping us to expand into Lancashire and Greater Manchester, perhaps wider.'

'That's great.'

She was bouncing on her heels, reaching for his hand that was thankfully not trembling any longer. 'We've still got a few minutes, let's go get a biscuit.'

Andrew let her lead him, enjoying the warmth of her fingers against his. He couldn't remember the last time he'd seen her this happy. Despite her history degree, she'd always wanted to work with young people. At one point after they'd got married, she'd talked about doing a post-graduate diploma to get into teaching. The problem, as with anything, was the money. As a couple, they couldn't afford it, and then they'd started to think about children of their own. This job gave her the opportunity to work with young people who needed help and she was clearly good at it.

They continued into the hall and were on the way towards the refreshment stall when Andrew realised Keira had stopped. Her fingers slipped from his, leaving him standing by himself. Andrew followed her line of sight and felt his heart flutter. Iwan was one thing but the man glaring at him was another matter entirely: the person of his nightmares, the reason why he and his ex-wife didn't have the life they had promised to each other.

Andrew's eyes met those of Keira's father for the briefest second, before Edgar Chapman uttered two utterly terrifying words.

'Hello, Andrew.'

26

Andrew had never been able to explain the magnetism of Keira's father. It was something that couldn't be taught, an intrinsic part of the man's make-up that made him the centre of everything. When he walked into a room, people turned to look. When he spoke, they listened. He had a build similar to Iwan's but it felt different because he was older.

He and Andrew were opposites in so many ways. Andrew was instantly forgettable, a normal face among a sea of mediocrity. Even Aunt Gem thought people were out of his league but Keira was the person who'd seen him as something else. They'd met in bizarre circumstances, become engaged in marginally stranger, and then run away to get married. They were made for each other and he'd never find better.

Keira's father continued to stare at Andrew. He was always cleanly shaven, with a full head of swept-back black and grey hair, and bristling dark eyes that could switch from welcoming to dangerous in an instant. Andrew had rarely been welcomed by them and they were certainly not pleased to see him now.

'It's been a long time,' Mr Chapman added.

Andrew nodded, unsure what to say.

'What is it? Eight years? Nine?'

'Yes.'

He demanded a specific answer: 'Eight or nine?'

Keira stepped between them. 'Daddy.'

Andrew cowered under his former father-in-law's glare, breaking the gaze and staring at the wall, the window, the vat of orange squash. Any-sodding-where.

'A word.'

Mr Chapman was thankfully talking to his daughter, not Andrew, who could only watch as they moved into the back corner. Father towered over daughter, hands out of his pockets. Andrew couldn't hear a word but the man's body language said it all. He pushed himself onto tiptoes to appear taller; he arched his shoulders forward, trapping Keira in the cramped corner; he nodded sideways towards Andrew; raised both hands palms upwards. He wasn't happy.

Keira didn't cower, maintaining eye contact and nodding along, not agreeing but not backing down either.

Around them, the break was coming to an end, with groups of youngsters drifting towards their next activities and coffee cups being stacked next to the sink. Andrew glanced through the window to where he was supposed to be working. There were already kids looking back to the main building, wondering where he was. He had to go but he was fixed to the spot. Other people had started to notice Keira in the corner, perhaps not realising the man in the suit standing over her was her father.

They'd been talking too quietly to be heard but Keira suddenly raised her voice, patting her father in the chest as she stepped away. 'I can look after myself, Daddy.'

She sounded annoyed, heading for the marquee, where Andrew cut her off.

'Are you okay?' he asked.

They glanced behind, to where Mr Chapman was making his way out of the main door, watching them over his shoulder.

'He's just worried,' Keira replied. She was close to tears, her voice wavering, eyes beginning to go red. 'After everything that happened, he's worried that I don't know what I'm doing.'

She dabbed a tissue underneath each eye, smiling thinly, breaking Andrew's heart. This was his fault.

'He doesn't want to see me hurt again,' she added.

Andrew started to reply but Keira was suddenly full of big, forced smiles. She peered over his shoulder towards the stupid Swedish man with whatever stupid problem he had. She squeezed Andrew's hand before heading into the hall. She put a hand on the Arsehole's shoulder. 'How can I help . . . ?'

27

SUNDAY

The four locks clunked open and then Gem opened her front door. She was wearing her Sunday best: a long pink dress covered in yellow and blue flowers that was probably older than Andrew, along with matching flat sandals. 'I thought you said half past two,' she frowned.

'It *is* half-two.'

Gem turned around to check the clock. 'You were brought up to be early.' She headed inside, leaving Andrew to take off his shoes and relock the door. The kitchen smelled of roast dinner, making Andrew's mouth water.

'Is everything working?' he asked.

Gem flicked the kitchen light on and off, as if to prove the point. 'He said it was something to do with the wiring. I hope he didn't charge too much.'

'Don't worry about it – as long as everything's working.'

She moved across to a saucepan, peering over her shoulder and talking while she stirred. 'Do you remember Douglas from the legion?'

Andrew sat at the kitchen table, holding a hand down to ruffle Rory's ears. 'I've never been to the legion.'

'But you know Douglas.'

'I really don't.'

'Anyway, it was his grandson's christening this morning, so he picked me up and we went to church. You'll never guess who I saw there.'

'Who?'

'Guess.'

'Gem . . .'

And off she went. Andrew spent a largely frustrating two hours listening to Gem's stories about what so-and-so at the legion was up to, or the latest rumours from bingo. He did his best to um and arr in the right places, slipping Rory a few pieces of lamb when he could. The pug lay at Andrew's feet, apparently bored with the topic of conversation too. This was the reality of life: people living in their own little worlds and finding happiness from those around them. It dawned on Andrew that he could scoff all he liked but he didn't have this. If it wasn't for Jenny in the office and his clients, he would go days without talking to anyone. Of the two of them, who was the most pathetic – the woman who looked on the bright side of everything and had friends all over; or the man with the money still trailing around after a woman he'd dumped years before?

'How's your little friend?' Gem asked as Andrew switched back into the conversation.

'Who?'

'Jenny, of course. She was round here yesterday, sitting where you are, telling me all about what's going on in her life.'

'What about it?'

'Oh, nothing. Just about her parents, her boyfriend.'

She never told Andrew about those things.

'You've spent more time with her than I have,' Andrew replied. 'I've not seen her since Thursday.'

'You really should think about settling down—'

'Gem—'

'Find a nice woman, someone who knows how to cook. I'm sure there are plenty of women out there who'd like that flat of yours.'

Andrew leant back, scaring poor Rory, as he squeezed the bridge of his nose and closed his eyes, wanting to be somewhere else. 'We've been through this.'

Gem was oblivious. 'I know, I know – I just want you to be happy. You're not getting any younger.'

'Thanks.'

'Take it from me, you don't want to be by yourself when you get to my age. Reg's next-door neighbour has a daughter who's in her thirties. I can put a word in if you want?'

'Please don't do that.'

'I'm only trying to help. She's very pretty, well apart from the nose but Reg says she used to play rugby when she was younger. I'm sure she'd like you, though. Why wouldn't she?'

Andrew let her continue for a few minutes until he couldn't take it any longer, interrupting with: 'Wasn't it Reg who knew the person that redid your wiring in the first place?'

Gem seemed annoyed at being cut off. She'd finished eating and rearranged her knife and fork on the plate so they were in line with each other.

'What about it?'

'I'd like to speak to the person who did it.'

'Why?'

'Because if he's putting people in danger, someone should say something.'

She stood, picking up her plate and carrying it to the sink, keeping her back to him. 'He's just a young lad trying his best. Everyone makes mistakes.'

'You can't make mistakes when you're doing a job like that, otherwise people get hurt. I'd still like a word. Who is he?'

Gem returned to the table, reaching across for Andrew's well-scraped plate, not looking him in the eye. 'Don't you go worrying yourself.'

'Kevin something – that's what you told me last time.'

She put his plate in the sink and started to run the water. 'I'll wash up,' Andrew said.

'Oh no you won't – you're a guest. You go and sit in the living room. I think there's some car racing on the telly.'

'What's Kevin's last name?'

'I don't remember.'

'I could go and ask Reg.'

Gem spun around, hands covered in soapy water. 'You'll do no such thing, Andrew Hunter. It's *my* flat and I'm telling you to leave things alone. I'm not as incapable as you think – now go in the other room and sit down.'

'I don't think you're incapable.'

She turned back to the sink, ignoring him.

Andrew peered down at Rory, who offered some doe-eyed sympathy, before plonking his head on the floor again. With little other option, Andrew traipsed through to the living room, where Gem's collection of tat seemed untouched. He flopped into the dog-scratched armchair and closed his eyes, knowing that hardly any of the weekend had gone as he'd wanted.

He felt Rory trot in and begin sniffing at his feet, before settling. In the kitchen, Gem was singing a Buddy Holly song out of tune. Andrew wondered what Keira was up to. He should probably message her but the spectre of her father hung over them both.

As he opened his eyes, Andrew felt himself drawn to a small stack of papers next to a snow globe from Vienna, a place that Gem wouldn't be able to pick out on a map. Andrew stood, glancing through the gap into the kitchen to see his aunt starting to dry up, still in full voice. He crossed the room and started to sort through the pile. Gem wasn't quite a hoarder but she wasn't far off. The pile had mail from months back: bills; catalogues; flyers from supermarkets and the Bargain Booze around the corner; a voting registration form; two postcards from Italy and another from Spain; an invitation to the church coffee morning; more bills; a bank statement; and, finally, a handwritten invoice from the person who'd done a hatchet job on the wiring.

The handwriting was abysmal, worse than Andrew's, with the numbers and letters blending into one enormous, barely readable scrawl. After peeping into the kitchen again, Andrew used his phone to take a photo of the bill and then arranged everything into roughly the way it had been. As he turned, Andrew noticed Rory staring at him accusingly from the floor.

He crouched and stroked the dog's back. 'You're not going to tell on your Uncle Andrew, are you, pal?'

Rory turned around, burying his head underneath the seat. Andrew's weekend had been such a write-off that even the dog had turned against him.

In the kitchen, Andrew apologised to his aunt for leaving early, saying that he had a few things to do for work before Monday. She fussed and protested, before letting him go with a hug, a kiss on the cheek, and a reminder that Reg's next-door neighbour's former rugby-playing daughter with the dodgy nose was single if he changed his mind.

Outside, Andrew checked the photograph, just managing to piece together the information. Kevin Leonard had charged two hundred and fifty quid for the privilege of wrecking the electrics in Gem's house. Andrew had no idea where she'd found the money but it had been signed off as 'cash – paid'.

He flicked through the dialled numbers in his phone until he found the one for the electrical company he'd paid to fix everything. After speaking to the person who'd put everything back together, Andrew was seething. The man told him that Kevin's botch-job was so bad, the flat was a 'fire waiting to happen'. Technically, Kevin *had* rewired – but he'd used cheap material and failed to earth it properly in the kitchen.

Andrew hung up, returning to the photograph until he'd deciphered the electrician's address and checked it against the map on his phone. He strode around the housing block, wanting to talk himself out of confronting the cowboy elec-trician, only to work himself up further.

He could still feel the twinge in his wrist from where Iwan had squeezed it; still feel the humiliation at being patted on the head; that emasculation as Keira's father marched her into a corner and told her exactly what he thought of her spending time with him.

The uselessness of not being able to stand up for himself.

By the time he was back at his car, Andrew could barely breathe properly. He wasn't an angry person, didn't pick fights, didn't look for trouble, yet there were legions of people who wanted to demean him. He might not be able to match Iwan physically, not to mention his former father-in-law. Even those kids on the roundabout close to Joe with the shoes' flat had taken the piss out of him. They were one thing, but this little shit, Kevin Leonard, couldn't be allowed to keep putting people's lives at risk, let alone charge them for the privilege.

Andrew stormed away on foot, crossing through the nearby park and cutting into the adjoining housing blocks. He knew *exactly* where Kevin lived: on the scroatish estate that had exploded into riots the previous year. By the time he reached Kevin's street, Andrew was almost running. He weaved around the parked cars, checking both sides of the road until he found the right number. He pounded on the door with his right fist, the noise echoing along the deserted street.

Thump-thump-thump-thump-thump.

Low grey clouds hung over the street, threatening to rain but not quite managing it. The weather forecaster's apocalyptic predictions of cold hadn't come true; instead Manchester was looking as it always did. A car grumbled to life on the next street over, the exhaust flaring loudly.

Thump-thump-thump-thump-thump.

A man's voice sounded from inside. 'All right, all right.'

The door opened to reveal a weasel of a man: pinched nose; stubble; twitching eyes that settled on a spot above Andrew's head. He was somewhere in his early twenties, wearing a Scooby-Doo T-shirt. The house stank of cannabis, tobacco and stale pizza. Andrew didn't exactly tower over him, but he was taller and brawnier.

'Who are you?' the man asked.

Andrew stepped forward until he was in the doorway. 'You Kevin Leonard?'

'Who's asking?'

'You rewired my aunt's flat and did such a bad job, it could have caught fire.'

Kevin plucked a can of Stella from a table next to the door, taking a swig. 'Piss off, did I.'

Andrew held up his phone. 'I've got the receipt with your name and address. You charged her two hundred and fifty-quid and could've killed her.'

He stepped fully into the house, making Kevin stumble slightly. The smaller man edged backwards, still holding his beer can. 'What about it?'

'I want you to give her back the money. An apology would be nice, too.'

Kevin laughed. 'Yeah, right, mate. You high?'

'Are you sorry?'

'For what? It's not my fault she lives in a shit-heap. Old people deserve what they get anyway, sitting on all that money, getting in the way. If that place had caught fire, I'd have been doing everyone a favour.' A sneer appeared on Kevin's face as he nodded at the door. 'Now piss off.'

Andrew didn't move, continuing to stare.

'Wanna be the big man, do you?' Kevin said, having another swig from the can.

'Give her back the money.'

'Want to make me?'

'If I have to.'

'What are you going to do about it?'

The words were out of Andrew's mouth before he'd thought about them. 'Go to trading standards.'

In the history of threats, it had to be the lamest.

For a moment, Kevin held Andrew's gaze before he burst out laughing. 'Christ, I thought you were going to try to beat me up. Trading standards?'

He had a point.

Kevin stepped forward, laughing in Andrew's face. 'You do that, pal. I'll tell you what, I've got a Yellow Pages out the back, I'll find you the number. You can use my phone. How about I go round there and offer her some energy-saving light bulbs? Twenty quid a pop – special offer – she'll lap them up. I know the sort that'll buy anything if you tell them they're getting a deal.'

Andrew lunged forward in fury, shoving Kevin in the chest and sending the beer can tumbling to the floor. He might have been bigger, perhaps stronger, but Andrew was no fighter. Kevin weaved sideways and cracked a punch into his jaw. The blow wasn't hard but it caught Andrew by surprise, making his head snap to the side. He stumbled into the table, keeping his balance but unable to avoid the second punch that thumped into his temple.

Kevin was dancing on the spot, giving an Ali shuffle as

he whooped in delight; fists high, like a boxer. 'Come on then.'

Neither of the blows had hurt anything other than Andrew's pride. He threw himself forward but had no idea what he was doing. The other man dodged left, kicking out a leg and catching Andrew painfully in the knee, cackling to himself.

'I could do this all day. Come on.'

Andrew was embarrassed. What the hell was he doing?

'Are you going to return my aunt's money?'

'No.'

It wasn't even about the cash: it was the principle, the fact that good people shouldn't be taken advantage of.

Andrew opened the front door again. 'Fine – I'll tell the police, trading standards, Citizens Advice, the safety council – anyone who'll listen.'

Kevin was still bouncing from foot to foot, shadow-boxing with added sound effects, as if he was whacking a punchbag. 'You do that.'

Andrew let himself out, hoping no one he knew had seen him, Kevin's joyous laughter ringing in his ears as he hurried along the street. He was such a wimp.

28

MONDAY

Jenny was already at the office when Andrew arrived. She peered over her glasses at him, sipping a cup of tea as he hustled through the door, trying to escape the cold and rain. 'You look like you've been fighting,' she said.

'I've not.'

'Well, you know what they say – you're either a lover or a fighter, so if you're not a fighter, that must mean . . .'

Andrew ignored her, heading for the already made steaming cup of tea on his desk. He'd filled himself full of painkillers but his head was still pounding. More than any physical pain, he felt embarrassed. If he couldn't defend his aunt against Kevin, or stand up for himself against Iwan or Keira's father, then what was the point?

'It feels like ages since I last saw you,' Jenny added.

Andrew logged onto the computer system, waiting as it went through its usual process of thinking about whether it wanted to boot up.

'How was your weekend?' she persisted.

'Okay. How was Gem?'

'She was good – excited to get home. She told me about all the things she's done in that flat, about her family and growing up. It was interesting. She wanted to cook me tea but I ended up doing it for her and Rory.'

That was it – no explanation for why she'd appeared at Andrew's flat, no hint of anything being inappropriate, because, in Jenny's world, it was perfectly normal to turn up at your boss's house while he was away and spend a day with his aunt. Sometimes her quirkiness was endearing; too many times it was just strange.

Andrew didn't get an opportunity to follow it up because she was already onto the next subject.

'. . . after I got home on Saturday night, my boyfriend dropped by unannounced, wanting to stop for the weekend.'

His computer finally got its arse in gear and Andrew logged into his emails. Jenny had forwarded him links to a list of articles about Thomas Braithwaite.

> Unions last night condemned a move that will put three hundred people out of work in the Hull area.
>
> A spokesman for Braithwaite Industries, which owns a manufacturing factory in Kingswood, confirmed that consultation had begun on a plan to make the entire workforce redundant before the end of the year.
>
> Unite Secretary, Ken Walters, held a four-hour meeting with the plant's owners on Monday. He said: 'This is a plan that will devastate the local economy. The truly appalling thing is that this is a factory that actually makes money. Profit last year was close to £300,000 but, when this was pointed out, the response was that the amount wasn't enough.
>
> The Braithwaite Industries spokesman refused to

confirm that figure, and would not comment on speculation that the move was down to planning permission being granted for a new factory being built in Sunderland.

A statement read: 'Management would like to thank the Hull workforce for their hard work and tireless dedication. Unfortunately, tough decisions have to be made in harsh economic times, and it is with much regret that we confirm the necessary consultancy has begun to close the factory later in the year.'

Mr Walters added: 'At the heart of this is pure greed. This decision is not about the lives and livelihoods of three hundred hard-working people in this community, it's down to the fact that making a large amount of money is not enough for some people. Three hundred families are going to be plunged into poverty through sheer gluttony.'

Andrew took a sip of his tea, only then realising that Jenny was still talking. '. . . anyway, after that he went home by himself. I don't know what his problem is. It's not as if we're married. Why are people so clingy?'

'I don't know,' Andrew replied, on autopilot.

'Right, I mean, it's not normal, is it?'

He returned to the emails he'd not had the time or inclination to read on his phone.

A local businessman last night condemned the 'witch hunt' against him, after a high-profile bribery case collapsed.

Thomas Braithwaite, owner of Braithwaite Industries, was due to stand trial alongside Gerry Conway, who represents the Norris Green ward.

Mr Braithwaite was accused of paying money to Mr Conway, who chairs the city's planning control board, in an attempt to force through plans for a new factory within the councillor's ward.

Both men pleaded not guilty late last year, with a trial due to go ahead next month. But a judge yesterday threw out the case following a pre-trial hearing, citing a lack of evidence and inconsistencies in the prosecution's documents.

Mr Braithwaite, who claims his company employs more than four thousand people nationally, said: 'This is complete vindication.

'I've spent the past eighteen months fighting against the vicious, untrue charges, which have put the jobs of around one thousand hard-working Liverpudlians in jeopardy. After all of that, when it comes down to it, the police do not even have enough of a case to take me to court.

'This has been a witch hunt against me and my family and I hope the people of this great city notice how the authorities around them choose to act.'

Mr Conway was equally scathing, accusing Merseyside Police of 'making up their own version of events and then trying to find the evidence to fit'.

A spokesman for the Crown Prosecution Service said they were 'astounded' by the judge's decision, adding: 'This was the culmination of many months of work and to dismiss the case before it can be heard before a jury is unprecedented.'

A police source claimed officers 'felt physically sick' when they heard the news, adding that there was a long trail of evidence, including recorded phone calls and financial documents.

There was plenty to read between the lines: Braithwaite setting himself up as a local hero in an us-versus-them battle with the police. Given the choice, plenty would side with him because so many people knew a person he employed.

Andrew realised Jenny had stopped speaking. He could feel her watching him from the side, turning to catch her smiling at him.

'Okay?' he asked.

'That's what I just asked you.'

'Oh . . . right.'

'I was wondering why Braithwaite might have turned on Sampson,' Jenny said.

Andrew took a moment to think. 'Any number of reasons. Perhaps Sampson arranged the robbery of his own shop with one of Braithwaite's rivals and Braithwaite was annoyed at being left out. Maybe Sampson went to Braithwaite, who got the Evans brothers to do it, but they then fell out over money?' Andrew flicked back to the first article. 'I'm not sure that's what really matters. It's like this piece about him closing the factory – everything's about business. If you're useful to him, making enough money and not causing trouble, then he'll let things go. If you cause a problem, that's the end of it. He heard the rumours about the killings of Owen and Wendy being linked to him because the Evans brothers once worked for him and he didn't like them. For whatever reason, he blamed Sampson, so now he's cutting him loose.'

'But if Braithwaite is the person we think he might be – and the police clearly think he is – why would he need us? He could make Sampson disappear, or whatever it is they do.'

Andrew shrugged. He couldn't admit the truth: he thought Braithwaite was after a new plaything and he'd accidentally provided it.

'I don't know,' he said.

Jenny removed her glasses and leant back in her chair. 'Let's say it was Sampson and Braithwaite. Sampson knows Braithwaite because he's Mr Brasso: he cleans up stolen jewellery and they've worked together in the past. He only finds out the expensive necklace is coming in from the production company first thing in the morning, so there's a window of three or four hours where it's going to be in the shop.'

'Right.'

'Whether he goes directly to Braithwaite doesn't matter because everything has to happen quickly. Either way, it's the Evans brothers who do the robbery. They're unreliable but perhaps they were all that was available because of the short notice. Braithwaite knew they'd stay quiet if they did get caught, so he wins in any case. They take the necklace, Sampson gets his insurance money *and* cleans the necklace so it can be sold on, probably with the jewels separated from the metal. He makes his money, the Evans brothers get a cut, as does Braithwaite, or whoever else it is he's working with. The police might have had an inkling about the truth but they couldn't prove anything and the Evans brothers were careless anyway. The police could have spent hours and hours peeling back the layers but, in the end, they had proof and three people in custody.'

'That explains the robbery,' Andrew said, 'but why the shooting? If Sampson was in on it all along, why not usher Owen and Wendy out when they entered the shop? He's got the CCTV camera, so the robbery would have been recorded. He didn't need witnesses.'

'Witnesses would be better, though – especially if the police were ever suspicious.'

Andrew nodded. 'Of course, so why were they killed? The robbery *happened* – the footage was on the news. Everyone saw it. When the Evans brothers were in court, it was played over and over. There were freeze frames in the papers. No one doubted it and the police would have found the brothers anyway. They weren't caught because of the statements Owen and Wendy gave, they were caught because they were stupid.'

Jenny was nodding. 'I don't think I've ever seen the video . . .'

Andrew wasn't listening properly. What had he missed? There must be something and he was pretty sure Braithwaite either knew what it was, or knew Sampson had done something he shouldn't. He wanted Andrew to find it, which was why he'd put him onto the jeweller.

'. . . I wonder if it's on YouTube,' Jenny added.

Her glasses were back on as she clicked the mouse.

Andrew wanted to focus but kept drifting back to Iwan's amusement and Kevin laughing in his face.

'It's on the GMP website,' Jenny said. 'They put it up for a public appeal and never took it down.'

There was the muffled sound of banging from Jenny's computer speakers as she watched the footage, before setting it to repeat.

'I had a good time with your aunt,' she said.

'So I heard.'

'I think she needs a holiday.'

Andrew finished his tea and pinched the top of his nose. He didn't feel well. 'I've told you – she likes Manchester. She's hardly ever left the city, let alone the north west. She doesn't have a passport.'

Jenny was uncharacteristically quiet, with the sounds of the CCTV footage continuing to play. Shouting, smash-smash, shouting, bang.

'When I was at her flat on Saturday, I did have a thought,' Jenny said.

Andrew wasn't in the mood to listen but had even less inclination to argue. 'Go on.'

'You know all the trinkets she has?'

'How can you miss them?'

'I was walking around the room and she was telling me about the teapots and the snow globes. Then she was showing me her postcards, the sticks of rock, the magnets and everything else, and it dawned on me.'

'What did?'

'Have you ever thought about what you *haven't* seen?'

'Oh, don't give her ideas. She'll be collecting dolls,

T-shirts, and God knows what else. The thimbles are bad enough.'

The CCTV footage started another loop. Shouting, smash-smash, shouting, bang.

'I don't mean that, I mean the places.'

'I think she wants something from South America,' Andrew said. 'She's got something from the other continents. Someone from bingo went on safari last year and brought her back a few bits from Kenya.'

Jenny's voice was as level as it had been throughout, no showing off, no being a smart-arse. 'You're missing it – you're seeing what's there, rather than what's not.'

Andrew finally turned, infuriated. He couldn't take another person talking down to him. '*What?*' he asked, fully intending the aggressive tone.

Jenny didn't look up from her screen. 'You say she loves Manchester, but there's nothing from the area. No teapots, no snow globes. Nothing with "Coronation Street" on it, no football stuff, none of those stupid teddies you get on Deansgate. Not even that "On the sixth day, God created Manchester" sign they sell. If she loves the area so much, why hasn't she got a single thing from around here? She even had Yorkshire teabags.'

Andrew wanted to answer angrily that he knew Gem better than her but the words stuck in his throat. He'd been visiting his aunt for as long as he could recall and she'd always collected tat – but he could never remember anything from the local area.

'I suppose she only collects things that people bring home for her,' he said.

'What if that's not it?'

'How do you mean?'

'What if she's been waiting her entire life to go on holiday to Spain, Greece, Egypt, or anywhere else she's got knick-knacks from?'

The footage started its loop again, with Jenny's eyes fixed on the screen.

'I've offered to take her away. She never wants to go anywhere.'

'That's what she always says. When you said you were going to take her to your flat, she argued for about five seconds and then caved. That's what she's like – she doesn't want to feel like a burden, so she *wants* you to give her no option. Instead of offering to take her away and letting her say no, she wants you to *tell* her you're taking her on holiday and she doesn't have a choice.'

There was a pause, the only noise coming from the speakers of Jenny's computer.

Oh, shit.

Jenny was right. All this time, all these years. Of course she wanted to go and see some of the places her friends had visited, that's why she covered her living room with it all. How had he missed what was right in front of him?

Andrew stood, crossing the room to stand behind Jenny as the footage began again. Wendy and Owen were on screen, peering into a cabinet when there was a squeal and three balaclava-clad figures burst through the shop door.

'How did you know?' Andrew asked.

Jenny shrugged. 'It's obvious, isn't it?'

Wendy hit the floor but Owen remained standing, as if

his legs weren't obeying what he wanted them to do. His knees crumpled slightly but he looked up to see one of the brothers pointing a sawn-off shotgun at his face. There was a stream of shouting and then the man thrashed Owen in the head with the butt of the gun.

'Where do you think I should take her?' Andrew asked.

'Say you're planning a holiday and you were wondering if she's heard of anywhere that's good. She'll come up with something and you can book it for the both of you. Either that, or I'll ask her.'

Owen slumped to the floor as one of the other robbers pointed a gun at Leyton Sampson, who was behind the counter. There was more shouting and then a crash as the cabinet on the far side of the shop was shattered.

'Why did you go around to my flat when you knew it was just her and Rory?' Andrew asked.

'I thought I could help. She seemed lonely.'

'Don't take this the wrong way, but . . . you don't really go out of your way to help people.'

'I know.'

'So, what's different?'

'I don't know,' Jenny replied. 'I like her.'

Owen was on the floor but looking up as Wendy reached for him. He glanced from Sampson to the robbers and back again. Sampson largely ignored him, turning to the bench and back to the robbers. At the front of the shop, the man without the gun – Paulie Evans – shouted at his brothers, just as another cabinet was smashed.

'Jen.'

'What?'

'Thank you.'

'Pfft. It's fine.'

The trio grabbed what they could, dumping everything into bags before rushing into the street. The entire thing had taken barely ninety seconds.

The screen faded to black, before displaying Greater Manchester Police's logo and a phone number to call.

'Again?' Jenny asked.

Andrew was chewing on the inside of his mouth, plucking a stringy piece of skin from his inner cheek. 'Yes.'

They watched in silence as the events played themselves out.

The footage repeated three more times before Andrew felt confident enough to point a finger at the screen, telling Jenny to watch.

'What am I looking for?' she asked.

'It's as you said. Have you ever thought about what you *haven't* seen?'

29

Jenny gasped when she spotted it, as strong a reaction as Andrew had ever seen from her. He didn't know if she was shocked it had happened, or stunned that she'd missed it.

'It's down to you,' Andrew said.

'You saw it.'

'Only because you kept going on about Gem. You put the idea in my head to ignore what was in front of me and look for what wasn't.'

She rested her head on his hip. 'We make a good team.'

Andrew was standing, with Jenny sitting, meaning her head was at an awkward height. Andrew didn't know where to put his hands. Should he ask her to move? Or step away and let her head drop? They'd had a brief hug after being rescued from Alkrington Woods a few months previously but that was at a time when Andrew thought they were going to die. This was . . . weird.

He was saved by the mobile phone on his desk starting to ring. Jenny lifted her head away as Andrew scuttled across the office, trying to forget what had just happened. The number was 'unknown', which meant it was almost certainly a telemarketer. He would usually ignore those calls, it wasn't as if the person ever left a message, but whoever it was had just saved him. He wondered what it would be, probably someone wondering if he'd been mis-sold a banking product. That was all the rage nowadays.

Andrew answered the phone with a deadpan 'hello', ready for the worst but utterly unprepared for the voice that spoke.

'I think we should talk.'

It was male, almost understated but demanding at the same time. Andrew felt a too-familiar chill on his back. He thought his former father-in-law was scary in person, but his voice had that distressing tone too. Andrew crossed to the sink, accidentally rattling a glass against the metal tap as he tried to fill it with water.

'Why?' Andrew asked.

'You know why,' Keira's father replied.

Andrew swallowed the water too quickly, making himself cough. His headache was back and he was suddenly feeling hot, even though it wasn't that long ago he'd been walking through the cold.

'I'm at work.'

'I'm aware. That's why I've come to you.'

Andrew spun around, expecting to see Keira's father behind him. But there was only Jenny, chewing on a pen as her fingers darted across the computer keyboard.

'You're here?'

'Come outside.'

Andrew had taken a step towards the door before he realised what he was doing, compelled by the other man's words.

Jenny turned and glanced up at him, mouthing 'Okay?'

Andrew cupped his hand over the bottom of the phone, nodding. 'I've got to nip out for a bit. I'll be back.'

She pointed at the video on the screen. 'Should I do something with this?'

'Not yet – let me have a think first.'

He grabbed his coat and headed out of the door, skimming down the stairs so quickly that he almost tripped. The rapidly decreasing temperature was matching his mood. He burst through the doors, expecting to see Mr Chapman standing and glaring, waiting with his hands on his hips in an expensive suit. Instead, the street was as empty as usual. In the building opposite, Tina peered up from behind the receptionist's desk and waved, all slender fingers and white-toothed smile. Her other hand didn't leave the keyboard. Andrew replied with a short nod, putting the phone back to his ear.

'How did you get my mobile number? I don't give it out.'

'Walk to the end the street, as if you were heading to the train station.'

'What if I say no?'

His former father-in-law laughed. 'You're a fool, Andrew, but you're not that stupid. Just do it.'

30

Andrew turned and started to walk, noticing the cold far more than he had earlier. It wasn't quite the end-of-days prediction he'd heard on the radio, but the wind had picked up and it felt like it might snow. The air was biting at his face as he hurried along the narrow path.

'Where am I going?' he asked.

'Keep walking until you get to the end.'

His fingers were beginning to stiffen from the cold, his gloves back in the office, along with his hat. He'd been in such a rush, such a panic, that it was lucky he'd remembered his coat. As Andrew neared the end of the path, the bustle started to increase. His office was barely a minute's walk from one of the city's main shopping areas but hidden away in the warren of age-old streets.

As Andrew reached the corner, a bus spluttered out a cloud of diesel, momentarily making it hard to breathe. There were voices, footsteps on concrete, a car horn, the beeping of a pedestrian crossing. Noise, noise, noise.

'Where now?' Andrew asked.

'Straight ahead, across the road.'

Andrew felt watched. He turned in a circle, then up towards the windows of the surrounding buildings, looking for Keira's father, but there was no sign.

'What am I looking for?'

'There's a pub. Come inside.'

Andrew started to reply but the call dropped, leaving him talking to himself. The place he was supposed to go wasn't a pub in the traditional sense: it had been bought out by a chain, plastered in identikit branding, and then reopened advertising cheap food and cheaper beer. It opened early enough in the morning that the alcoholics could roll right in, and stayed open late enough that students could flock around the tables and drink themselves stupid on the way back to halls.

As soon as he stepped inside, Andrew felt his shoes sticking to the floor. Ick. In the corner, the fruit machine was ding-ding-dinging as a skeletal bloke in a baseball cap piled pound coins into it. His girlfriend sat at the table next to him, cradling a near-full pint of something cloudy. There were three empty glasses on the table in front of her and it wasn't even lunchtime.

The usual types were at the bar: four unshaven blokes in long coats with blotched red faces, mumbling nonsense but set for the next eight or nine hours of drinking. They'd be gone whenever they were judged as too drunk to be served, or they ran out of money. The smell of microwaved fried breakfasts drifted through the high-ceilinged room, making Andrew gag. It might only cost three quid a meal but he valued his intestines enough not to subject them to that. He tried not to be a snob but had a rule that if a meal cost less than, or equal to, a ream of paper, then he'd probably be better off eating the paper.

The pub was spread across two levels, with a few steps up to a seated area close to the window, offering a view towards the shops. Edgar Chapman was at a small table in the bay, sitting by himself, legs crossed at the knees. His crisp, pinstripe black and white suit made him stand out instantly, even before Andrew noticed the pink tie with the giant Windsor knot. He sipped from a tiny espresso cup, wincing slightly, before putting it back on the table.

For a moment, Andrew thought his clothes were shrinking. It was only as he gasped that he realised his chest felt tight, his nose blocked from the cold. He crossed the room, sliding into the chair opposite Keira's father without a word.

The other man was reading a broadsheet and didn't look up immediately, turning down the corner of the page, folding it, and flipping the newspaper into a leather satchel. He took another sip of the espresso, grimaced once more, before finally acknowledging Andrew.

'Don't order the coffee,' he said. 'I hate these bloody places. Cheap shit for cheap people.' He pointed at the cup, not even having the grace to smile as he took the piss. 'Want one?'

'I'm not staying.'

'So what does a private investigator do with himself?'

'Is that what you came to ask me about?'

Andrew's former father-in-law shook his head. 'Not particularly, I'm interested in what you're doing with *my* money.'

'It's not your money.'

Finally a smile, albeit one so thin-lipped that it barely counted. 'We had an arrangement, Andrew.'

'All arrangements can expire.'

'Not this one.' He reached for the cup again, sipping the dregs, scowling, and then standing. 'Are you sure you don't want something?'

'I'm fine.'

Keira's father walked toward the bar, the light glinting from his shiny black shoes. Heads turned to look, probably in confusion why someone who could afford such clothes was in a place like this. He'd left his phone on the table, filling Andrew with visions of taking it and . . . he didn't know what. Perhaps there would be interesting emails from a secret lover? Something Andrew could use against him. He knew it was ridiculous, that the phone had almost certainly been left there to tempt him, yet he couldn't rid himself of the thought.

Mr Chapman soon returned, placing two espresso cups and saucers on the table and pushing one towards Andrew. He relaxed his large frame into his seat. 'I got you one anyway.'

Andrew pushed the saucer away as his former father-in-law sipped from the cup, pulling an anguished face again. 'Jesus, that's awful.'

'Why did you get another one then?'

He smiled properly this time. 'When you bring yourself down to the level of pigs, Andrew, you can't complain about wallowing in shit.'

'Charming. Is that from Nietzsche? Descartes? Aristotle?'

'Are you interested in philosophy now, Andrew?'

'Stop calling me that.'

'Andrew? It's your name, is it not?'

'Just *stop*.'

Keira's father seemed delighted at the reaction. Andrew knew he should've ignored it but the way the other man said his name grated on him, making him shiver each time. He reached forward, snatched the coffee cup and downed the espresso in one, instantly realising why Chapman had been wincing. It was *awful*.

'As I was saying,' the other man continued, '*this* agreement does not expire. You have everything: your flat, your business, your pretty young *"assistant"'* – bunny ears – 'because of the money I gave you.'

'She works for me, that's all.'

'Good for you. Easy on the eye. Nice choice. What's her name?'

'None of your business.'

'Jenny, isn't it? She has a nice little Volkswagen Beetle. Purple. It's interesting how she gets to work before you, yet you only live around the corner.'

Andrew was sick of people spying on him. First Braithwaite and Iwan, now Keira's father. He was supposed to be the one poking his nose into other people's business but everything was upside down.

'Stay away from my life and leave Jenny alone.'

'Aah, so you're feeling protective over the women in your life. Finally, that's a trait I can admire.'

'What do you want?'

'Is that your type now? Downmarket, wide-eyed, inner-city types?'

'Jenny isn't like that – and, even if she was, so what? We're all people. What does it matter where you come from?'

The other man stood again, finishing his drink in one and wiping his mouth. 'My bowels are going to make me pay for this later.' He picked up Andrew's cup. 'Another?'

'Just sit down and tell me what you want, so I can go.'

'*This* is what I want, Andrew. I want you sitting at my feet, waiting for me to click my fingers to tell you you're dismissed. Now sit still like a good little boy and wait for the grown-up to return.'

Keira's father ambled across the floor, this time taking his time, knowing Andrew would be watching. Knowing he'd be seething. Each day brought a new indignity, like the old days of being bullied at school by the bigger kids for being fat or ginger. He'd spent years describing his own hair as 'sandy', before finally realising that it was their problem, not his. He was thirty-five years old and all it took was a few bigger men to make him feel eight again.

His former father-in-law strode back across the floor, two more espressos in hand, before placing them delicately on the table and sitting again. Andrew was silent and didn't dare reach for the cup, knowing his hand would be shaking. Keira's father had no such problems, holding the dainty handle between his thumb and index finger and sipping softly. He even managed to avoid grimacing from the acid taste.

'"What does it matter where you come from".' He repeated Andrew's words and then breathed in heavily through his nose. 'That's where you and I differ, Andrew. If you, or anyone else, imagines for one second that I'm leaving my fortune to someone of whom I don't approve, then you're going to have another think coming. You already stole my daughter once, took her away to some casino-ridden hellhole to marry her, and it's not happening again.'

'Vegas was her idea.'

'Like hell it was.'

'I don't care if you believe me – it was. We sat in a muddy field surrounded by people covered in filth who were half-naked and carrying toilet rolls. Someone in a tent close to us was smoking dope, someone else was on his third can of lager and it wasn't even eight o'clock in the morning. She said she wanted to go to Vegas because you wouldn't be able to get to us there.'

It got the reaction Andrew had hoped for. The other man's fingers started to tremble in rage, rattling the cup back onto its saucer.

'This isn't a discussion. When I paid you, that was go-away money, yet you're still around. Do you not understand what going away means?'

'I don't want to go anywhere.'

'Do you want me to tell my daughter that you took the money over her?'

'If you do that, you'll have to tell her that it was you who paid me.'

Mr Chapman nodded. 'I'll tell her *you* asked. You came to me saying you'd disappear – you'd abandon her – if I paid you off. I cared for her so much that I agreed to the blackmail to make her happy.'

'She won't believe you.'

'I'm happy to see what she believes. I've been in her life for the past nine years. I'm funding the work with those damned street kids that she so dotes upon. What about you?'

'You gave me no choice but to take that money. You said you'd break us up anyway, make my life miserable, target my parents, leave me with nothing.'

Keira's father nodded. 'Do you still believe that?'

Andrew pursed his lips, breathing in, wondering what his answer should be. He snatched the cup and downed the espresso in one, wincing again as the bitterness scratched at the back of his throat. 'I don't know.'

The other man leant in, close enough that Andrew could smell his aftershave, which reeked of wealth. It was probably called 'Money' and cost ten thousand for a tiny bottle.

'Tell her you've made a huge mistake,' he said. 'Tell my daughter that *this* is all over for a second time. That you were right back then and you have no future together. Do that, or I'll take away everything you've got.'

'What if I don't?'

Keira's father leant away again, peering out of the window as a woman with a pushchair struggled past, fighting into the snarling wind.

'I take it your phone can access the Internet?'

'Yes.'

'Search for the name "Tanjir Ahmed".' He spelled it out as Andrew did as he was told. The atmosphere had changed from edgy to plain hostile. 'What's the top link?' he asked.

'A news report from last month,' Andrew replied. 'Father-of-three jailed for child porn offences.'

'Read it.'

A Slough man was yesterday jailed for downloading more than four thousand images of child pornography onto his laptop.

Tanjir Ahmed, a father of three, was sentenced to five years in prison at Reading Crown Court under the sexual offences act.

Ahmed, forty-four, a former banker at Hughes Lawton in the City of London, pleaded not guilty to possessing indecent images of children last month but was convicted by a jury after a trial lasting three weeks.

He was arrested in March last year as part of the wider Operation Haslington investigation into child abuse.

Ahmed was described by the prosecution as 'possessing level five material that included some of the most serious levels of abuse ever witnessed'. He insisted throughout the trial that he had no idea the images were on his computer and that he did not know how they got there. The prosecution called his defence 'utterly implausible'.

Ashwell Graves, defending, pointed out that there was no suggestion Mr Ahmed attempted to distribute the material.

In handing down the sentence, judge Roger Macklin told Mr Ahmed: 'It is time you face up to the seriousness of what you have done. No one has alleged that you were party to any of the abuse witnessed in those images, but by downloading them, you are creating a market for material of that type to be generated. Real people, real children, are impacted by this and, for that, imprisonment is the only option.'

Ahmed, who has been prevented from seeing his own children, wept throughout proceedings. He was also served with a Sexual Offence Prevention Order, which will last indefinitely, severely restricting his access to computers and children.

Upon release, he will be required to register as a sex offender for eight years and has been banned by the Disclosure and Barring Service from any work with children.

Andrew read the article twice, his eyes sticking on two words that most people would skip past: 'Hughes Lawton'. It was the bank where the man opposite him worked; the bank whose charity was currently funding Keira's work.

Slowly, he looked up, trying to meet the stern gaze of his former father-in-law. Another chill rippled through him, nothing to do with the weather.

'What are you showing me?' Andrew asked, hoping it wasn't what he thought.

Keira's father wouldn't meet his eye. 'What do you think?'

'Tell me.'

A flash of eye contact and Andrew knew exactly what had happened. He didn't know how but that didn't matter.

'I'm smarter than you, Andrew. Better. I have money, contacts, and can make things happen. I'm trying to look out for you, son—'

'Don't call me that. You've never called me that.'

'I'm trying to look out for you, *son*. I wouldn't want anything unfortunate to happen.'

Andrew glanced at his phone again, holding it up. 'What did he do to you?'

'It doesn't matter.'

'It does to me.'

Andrew thrust the phone forward until it was under the other man's nose, almost pressing against his top lip.

Keira's father went cross-eyed as he peered towards it, before slapping Andrew's hand away. 'Mr Ahmed was a thief who thought he could get away with it. I suppose he did get away with it in some ways. Not in others.'

'Did you do this?'

'I can do many things.' He downed the rest of his drink and then rattled the cup back onto its saucer, standing in one movement and plucking his phone from the table, before picking up his satchel. 'You *will* do what you're told, Andrew – *son* – and don't even think about pushing me.'

31

Andrew parked his car on the opposite side of the road from Margaret Watkins' house and switched off the engine.

'Are you sure you're all right?' Jenny asked.

'I've told you, yes.'

He could feel her peering at him from the passenger seat. Of course he wasn't bloody okay. Being tied up in the woods at night with a knife pressed against him wasn't as scary as what he'd just been through. It had taken him five minutes to stop shaking before leaving the pub. If anyone else had told him to check that link and then hinted all was not as it seemed, Andrew wouldn't have believed them. With his former father-in-law, he believed every word. Was he really going to have to walk away from Keira again?

'Do you want me to do the talking?' Jenny asked. She had one hand on the door handle.

'No, er . . . we'll play it by ear.'

Time for another humiliation.

Andrew and Jenny crossed the road and rang the doorbell. Margaret flung the door open moments later, only for her face to fall instantly. Her hair had been tamed slightly. Instead of sprouting in all directions, it was just big.

'Oh,' she said, taking in Andrew and Jenny before poking her head out of the door to stare at the road beyond. 'I didn't realise you were coming.'

'We were in the area,' Andrew said. 'Can we come in?'

'I'm . . . busy.' She focused back on them. 'I've got something on. Can you come another time? Tomorrow perhaps? I'll be in all day.'

'We only need a few minutes.'

She glanced past them again before pulling the door open. 'All right.'

The manic hand-flapping wasn't in evidence as she led them into the living room. Geoffrey was nowhere to be seen, although he could be in casualty given that he lived in constant danger of getting clattered in the head.

'I'm afraid I have an apology to make,' Andrew said, nodding towards the giant canvas on the wall. 'We've been trying to look for your cats but leads have been hard to come by. Jenny's done an awful lot of work behind the scenes; we've tracked down vets; other breeders; traders. We've followed a few threads but there's really not very much for us to go on.'

Margaret nodded knowingly. 'I feared as much.'

'Things don't usually end like this. I'm a little embarrassed but I'm not sure using more time – and money – is going to be worthwhile for either of us. We've still got a few informal inquiries going on, so it's not the end entirely. We could get a hit, though we're not hopeful.'

'I understand.'

He took out a sheet of paper, sliding it across the coffee table between them. 'We've got a list of expenses, but—'

She didn't look at it. 'Just leave the bill.'

'I was going to say that we'd waive part of it because of the outcome.'

'It's fine. I'm sure you did your best. I knew it was a long shot – the police didn't find anything, so I'm not sure why I expected anyone else to.'

Margaret's gaze shot past Andrew to the door beyond. He followed it to where there was a clock hanging on the wall. By the time he turned back to her, she was looking at her watch.

She started to stand, one hand on her back, seeming older than she had when they'd first met a week ago. 'You should have called ahead,' she said, glancing at the clock again.

Andrew and Jenny stood. This wasn't the reaction he'd expected. He'd thought there would be disappointment, perhaps even anger, but instead it was resignation.

'Are you okay?' Andrew asked.

Margaret was practically shoving them through the living-room door, back into the hallway. 'I'm fine.'

Andrew allowed her to shoo him, but Jenny stopped at the bottom of the stairs. 'Do you mind if I use the toilet?'

There was a momentary pause but no one ever said no in that situation.

'It's . . . upstairs. Second door on the left.'

Jenny offered a sweet-sounding 'thank you' and then followed the directions. Andrew wondered what she was doing. It was clear Margaret wanted them out of the house and Jenny was only prolonging that, revelling in how uncomfortable it was.

Andrew stood awkwardly in the hallway, peering up the stairs. He offered a weak – returned – smile to Margaret, before glancing away again. The space was covered with family photographs: Margaret, Geoffrey and Edie, with the two Bengals front and centre in almost every picture. There they were in the back garden; with ribbons at a competition; in a park; dressed up in red and green for Christmas.

'Sorry,' Andrew said.

Margaret nodded and checked her watch, the silent question passing between them: what on earth was Jenny doing? Another mutual, awkward, smile – and then a lot more wall-gazing. Andrew tried to think of something to say that wouldn't make him sound like a complete idiot. Everything that had gone wrong in the past week had happened because he was too soft. He shouldn't have taken on the case in the first place, knowing the moment Margaret had started talking about cats that they were going to get nowhere.

Finally!

The sound of a toilet flushing was like church bells on a crisp Sunday morning. The taps gushed and then, moments later, Jenny was walking down the stairs, all smiles and thank yous.

Margaret held the front door open for them and Jenny patted her pockets and turned back inside. 'I think I left my phone in your living room.' She offered an apologetic smile and then ducked under the other woman's arms, heading back inside. Andrew didn't know where to look, but Margaret did: at her watch.

Jenny emerged again, holding her phone in the air. 'Sorry!'

Andrew was halfway along the path when Jenny slotted in next to him. 'It's exactly four o'clock,' she whispered.

'So?'

'She obviously wanted us out of the house. People usually arrange to do things on the hour, so if anything's going to happen, it'll be about now.'

They'd taken two strides when a car pulled to a halt at the end of the path. It was at least twenty years old, with rust around the wheel rims, dark-tinted windows and an exhaust that sounded like a noise pollution enforcement notice waiting to happen.

The rear door opened, revealing a flash of black, purple and green, before closing quickly. A man in a beefy-looking army jacket clambered out, wearing sunglasses and a camouflage beanie hat. It was difficult to judge whether he was thickset, or if it was the size of the coat. He stepped around to the boot, opened it, and then removed a black animal carrier. The weight was almost too much for him as he leant to the side, before softly closing the boot.

Without paying any attention to Andrew or Jenny, he strode along the path and planted the carrier next to the front door. Margaret crouched, tears in her eyes as she glanced inside, before heading into the house. She emerged moments later with a thick padded envelope and handed it across. The man lifted the envelope flap, peered inside, nodded, and then returned to the car.

The second animal carrier was placed carefully next to the first, before the car pulled away, leaving a slight ringing in Andrew's ears.

Margaret caught his eye, still slightly teary. 'They called last night,' she said, crouching to open the first carrier. Tentatively, a tan and orange cat emerged, a galaxy of beautiful black and gold markings on its back. A similar creature

266

poked its head out of the second, sniffing the air before heading into Margaret's waiting arms. They were too heavy for her to lift them both, so Andrew helped, picking up the cat and taking it into the house. Jenny brought in the carriers, using the sleeve of her top to pick them up, before leaving them against the hallway wall.

'They might have fingerprints on,' she said.

Margaret shook her head. 'I don't care.'

Once inside, the two cats strutted through to the living room, noses and tails in the air. Margaret followed them through, sitting on the carpet and stroking the nearest one. 'Come to Mummy, Presley. What have the naughty people done to you, Elvis?' She reached underneath the coffee table and pulled out a basket, taking out a brush and running it along the cat's back.

'How much did you pay?' Andrew asked.

For a moment, he didn't think he'd get an answer, then Margaret opened her mouth, not turning from the cats: 'They asked for three-thousand a cat . . . I was going to phone you, but . . .'

Presley crossed the room to join Elvis. The two cats seemed unperturbed by whatever had happened to them, tails curling as they purred in pleasure at the attention.

'Geoffrey didn't understand. He said we should call the police but I just wanted them back. Edie doesn't get home from school until five, so it's just me.' Andrew didn't reply but she must've known what he was thinking, adding: 'You can't put a price on a family member.'

'But that's exactly what they did. The police could have been here waiting if you'd contacted them.'

'They said they were watching the house and that they'd know. If I got the police involved, they wouldn't show up and I'd never see my boys again. They said they knew I could get cash and that they wanted it in an unmarked envelope. It's why I was so worried when you turned up. I thought you'd put them off but I guess they know you're not police.'

'Who called you? A man? A woman?'

'It doesn't matter.'

Andrew exchanged a glance with Jenny, wondering if she'd seen what he had. He couldn't read her face. 'What would you do if I found out who did this?' he asked. 'If I gave you a name?'

Margaret didn't look up from her cats. 'I don't care. I'm just glad I have them back.' She picked up one of the cat's feet. 'Oh, Elvis, look at your nails. They're going to need a trim. It's baths for the pair of you tonight, too. I don't care how much you complain.'

'Margaret . . .'

She peered up at him, smiling softly, looking shattered. 'Just leave your invoices, your bill, whatever you want. You don't need to knock any money off, I trust that you did the work. I'll pay it within seventy-two hours, I just need to move a few things around.'

'There's no need . . . we're . . .' Andrew was struggling. 'Is there anything else we can do?'

She shook her head. 'Just go.'

32

'Did you see it?' Andrew asked.

Jenny was fiddling with her seatbelt as he pulled away. 'On the back seat of the car?'

'Yes.'

'I was going to ask you the same thing. I thought Margaret might have spotted it but it was only because we were halfway along the path that we had the angle. What do you think we should do?'

Andrew checked his mirror as he reached a T-junction and turned left. 'I'm not sure I trust my judgement much at the moment.'

Jenny smacked her lips together. She could have commented but didn't. 'Perhaps we should just have a talk? See what our thief has to say for themselves.'

Andrew's eyes flicked to the mirror again. As he'd turned left, two vehicles had slotted in behind from the right. A silver Vauxhall was hanging on his bumper, with Andrew trying to peer through its windows to the car beyond.

'Someone you know?' Jenny asked.

'Maybe . . .'

Andrew slowed slightly, allowing the Vauxhall to get even closer. There was a child seat strapped into the passenger's side, while the female driver was either talking to the baby or on hands-free. She was flapping a hand in Andrew's direction, wanting him to speed up, even though he was only just below the limit.

'Jen.'

'What?'

'If I drive a little bit like a dickhead, could you not call me names?'

She twisted in her seat, checking behind.

'I can probably manage that, just look out for the speed patrols.'

'Fine.'

Andrew slowed even further until he was doing twenty in the thirty zone. Behind, the mother was becoming increasingly agitated, holding one hand out to the side in the universal 'stop driving like a knobhead' pose, easily confused with the 'what are you doing?' stance.

Slow . . . slow . . . slower . . .

Fifteen miles an hour. Ten. It felt like they were barely moving. Down to second gear.

'Ready?' Andrew asked, still looking in the mirror.

'Yep.'

Go!

Andrew stamped on the accelerator, wrenching the car right and barrelling along the side street, before taking the next left. He was lucky nothing had been coming the other way but the short burst had been enough. The Vauxhall driver had been so taken by surprise that she'd stopped in the middle of the road, blocking the car behind. By the time he'd gone left, she still hadn't passed the junction where he'd turned in the first place.

He eased off, taking two quick rights and waiting at the T, staring towards the main road.

'Anything?' Jenny asked.

'No.'

'Who was it?'

Andrew didn't answer, edging along the side street, back in the direction he'd headed originally, glancing quickly from one side to the other.

'What are you looking for?'

'There was a black car behind the silver one, biggish, I don't know the make. It's shiny.'

There was no sign of anything at the first turn, so Andrew took the next one, keeping to the residential twenty-mile-an-hour limit now he was off the main road. Vehicles were parked on both sides, making it hard to manoeuvre, but that meant it was easier to keep an eye on what was ahead. He was almost at the turn back to the main road when Andrew spotted what he was looking for. He parked in between two cars and switched off the engine.

'Who is it?' Jenny asked again.

'No one you'd know.'

'I think you should tell me.' She was firm but polite. Not pleading, not angry, just honest.

Andrew was chewing the inside of his mouth again, a bad habit that was developing. Psychologists would probably have something to say about it: nervous tension; unfulfilled childhood; unresolved guilt at dumping his ex-wife, with whom he was still in love, that sort of thing. They could find fault with anyone if they put in a bit of effort. Gandhi? His bald head was clearly a symbol of insecurity. Mother

Teresa? Her lack of height was clearly down to a lack of ambition.

'His name's Iwan,' Andrew said. 'He works for Thomas Braithwaite. He was in Cheshire over the weekend. I was pretty sure I was being followed then, now it's obvious.'

'What does he want?'

'Let's find out.'

On one side of the road was a small community park, a row of empty benches facing the street next to it, and a long terrace of houses on the other. Andrew opened the door and strode along the pavement. When he reached the black car, he crouched slightly to see Iwan sitting inside, phone clamped to his ear. He rapped hard on the glass, enjoying a twinge of pleasure as the brute inside jumped. Iwan's head twisted so that he was peering up and then he muttered something into his phone before dropping it onto his lap. Jenny arrived at Andrew's side as the window hummed down.

'I thought I made myself clear about being followed,' Andrew said.

Iwan shifted in the driver's seat, tilting his head so that he could see them both. 'And I thought I made myself clear that Mr Braithwaite is expecting an update.'

'You haven't given me a way to contact you.'

'I'm here now.'

Andrew willed Jenny not to say anything about what they'd found within the CCTV footage. He wasn't ready to divulge it and didn't like being bullied. 'We've been busy doing other things,' Andrew said.

Iwan gritted his teeth, nodding. 'That sounds very disrespectful compared to the welcome Mr Braithwaite gave you.'

'If you keep following me, then you'll get nothing. I'll tell the police before I tell you.'

That did it, as Andrew knew it would. It was as if the previous week had all been part of one long self-destruct mission. The car door opened, forcing Andrew to step backwards towards the nearest house. Iwan seemed bigger than Andrew remembered, dressed in a tight-fitting black suit with a white shirt. His chest and arms bulged, eyes boring through Andrew.

'That really wouldn't be a good idea.'

'How about I tell them what you told me about Sampson the jeweller? I'll tell them who gave me the information. Let them know how you followed me to Cheshire to keep an eye out.'

Iwan smiled, taking a step forward.

Andrew opened his mouth to say something else stupid but Iwan's mitt was already around his throat. He tried to kick his legs but his back slammed into the wall, stealing his breath. Iwan let his throat go, but pressed a forearm across Andrew's chest. He jabbed the bump on Andrew's head with a sausage-like finger.

'Been pissing someone else off, have we?'

The wound had stopped hurting while they'd been at Margaret Watkins' house but Andrew grunted as jolts shot through him. It was more painful than when Kevin Leonard had hit him in the first place.

Iwan poked it twice more. 'Where'd this come from?'

Andrew tried to struggle but his strength was nothing compared to the other man's. He was struggling for breath as Iwan's forearm crushed the top of his ribs.

'What are you going to do, big man?' Iwan taunted, ready to poke the injury again. 'Mr Braithwaite might be tolerating you, but I'm not.'

The pressure increased on Andrew's chest, leaving him gasping, unable to breathe.

'Oi!'

Air spilled back into Andrew's lungs as Iwan turned to where Jenny was standing next to the black car. He twisted between the two of them, grinning. 'You need a girl to fight your battles?'

Andrew couldn't reply, coughing as he slumped along the wall. His head was pounding and he felt light-headed from the lack of oxygen and subsequent panic.

'How about you come and work for a real man, darling?' Iwan said.

Jenny was returning his stare, unruffled. In a flash she reached through the open car window and snatched the keys from the ignition. Iwan straightened up, unsure what was going on.

'What do you think you're doing?' he said, taking a small step forward.

Jenny held them up, angling towards the small park across the road.

'Don't you—' Iwan began, but he was already too late as Jenny reared back, grunted slightly, and threw the keys into the hedge that ran alongside the green on the opposite side of the road. There was a metallic jangle and then silence as they lodged somewhere among the mass of twigs, mud and leaves.

Iwan didn't know where to turn, staring open-mouthed at the hedge, then the car, then Jenny. She was wearing flat black shoes, tights, a pleated dark skirt and a jacket, but didn't shrink back, even though he towered over her. She stood with one hand on her hip, top lip curled into an amused sneer, daring him. Andrew pulled himself to his feet, still short of breath but far more shocked by what Jenny had done.

'I've seen some nutters in my time but you, darling, are a right psycho.'

Iwan took a step into the road, heading for the hedge but Jenny's features changed completely. The confidence was gone; the smile changed into aggrieved fury. With a screech, she threw herself forward, leaping onto Iwan's back. In other circumstances, she would have bounced off, but Iwan had one foot in the road, one on the pavement and was off-balance. At Jenny's frenzied cry, he stumbled sideways, landing face-down with Jenny on top of him. She was smashing clenched fists into the back of his head, tears streaming down her face as she clattered his ears.

Andrew was so surprised that it took him a few seconds to realise what was going on. He darted across the pavement and grabbed her around the waist, heaving her up and away from the suited man. Her legs flailed as she hissed and spat. He'd never seen her like this before: she was always composed, even standing up to men with knives.

'Jenny!' he shouted, trying to calm her.

The entire episode had lasted barely two or three seconds,

with Iwan using the kerb to pull himself up. There was a mud streak across his front, with flecks of grit stuck to his breast pockets. He brushed himself down and rubbed his ear, where a crease of blood was beginning to dribble, twisting towards his mouth. He peered at the red on his finger and then stared towards Andrew and Jenny, who had finally stopped kicking. Andrew lowered her to the pavement, but kept his arms across her shoulders, holding her back. Or, if interpreted another way, using her as a human shield.

Iwan touched his face a second time, smearing the blood slightly, before he pointed a thumb towards them. 'You're to come to the house tomorrow afternoon. Don't make me come and find you.'

Andrew didn't reply, waiting until Iwan had his head buried in the hedge before grasping Jenny's hand and leading her back to the car. She was panting, sweat streaming from her forehead, despite the cold. He opened the passenger's door and she climbed inside, not looking at him, eyes unfocused.

By the time he'd started the engine, Jenny hadn't moved, so Andrew reached across and pulled the seatbelt across her, clicking it into place. Iwan was still searching for his keys in the hedge as Andrew drove past, neither of them bothering to look at each other. He reached the end of the street and pulled onto the main road, driving as carefully as he could as the traffic started to back up.

'Jenny.'

No reply.

'Jen.'

Nothing.

'What was that about? You could've been hurt.'

Andrew glanced at his own reflection in the mirror, remembering she'd only intervened because he was getting the shite kicked out of him. Again. The small gash on his head had become a larger, rounded wound. It wasn't bleeding but there would be one hell of a bruise.

'Jen.'

'I'm not a psycho.'

'I don't think you are. It was just something he said. He doesn't even know you.'

No reply.

'Jen.'

'What?'

'No one thinks you are.'

She shook her head slightly, still not shifting her unblinking gaze from the road, her lips barely moving. 'I'm not a psycho.'

33

TUESDAY

Jenny was deliberately not looking in Andrew's direction. She was staring at the road, the lines of students, the arriving and departing coaches – anything but him.

'You can stop watching me,' she said, not harshly but with a distinct edge.

'Do you want to talk about it?'

She started playing with a fingernail. 'No.'

This was the first time Andrew could remember picking her up in the morning when she'd not been eating. Usually, there were slices of toast on the go, cereal bars, biscuits, bars of chocolate, occasionally an apple. When she was in the office, the first thing she normally did was stick the kettle on and then raid her drawer full of biscuits and cakes. She ate for large parts of the day, showing off a superhuman appetite and metabolism. Not only had she failed to eat for the entire half-hour journey, she'd barely spoken. He doubted she'd left her house since he dropped her off the previous afternoon.

'I'm not a psycho,' she said softly.

'I don't think you are.'

'I don't like being called one.'

'I understand.'

The morning was cool, but, compared to recent weeks, it was positively tropical – at least one or two degrees above freezing with no wind and barely even a hint of rain. The sky was still washed with a murky greyness but that was normal. Anyone who spent any time in Manchester could distinguish between rain-grey and gloomy-grey. This was distinctly gloomy. Newborn Mancunians were issued a colour chart comprised entirely of shades of monochrome, helping them to learn the names of various greys long before they could start counting.

Andrew and Jenny were sitting on a wall watching groups of young people pass by on their way to school. If he had been by himself, there would have probably been a catch-the-paedo riot squad deployed by now, but nobody was paying the pair of them any attention.

'Thank you for being concerned,' Jenny whispered.

'If it wasn't for you, I'd have had my arse kicked by Iwan.'

She smiled slightly. 'You had him right where you wanted him.'

A giggle, which was nice, even if she was joking about him getting beaten up.

'There's no way you can come along this afternoon,' Andrew said.

'I know.'

He had expected more of an argument and had spent almost an hour in bed that morning rehearsing the best way to tell her that, though he valued her input, he didn't want her anywhere near Braithwaite's house.

'What are you going to tell him?' she asked.

'That depends what we find out when we go to the university.'

A group of girls traipsed past, skirts around arses, blouses a size too small: all make-up and 'y'know's.

'. . . well I had five Valentine's cards this morning but I think one of them's from that Ian kid.'

'Eew. That is soooo gross.'

'I know. I was all, like, this is totally weirdsville. Just 'cuz he lives on my road, he thinks we should totally be together. As if I'd ever go out with a ginger. It's, like, totally disgusting, and that. It might be catching.'

'Did you get anything from Stephen?'

They rounded the corner, denying Andrew the chance of finding out if the ginger-hating mini-Hitler had a card from Stephen. He realised he was rubbing the top of his head and stopped himself. The past week had gone so badly that even teenage girls he didn't know were giving him a hard time as he listened in to their conversations.

Jenny laughed quietly. 'They're why I didn't have many friends at school.'

Andrew sat up straighter as he caught sight of the reason they were there. Jenny spotted it too, brushing her skirt down and hopping into a standing position.

Edie Watkins was walking along the street with two identikit lads, each with spiky dark hair and black rucksacks. The minute they were out of school, it'd be nipple ring-this, and emo tattoo-that. The other girl with them had long black hair, a clown-load of make-up and was wearing a skirt that was ripped at the bottom. Edie stood out because she looked like she'd barely made an effort: uncrumpled school uniform, straight blonde hair and dark rucksack covered in purple and green badges slung over her back.

Andrew caught her eye from a distance but she looked away instantly. It was only when she was level with Andrew and Jenny that she stopped again, telling her friends that she had to tie her lace and that she'd catch them up. They shrugged and disappeared around the corner.

The moment they were gone, Edie stood, looking between Andrew and Jenny. 'What do you want?'

'How old are you?' Jenny asked.

'What's it to you?' Edie snapped.

Jenny patted the wall and sat. Edie glared at her but did the same anyway.

'You know what this looks like, don't you?' she said, nodding at Andrew. 'I'm sixteen – *sixteen* – and you're a grown man.'

Jenny talked across her. 'You're having a conversation with me, Edie.'

The teenager stood again. 'No, I'm not.'

'Fine, we'll have this conversation with your mum.'

The two young women stared at each, neither wanting to give in, until Edie eventually plonked herself back on the wall next to Jenny.

'Who was the lad?' Jenny asked.

'What lad?'

'The one with the army coat and stupid sunglasses. And who was driving?'

Edie started to stand again. 'I don't know what you're—'

Jenny gripped her arm and pulled her back. 'Sit! We know, all right? We saw your rucksack on the back seat of the car. The purple and green badges were quite the giveaway. We've come to talk to you before we do anything else. If you want to be Miss Know-It-All, then walk away and we'll have to tell other people. If you want to have a conversation, then stop messing around.'

Edie took her phone from her pocket and pressed the screen. 'I've got to be at registration in fifteen minutes.'

'So hurry up. What are you going to do with the six thousand you stole from your mum?'

'What six thousand?'

Jenny leant forward. *'Really?'*

Edie threw her hands up. 'Fine. It was supposed to be a joke, to teach her a lesson but it all . . . got a bit out of hand.'

'So tell us.'

Edie sighed. She dropped her bag on the floor and stared at her feet. 'There was this big cat show last month in Brighton. Mum and Dad went down on the Friday evening, leaving me alone for the weekend. When I was younger, they'd make me go but I started causing problems to get out of it. I'd moan the whole way down, or spend ages talking on my phone, that sort of thing. You'd do the same if it was you – it's so boring, just lines and lines of bloody cats parading up and down. Then some old bag picks a winner and everyone spends the next six weeks moaning about the decision until the next competition. It's ridiculous.'

'So you had the house to yourself while they were in Brighton?'

'Right, and I invited a few mates over.' She pointed in the direction in which her friends had gone. 'There were a few from school, plus a few older lads we know. Nothing stupid but we had some cider and a bottle of vodka. We were mucking about.' She nodded at Jenny. 'You know what it's like, yeah?'

Jenny nodded, though Andrew wasn't convinced that she did.

'It wasn't actually that messy. We had this party round Frankie's house last year that got well out of hand. Jessie was sick everywhere, then Tia got grounded because she was really pissed and called her mum a bitch. Frankie's parents went mental, so we kinda learned our lesson. You still want to get shitfaced, just not so that our parents kick off.'

The way she explained it made it sound perfectly logical.

'Anyway, we were mucking around and Frankie was like, "Your mum and dad love your cats more than you." I just remember throwing this cup of vodka over him but then I was in the toilet later on and . . .' She paused, gulping and licking her lips. 'Well, he's right, isn't he? They do.'

'I'm sure that's not true,' Andrew said, speaking for the first time and getting a scowl for his efforts.

Edie turned back to Jenny. 'We'd been drinking and Frankie was like, "Why don't we do something about it?"'

Jenny nodded. 'You could have just talked to her.'

'Have you ever tried having a conversation with my mum? Everything she says revolves around those cats. That's if she's not taking Dad's head off, or knocking things over.' She checked her phone again. 'A few years ago, I used to be interested in dancing.' She laughed humourlessly. 'I have no idea what I was thinking. The only people at school into dancing, drama and all that shite are the hippie lot always banging on about government-this, or let's legalise drugs-that. You should hear them. Anyway, I was twelve or thirteen and one of my old friends, Katie, got me into it before she moved away last year. We'd practise in her garage and had this whole routine worked out. There was this talent competition at the school one Saturday and we wanted to enter. It was all right, just a bit of fun, a bit lame now, but we finished second. There were loads of kids there and Katie's mum was at the back taking pictures. Wanna know where my mum was?'

She didn't wait for an answer.

'Bristol. She and Dad had pissed off for some cat competition and didn't return until the Sunday evening. When she got back, what do you think she said? Do you think it was, "How was your competition, Edie?" or, "Sorry I didn't call, Edie, what was it like staying at Katie's house?" Or do you think it was, "Elvis and Presley were robbed by some judges who voted for a different cat"?'

She threw her hands up, jabbing a finger in Jenny's direction. 'You want to know where her six grand is, well, bollocks to her. I earned that money by sitting at home by myself while they pissed off around the country doting on those bloody things. When I wanted new shoes to dance in, she said they couldn't afford it – but when she wanted to get security trackers for the cats, they miraculously found the money.'

Jenny had recovered her usual composure, speaking reassuringly. 'It's still stealing, Edie.'

'Too right it is. I'm not giving that money back. If you want to report me to the police, then do it. If you want to tell my mum, do that too. I couldn't care less. I'll tell everyone who wants to know what I've had to put up with.'

Jenny's gaze flickered to Andrew, and he knew this was a call he'd have to make. He wanted to be the adult, to stamp his foot and say that stealing, blackmail, kidnapping, whatever anyone wanted to call it was wrong, but, if anything, he was on Edie's side. He'd taken plenty of grief over the past week but it sounded like Edie had been putting up with it for most of her life.

'How did you get the tracking chips out?' Andrew asked.

Edie turned to him, frowning. The flow of students passing the wall had become a trickle as it was almost time for the school day to begin.

'I thought you didn't care?' Andrew added.

'I don't, but . . .' Edie swallowed, staring back at her shoes. 'Look, I've got exams in a few months. It started as a stupid idea when we'd been drinking and got a bit out of hand.'

'So how did you get the tracking chips out?'

She shook her head. 'It wasn't me. Frankie knows this girl who's training to be a vet at Manchester Uni. He reckoned she owed him a favour, so she did it. It was all really sterile, with gloves and cloths and . . . I don't know, whatever else vets are supposed to use. She knew what she was on about, plus she wasn't going to say anything afterwards, because she'd get chucked off her course.'

'What happened then?'

'Why do you want to know?'

'Because I'm interested.'

She huffed and stamped her feet almost cartoon-style.

'There's this lad called Ricky who's got a thing for me. He's a couple of years older and lives down the road from Frankie. I'd only met him a few times.' She turned to Jenny. 'You know what it's like when a lad keeps asking you out.' Back to Andrew. 'I told him that if he helped us look after Elvis and Presley, I'd go out with him.' Andrew opened his mouth but she cut him off with a frown. '*Just* go out. That's all.'

'I wasn't going to ask that.'

She wasn't convinced. 'It seemed like a good idea at the time but we'd not really thought it through. Ricky couldn't let Elvis and Presley out of his house in case they ran away, or someone saw them, but they kept shitting everywhere because they were stressed out and he didn't really know how to look after them. I went round each evening to make sure they were fed. They weren't mistreated, or anything. They just wanted to get outside. At first, we were going to leave them on the driveway in those carriers for Mum to find, figuring she'd learned her lesson, but then you got involved.' She checked her phone again and pushed herself up from the wall. 'I've got to get going. I'm going to be late and I'm already on a warning.'

'Why did me being involved change things?' Andrew asked.

Edie didn't look up. 'How much has she paid you?' Andrew fluffed his words, taking a step back as Edie picked up her bag and rounded on him. 'Exactly. I don't actually care – it's just more money she was happy to spend on them. What's new? I figured it was about time I got something for myself.' She pushed past him, striding towards the corner, turning and scowling. 'Look, tell her, don't tell her. I really don't care any more. If you want to mess up my life and you can live with that, then it's up to you.'

She stormed around the corner, leaving Andrew and Jenny alone on the wall.

For a moment, neither of them spoke. Jenny broke the silence. 'I like her.'

Andrew laughed. Really laughed. If he'd been drinking milk, it would be spewing from his nose. 'That's perhaps the least surprising thing I've heard this week,' he said.

'What are you going to do?'

Andrew turned, heading for the car and sighing. He didn't want to make decisions like this. Edie was right – if he told her mum or the police, it probably would wreck her exams in a few months. Regardless of the money, Margaret Watkins had seemed happy the previous day when the cats were returned.

'You're going to let her keep the money, aren't you?' Jenny said.

Andrew rubbed the mark above his eye. It had been aching non-stop since Iwan had jabbed it. 'I've not decided yet.'

Jenny squinted at him, not saying it but confident she knew what he was going to do.

'What next?' she asked.

'Now it's time to get justice for Owen, Wendy and Fiona Methodist.'

'How are you going to do that?'

Andrew took a deep breath. 'First, there's someone we need to speak to – then I sell my soul.'

34

'Roses are red, violets are blue, you've got big tits, let's go screw.' Jenny giggled, peering up from the small yellow heart in her hand. 'It does have a sort of poetry to it.'

They were waiting inside a university building just off Oxford Road, where there was a giant pink heart attached to the wall. On a table nearby was a stack of heart-shaped yellow and blue sticky labels. The idea was that students could write romantic messages on the stickers and then pin them to the bigger heart for one another to discover. True love would be found and everyone would live happily ever after. Ahhhh . . . .

Unfortunately, or fortunately, depending on an individual's viewpoint, as with so many well-meaning events and celebrations, it had rapidly descended into a tsunami of filth, with people leaving increasingly disgusting or hilarious messages and no one in authority noticing.

Jenny plucked another yellow heart from the board. 'There once was a girl from Billinge, who had a really long fringe. She had so much hair, that it didn't stop there, it went right down to her . . . oh.'

Andrew picked up a blue heart and flipped it around, reading something about 'Sticky Vicky'. He pinned it back on the board. 'Some of these kids aren't even trying.'

As Jenny continued looking through the messages, sniggering to herself, Andrew gazed around the rest of the reception area. Usually, he would have felt out of place but there were people of all ages hurrying through and heading to class. Meanwhile, the university campus was a mass of purple and pink banners advertising that night's Valentine's Ball, which clashed with a speed-dating event and a separate thrash metal gig at the Academy. Of the three, he'd have probably gone for the thrash metal.

Andrew was watching Jenny skim through the Valentine's board when a tap on his shoulder made him jump. An Asian lad wearing jeans and a long-sleeved Man City goalkeeping top was nervously bobbing from one foot to the other. 'Are you Andrew?'

'Ishan?'

'Yep.'

They shook hands, with Andrew calling Jenny across. She made eye contact with Ishan, smiling and showing off her dimple. He was instantly nervous, avoiding her gaze and turning back to Andrew, who pointed towards the lounge area next to the coffee bar.

'Do you want something to drink?'

Ishan shook his head. 'I've got another lecture in half an hour.'

They sat anyway, with Andrew doing the talking. It wasn't always easy to judge lads in their teens or early twenties. Some preferred to talk to Jenny, bragging and spilling everything they might usually keep to themselves. Others, like Ishan, were anxious around girls and drawn to Andrew, spotting one of their own.

'I'd like to ask you about the day Owen and Wendy died,' Andrew said.

Ishan shuffled nervously. 'You said on the phone this was to discuss putting together a team for the mathlete Olympics.'

Andrew glanced at Jenny – her idea.

'I'm trying to find out what happened on the day Owen and Wendy were killed,' Andrew said. 'You were there.'

Ishan stood but Jenny was on her feet quickly too. 'Please don't go, Ishan,' she said. 'It's really important. This is just the three of us sitting on a couple of sofas chatting. Nobody needs to know what we're talking about. Andrew's a private investigator and I help him out. We're trying to find out what happened.'

He glanced between the two of them, then Jenny placed a friendly, perhaps flirty, hand on his shoulder. Ishan shivered nervously then lowered himself slowly back onto the sofa. 'How do you know I was there?' he said.

Andrew nodded at Jenny, who reached into her rucksack, the amusement from before now gone. 'There was so much written about the shootings that it was really hard to find out much of anything. The papers and Internet sites pretty much all quote the same police press conferences and wire copy, which only mention two witnesses being on the scene.'

Ishan couldn't sit still, staring towards the cafe counter and the door, fidgeting constantly. 'They kept my name quiet because of *them*.'

'Owen and Wendy?' Andrew asked.

'They'd been on the news and all over the Internet as

witnesses to that robbery. That gang knew what they were called and where to find them. When the police arrived and took my statement, they said they wouldn't release my name to the media, just in case. Throughout the inquest, I was known as "Witness I".'

Jenny plonked half a ream of print-outs on the table, brushing some loose hair from her face and grinning. 'I know. I spent long enough searching for you the other night.'

'But how did you find me? Most of my friends don't even know I was there. I know it's a miracle that the other people who showed up have kept their mouths closed, but—'

'It was you,' Jenny said.

Ishan threw a hand up, confused. '*What* was me?'

'Who did you tell?'

'My parents, my sister, one of my flatmates. Some of the people on my course know because they were there, too.'

'Who else?'

'No one.'

Jenny sifted through her papers and handed him a page. 'You wrote about it on this online maths forum. It only has your first name, but it wasn't hard to find out the rest.'

Ishan scanned the page, clearly unhappy. 'This is a private forum, though. You have to answer a dozen complex equations to be able to register, let alone be approved.'

'Yeah . . .'

'You've got to be interested in maths.'

'Yeah . . .'

'It's for, well, nerds, I suppose.'

Jenny shuffled her papers until they were all in line and then dropped them back in her bag. She beamed at him. 'What's your point?'

For a clever person, it took a few seconds for it to drop. '*You* like maths?' Ishan asked disbelievingly.

'My degree's in ICT but I did two maths modules, one in functional analysis, another in algebraic topology.' Andrew didn't dare ask what either of those actually was. 'I've been a member of that forum for about four years,' she added. 'I *knew* I'd read a first-hand account of the incident somewhere and thought it must have been on a news site. I waded through all those articles until remembering it wasn't that at all. It took me ages to figure out where, and then I stumbled across your post. I wish I'd thought of that before reading through a hundred news stories.'

Ishan suddenly seemed a lot more interested in Jenny than he had been before. He relaxed into the sofa, making eye contact with her for the first time. 'I still don't understand what you want to know.'

'We'd like you to tell us what you remember. I read your post but it's more about the aftermath and how you were dealing with everything.' She gave him a sympathetic smile. 'Everyone on there was really nice and supportive.'

'It's a decent community.'

'I know.'

Ishan had relaxed to such a degree that he was almost sitting still. 'I told the police everything I saw at the time but I've forgotten a lot of it now.' He stopped, clearing his throat. '*Tried* to forget.'

'Can you try to remember?' Jenny asked. 'For me?'

He looked from one of them to the other. 'It's not for some book, is it?'

'Why would it be?' Jenny replied.

'Because everyone I know's writing a bloody book. It's an epidemic.'

'It's not for a book.'

He pinched the top of his nose, much in the way Andrew did, and then peered towards the coffee bar. 'I think I need something to drink after all.'

Jenny turned to Andrew, raising her eyebrows. *Go on then.*

'What do you want?' Andrew asked, standing to do as he hadn't been told.

'Green tea and a muffin,' Ishan replied.

'Jen?'

'A hot chocolate, almond croissant, blueberry cupcake and one of those dippy things. Oh, and an apple.'

'"Dippy things"?'

'You dip them.'

Andrew didn't feel as if he had enough information, but headed to the counter anyway, ordering everything, plus a coffee for himself, and being shocked that he got change from twenty quid. That could only happen in a university building – cross the road and go into Starbucks and he'd need a second mortgage. The dippy things turned out to be piped shortbread with chocolate on either end. Apparently, it was only Andrew who had no idea what they were. As soon as he mentioned 'dippy thing' to the waitress, she plopped it on a plate and gave him a sideways glance as if to ask what he'd been wasting his life on.

As the waitress stacked up the calorific collection of diabetes-inducing items, Andrew watched as Jenny worked Ishan perfectly. They didn't want to use him – it had taken them long enough to find him – but they needed him to be relaxed in order to talk about the trauma he'd seen. He'd gone from not being able to look Jenny in the eye to smiling and mirroring, touching his hair when she touched hers. It wasn't just him who had changed. Barely a day ago, Jenny had been snarling, scratching and kicking. If Andrew hadn't stopped her, she would have kept fighting until Iwan had done her some serious harm.

I'm not a psycho.

She might be right – but not many people had to go around telling others what they weren't. It was largely implied by the way they acted.

Andrew crossed back to the seating area, balancing the cups and plates. Jenny instantly launched herself into the croissant as Ishan sipped his tea.

'Ishan was telling me that he was in a maths lecture when he heard three shots,' Jenny said, not looking away from the student.

Ishan nodded. 'It was a normal Monday. I was a bit tired and there's this lecturer who just bangs on and on in the same tone the entire time. It's really hard not to fall asleep.'

'Where were you sitting?' she asked, taking control again.

'At the back.'

'How did you know they were gunshots?'

'I live close to Longsight and you recognise things like that. Not often. Me and my friend Vik were chased by this gang one time. We got away but . . . you don't forget.'

'What did you do when you heard the gun?'

Ishan bit a chunk from his muffin, chewing and playing for time. 'I wasn't really thinking but I knew something bad had happened. I went out of the back of the lecture theatre into the corridor where there's a glass door that leads out to this courtyard area.'

'I know it.'

'Right. When I think of it now, I don't know why I went out there. Whoever had the gun could have still been roaming around, picking people off. That's what you hear about whenever there's another shooting in America – some maniac with a weapon wandering around taking pot shots.'

'But you went out there anyway?'

'I know – it's not the sort of thing I'd usually do. I'm not some sporty, athletic hero-type. I do maths because my mum and dad want me to.'

'You must've been brave to go out there.'

Ishan took the compliment well, smiling gently and having another bite of his cake. 'I felt drawn to it. The tiles are bright white but there was this red. You could see it from way back.'

Jenny had stopped eating and was nodding along. 'The papers said there were witnesses on the scene within seconds.'

'That was me. It felt like I was being pulled. There were three of them on the ground. I know the names now but I didn't then. I remember staring at the lad's – Owen's – hoody, because I have one just like it. There was a voice in my head saying it could have been me. Then there was the soldier in all his green stuff. I remember him seeming really big but he wasn't really, it was just in comparison to the other two. There was so much blood from the three of them, all running together.'

'Did you call the police?'

He shrugged. 'It's in the statements and they played the 999 call at the inquest. It's weird because I know I did – but I don't remember any of that. I remember the noises around me. People were screaming, crying, but there were also a few seconds where it felt like everything had stopped, even the buses and the traffic.'

'The report says "witnesses".'

Ishan nodded.

'How many were there?' Jenny asked.

'It's complicated. Lots, I suppose, because there were people in the windows and others coming out of the lecture theatres.'

'But how many of them were next to the bodies? The reports imply there were only two – one of them is you.'

'I was the second one there. By the time I arrived, Professor Steyn was already there.'

It was the first time either Andrew or Jenny had heard the name. She glanced up, catching Andrew's eye, letting him know she was still in control.

'If he was there first, what was he doing?'

'He was a mess.' Ishan glanced between them. 'You sort of expect older people to be the ones in control, don't you? Especially when things start going wrong. It's like when you're a kid. You assume your mum and dad have the answers to everything because they're the grown-ups. It's only when you grow older yourself you realise that it's not like that. You only know the answers through education and experience. Most of the time, you're guessing and hoping for the best.'

'What was Professor Steyn like?'

'He could barely speak. He had his hand over his mouth and was stumbling along, like his knees couldn't hold him up. He was trying to help her.'

'Who?'

'Wendy. I think he thought she was still alive but she was long gone. The police said she died instantly. He tried to turn her over and then he was sick everywhere. All over himself, all over them. I think he saw the actual shootings.'

Andrew was now the one fidgeting. If that was true, it had never been divulged in the papers. If it had been brought up in the inquest, it had been kept secret, most likely to protect Steyn's identity.

'Did he say anything?' Jenny asked.

'The professor? I don't know. He was slurring his words. I took a module with him in year one but I don't think he remembered me.'

Slowly, Jenny had gone from smiley, happy look-at-me maths friend to interrogator. Her eyes locked with Ishan's, voice calm. 'Think about what he was slurring. If he saw what happened, what did he say?'

Ishan scratched his head with one hand, holding his tea steady with the other, transfixed by her. When she wanted to command a conversation, Jenny could be as good as Keira's father.

The student's voice was a whisper. 'He said, "he shot them both".'

'But you didn't actually see the gun fired?'

'No, it was on the ground next to the soldier when I got there. I heard it.'

'And Professor Steyn definitely said, word for word, "he shot them both"?'

'Yes . . . and then . . .' Andrew could see the light bulb going off in Ishan's mind. He sat up straighter, putting down his cup, his hands becoming animated. 'It's strange because that's how I remember it. He said "he shot them both" and then a few of the others who came out started repeating it.' He clicked his fingers. 'I remember it now – that's what I told the operator on the phone. She asked what I could see and I spelled out the name on the soldier's coat, then I said that he'd shot both of them, then himself. The gun was next to his hand but the only reason I thought he'd shot them is because Steyn told me.' His eyes widened, turning from Andrew to Jenny. 'Is something wrong?'

Andrew told Jenny the answer with his eyes and a barely perceptible shake of his head.

'Not at all,' she said. 'You said the professor didn't recognise you but what was the module you did with him?'

Ishan's voice was starting to crack. 'He's not really a lecturer,' he said. 'I think he used to be but he does a lot of research now. He teaches a first-year elective in African Studies. That's all I know. I've not seen him since.'

He buried his head in his hands, tears suddenly coming, words almost inaudible between his gentle sobs. 'You can't un-see things.'

If Andrew didn't feel bad enough, Jenny leant forward and drew Ishan's head onto her shoulder, catching his gaze over the poor kid's back. Whether or not Andrew had meant to, he'd used the pair of them to find out what he needed.

35

Andrew didn't have to wait for Iwan to open the gates on his second visit to Thomas Braithwaite's mansion. By the time he had parked his car and crossed the road, the gates had already unlocked themselves and swung inwards. If anything, that only added to his sense of unease.

He feels he's trusted you and brought you into his inner circle.

This was an inner circle of which Andrew didn't particularly want to be a part – but it was already too late for that.

Gloomy-grey was just about clinging on in the battle against rain-grey but the temperature was beginning to cool as Andrew walked steadily along the drive, peering both ways and trying to absorb the scene around him. Afternoon was caving in all too easily, giving way to early sunset and the onset of evening. It really should grow a little backbone.

The garden was hauntingly still, leaving Andrew with an increasing sensation that he was walking to his doom, one plodding step at a time. When he reached the fountain and expensive cars, he continued towards the rear of the house in the way Iwan had directed him on his previous visit. He was so busy keeping an eye on everything around him that he almost bumped into the locked gate blocking the archway cut into the hedge. He squinted through the gap in the metal towards the stable at the back of the garden, cupping his hand over his eyes, but there was no one in sight.

Andrew turned, staring up at the house for any sign of a camera. He felt watched. Like one of Pavlov's dogs, already conditioned to act in a certain way.

Hands in pockets, trying to appear casual, Andrew returned to the front of the house, passing the Bentley and red sports car, feet crunching across the gravel until he reached the front door. This time, he did have to ring the bell, standing and waiting, until it opened a crack to reveal Iwan's towering bulk. Andrew gripped the strap of his satchel that was slung across his front. It wasn't much of a shield but it was better than nothing. If people with clenched fists weren't supposed to hit a man with glasses, then surely they couldn't pick on a bloke with a satchel strapped across his chest?

Iwan tugged on the sleeve of his suit, eyes staring through Andrew. He turned, but not quickly enough to hide the blood-red scratch that linked his ear to his eye.

Jenny had literally left her mark.

Andrew closed the door, entering into a vast hallway, decked out in a mix of echoing shiny tiles and antique wood. A staircase spiralled up to the first floor, with an enormous canvas painting of someone in a red coat riding into battle hung on the wall in front.

Iwan's footsteps clip-clopped across the hard floor, heading out of sight into another room. Andrew had to hurry to catch him, almost sliding into the kitchen, where Braithwaite was sitting at a high stool next to a counter in the centre of the room. The counter tops were carved from thick white marble, with rows of glinting pans hanging above and an oven that was three times as wide as the one in Andrew's flat.

Braithwaite turned, that ice-blue stare fixing on Andrew for a moment before he broke into a smile. 'Mr Hunter, it's so nice to see you again.' He offered his hand, leaving Andrew with little choice other than to shake it. There was having self-respect and there was being stupid. Braithwaite nodded at the stool next to him, wanting Andrew to sit, and then peered over his shoulder towards the doorway. 'That'll be all, Iwan.'

'Sir.' The man in the suit turned and headed back into the hallway, footsteps echoing loudly behind him.

Braithwaite had been reading a broadsheet but folded it in half, pushing it towards a thick wooden chopping board in the centre of the unit. The similarities between him and Keira's father were uncanny. Different men who moved in different circles, yet both steeped with the aura of power. He indicated towards the door through which Iwan had departed.

'I understand there was an incident yesterday. I can only apologise if things got a little out of hand. I've had a word with Iwan. It shouldn't happen again.'

'You've had him following me.'

Braithwaite pressed his lips together, nodding slowly. 'Do you cook, Mr Hunter?'

'Er . . .'

He pointed to the pans above their heads, holding both hands aloft. 'I took it up last year, when I retired. My wife used to do the cooking, or we'd sometimes get professionals in. I'm slightly ashamed to say that I always thought of it as women's work. I come from that age where women still knew their place but, alas, time moves on, so with it we must move.' He plucked a muffin tray from underneath the counter and placed it between them. 'So, do you cook?'

'Not . . . really. Only simple things.'

'There's nothing wrong with simple things, Mr Hunter. Everything today's about trying something new: Vietnamese food, Thai curries, Moroccan. It's something different every month but you can't beat a good British roast.' He stabbed at the tray. 'Do you know the secret to a really good Yorkshire pudding?'

'No.'

'It's nothing to do with the batter. Whatever you come up with is a mix of flour and either water or milk, with a pinch of salt. I like to use egg but that's just me. The thing that really matters is the planning. You've got to coat your pan with oil, get your oven up to the hottest temperature it can reach, and then put the pan in. You wait for the oil to start smouldering and then remove it again, pouring your batter in quickly to the perfect level, before getting it back into the oven on a lower heat. It sounds simple but it's about timing and it's the temperature that's critical. Too hot and it'll burst free from the pan, too cool and it won't rise. Some people like Yorkshires when they expand.' He shook his head, tapping the pan. 'Not me. I like them to be just the height of the tray, no higher. Getting it right is all about making an investment and then sticking with it, even if it means sitting in front of the oven and watching everything meticulously.' He focused on Andrew, both arms out as if they were going to embrace. 'When I make an investment in anything, Mr Hunter, including people . . . *especially* people . . . I like to know what I'm getting in return. Just like my Yorkshires, it's all about timing, groundwork and dedication. I want assurances that other people are putting in the time and the preparation that I do. I don't want them bursting free and doing their own thing.'

He continued staring at Andrew for a few moments, before returning the tray to underneath the counter.

'Do you understand?' he added.

Yes, Andrew thought, that you're a sodding nutter.

'I can't work properly if I'm going to be followed everywhere I go.' Andrew pointed a thumb over his shoulder. 'Especially by him.'

Braithwaite was nodding slowly again, absorbing the words. 'I realise that Iwan and yourself haven't got off to the best of starts. He can be slightly headstrong. You have my assurance that he will not follow you again.'

It wasn't exactly what Andrew wanted – the words had been chosen carefully enough that it meant Braithwaite could get any of the other seven billion people on the planet to follow him, but at least Iwan should steer clear.

'How is your aunt and her electrics?' Braithwaite asked, taking Andrew by surprise again.

'Sorry?'

'The last time you were here, you said something about a "cowboy" making a mess of things.'

'Oh . . . right . . . she's fine. It was so bad it could have caused a fire but I got someone to sort it all out.'

'I have a number of skilled people who work for me. I

could arrange for someone to check everything over. It'd be peace of mind, I'm sure.'

'Thank you for the offer but it's all been sorted.'

'If you're sure . . . I should probably ask for the name of your "cowboy".'

Andrew was avoiding eye contact but he could still feel Braithwaite's stare. 'Why?'

'I have tradesmen working for me all over the country, the north especially. If there's someone doing dangerous work out there, I'd rather know.'

'You wouldn't need to worry about him. He's this small-time kid.'

'I'd still like the name, Mr Hunter.'

Andrew could feel the mark on his forehead itching, from where Kevin had punched him and Iwan had jabbed it. 'He's a nobody.'

'The name, Mr Hunter.'

'It's Kevin. Kevin Leonard. He's just some scally, no one you need to bother about.'

'Noted. Now, shall we get to business?'

Andrew removed the laptop from his bag and placed it on the counter top between them. He had to fiddle with the settings to link it to the wireless on his phone, figuring Braithwaite wasn't the type of person who knew about Wi-Fi connections.

'This is the CCTV footage from the robbery,' Andrew said, loading the police's website and setting the video running.

Braithwaite watched in silence before turning to Andrew. 'What's your point?'

'Everyone missed it, even though it was in plain sight the entire time. Watch the far left of the screen.'

He replayed the footage again, only to get another similar blank look, which wasn't entirely surprising. Andrew could have told Braithwaite what to look for but it was nice to feel superior for a change. *He'd* seen it. Not the police, not Braithwaite, not even Jenny.

'What am I looking for?' Braithwaite asked, a tad annoyed.

'When Owen and Wendy enter the shop, Sampson is working at a bench behind the counter. We already know that he's busy fixing a necklace for a film production company. It's really small but you can just about make out a shiny loop on the footage. It looks white.' Andrew pointed towards the blob on the far left of the screen, almost out of sight. 'Now watch,' he added, starting the footage again.

As Owen and Wendy browsed the cases, the shop door burst open, with the Evans brothers piling inside. Shouting, smash-smash, shouting, bang. Andrew had seen it so many times that he knew the movements of everyone involved. Without watching, he knew the exact moment that Owen made eye contact with Sampson, who then looked away.

Braithwaite almost rocked himself off his stool when he saw it: 'They stole the wrong thing.'

As the Evans brothers left the shop, Braithwaite pointed to the white blob on the left of the screen, in the exact same position it had been in throughout.

Andrew set the footage replaying from the beginning again, spelling out what the screen was showing. 'The robbers clear out the counter and smash the other one bu

Sampson's constantly trying to catch their eyes and glancing back to the bench. If someone's pointing a gun at you, you'd be looking at the gun, or the person holding it – not peering behind. He's trying to give them the message where the expensive necklace is – but failing completely because they're too stupid. Sampson could hardly clear off the bench and dump everything in their bag because it'd be obvious.'

'Everyone missed it . . .'

'Because you naturally look for what *is* happening, not what isn't. That footage is blown up to full-size on my screen and you can only just about pick out the white blob. Most people wouldn't have seen it like that, if they watched it at all. It's been on the police's own website for over a year and they missed it. The people who might have noticed were Owen and Wendy because they were there. Sampson knew straight away the wrong thing had been stolen, so he panicked.'

Braithwaite's features were a strange mix of admiration, intrigue and amusement. 'I knew there was something not quite right. The sly bastard.' He turned to Andrew again. 'So how did he get Methodist to shoot them?'

Andrew closed his laptop lid and slipped it back into his bag, just as one of the Bengals crept into the kitchen, tail twisting and curling as it let out a gentle mew. Braithwaite held his hand out for the cat and began stroking its back.

'I'm not sure yet,' Andrew replied. 'I need time. I had to come here this afternoon, else I could have been getting answers.'

Braithwaite smirked slightly, lifting the cat onto his lap. 'Point taken.'

'I've got things to do this evening – and tomorrow. I'll come back to you when I have answers. *If* I have answers.'

'Understood, but . . . I only need to know what our friend Mr Sampson has been up to.' Braithwaite gazed into Andrew's eyes, the message clear. The Bengal began to purr as it was stroked. Braithwaite looked like a Bond villain who had a designer kitchen. 'I could use someone like you,' he purred, as if imitating the cat.

'I'm not for sale,' Andrew replied.

'I can find out all sorts of things about people but I have no idea how you managed to accrue such a lifestyle, nor why you'd continue to work. Someone who lives in an apartment like yours, with the money that implies . . . you must have demons in your past.'

'We all have our secrets.'

'That we do.'

Andrew stood and picked up his bag, his sudden movement spooking the cat, who leapt from Braithwaite's lap and bolted for the door.

In the moment of scratching, sliding claws on tile, Andrew seized his moment, whispering delicately enough that there was no risk of anyone overhearing. 'There might be a professor involved.'

Braithwaite studied him, sucking in his cheeks, eyes narrowing. For a moment he said nothing, then he scratched furiously at the dusting of stubble on his chin. 'Why would you be telling me that? I told you that I only needed to know about our friend, Mr Sampson.'

This time it was Andrew who locked them into a stare. 'You know why.'

A short nod, a thin smile. Mutual understanding. Soul sold. 'If you give me the name, I'll look into my options.'

Andrew shook his head. 'Not today. What would you do?'

'What do you think?'

'I don't want *that*.'

Braithwaite seemed amused, toying with his new plaything, offering a pat on the head with a look, rather than a hand. 'What *do* you want?'

Andrew turned to leave. 'Give me a day. I learned a thing or two from my former father-in-law.'

36

The clouds of earlier in the day had broken, leaving space for a wonderful bright moon to beam white light across the city. Andrew stood in the window of his apartment, staring across the vast ocean of people going about their lives. Vehicles were dribbling in and out of Manchester, with the endless stretch of buildings lit up far into the distance.

Because he saw it every day, Andrew often felt desensitised to the view. There was a strange beauty to the organised chaos. The confusing web of centuries-old highways and towering glass structures, like the one in which he lived, existed side by side. The canal wound its way through the city as if it had always been there, but it wasn't even a century and a half old. Everything would keep expanding, continuing to change. When he stood in this spot, peering down upon the world below, it was hard not to feel the urge to press his nose hard against the glass and keep pushing. To feel the rush of the wind, the thunderous roar of the elements.

'Andrew . . .'

He turned at the sound of Keira's soft voice. She was standing next to the sofa, glass of wine in her hand, stunning in a black cocktail dress with matching shoes that she hadn't kicked off. He was embarrassed at the effort she'd made when he was wearing loose-fitting dark trousers, socks, and a shirt that hadn't been ironed. She could go out on the town, he could do knee-skids on the hard floor as if he was a kid at his first school disco.

'Whatcha thinking about?' she asked, click-clacking across the room and linking her arm through his. She put her wine glass on the ledge and rested her head on his shoulder, staring towards the eternity beyond the glass.

'Just . . . life.'

'That's deep. I thought you were going to say you were wondering if we should order in a takeaway and, if so, did I want Chinese or pizza.'

He squeezed her tighter. 'That's what I'm thinking about now.'

'So? Chinese or pizza?'

'We could go out?'

She stepped away from him, bending her knees slightly in a half-curtsey, holding her hands out. 'Does it look like I'm dressed to be outside in temperatures like this?'

It gave him an excuse to look at her bare legs, the thin straps of her dress hooping over her shoulders, the low U-shape in the centre. More flesh. If she hadn't got so dressed up to go out, then there was probably only one reason.

She stepped back towards him, wrapping an arm around his waist. 'The city looks completely different from up here. When you're on the ground, it's just noise and people, cars and fumes. From here, there's a sort of organised chaos to it all.'

The hairs stood up on his neck as she used the exact phrase that had been flitting around his mind.

'There's a sort of magic to it all,' she added. 'You've done so well for yourself.'

Andrew didn't know how to respond. He was embarrassed: he'd not done well for himself at all. He'd been bought.

'It's been lovely living in the country again,' Keira continued. 'There's a prettiness there – the green, the trees, the walks, the peace . . . this is beautiful but in a different way. You could sit here for hours and not get bored.'

'Anything's better than watching ITV.'

Keira laughed.

'It's not always like this,' Andrew added. 'When the riots happened last year, you could see the fires in the distance and flashing blue lights from the police cars and ambulances heading towards them.'

She tickled him slightly, making him gasp. 'You always were the smooth talker. Is that your sexy talk? Riots?'

'Sorry. I was thinking out loud.'

Because of the heels, she didn't have far to reach, pressing her lips into the nape of his neck. It only lasted for a moment but was plenty enough to make Andrew tingle. He'd been waiting almost nine years to feel this chemistry.

Keira stood on her toes, breath brushing his ear seductively. 'Chinese or pizza?'

She burst out laughing, wobbling slightly and falling into him. Andrew held her close, resting his head on her hair, breathing her in. She was slightly tipsy already and hadn't even finished her first glass of wine. Either that or she was happy. He couldn't tell the difference.

'Can we talk first?' he whispered.

'We are talking but I'm hungryyyyyyyyy.'

Andrew took her hand and led her across the room to the sofa, where she flopped into the corner and started giggling. She crossed and uncrossed her legs, trying to get comfortable.

'We could just go to the bedroom,' she whispered silkily.

'We should talk.'

She reached out and grabbed his hand. 'We can do that after.'

Anything up to ninety-nine per cent of Andrew's body was more than happy to go along with that suggestion but there was that pesky little conscience in the back of his mind whispering its malicious spoilers. What a heartless bastard it was.

'We need to talk about what happened when we broke up.'

Keira pressed a finger to his lips, shaking her head, the giggles gone. 'No.'

He opened his mouth anyway: 'I should have told you then.'

'We were different people then, kids, we got married too soon. We had too much, too young. I get it. We've grown up now.'

'It's not that.'

She took his wrist, running her slender fingers across the back of his hand, tracing a pattern. 'Shh . . .'

'Keira . . .'

'Do you know why I fell for you?' she said. Andrew gulped, wondering if he was going to bottle it. He shook his head. 'My friends thought I was crazy for going out with you. You'd dumped all that food on me in the refectory and then acted like a bit of a dick about it.'

'I was trying to make you laugh.'

'Then you gave me your number because you wanted to pay for any cleaning bills.'

'I thought it'd be chivalrous!' She raised an eyebrow at him. 'Okay, I was hoping to get your number and I thought that might be the best way.'

'I texted you a very simple message, which I thought couldn't be misinterpreted—'

Andrew completed her sentence: '"How are you going to make amends?"'

Keira nodded. 'Exactly,' she said. 'I thought you might offer to take me out for a nice dinner, perhaps for cocktails, some dancing, that sort of thing. But where did we end up?'

Despite his mood, Andrew couldn't stop himself grinning. 'I thought you literally meant "make amends".'

She rolled her eyes. 'So we're in the launderette doing my washing, you've fed a quid fifty into the machine and we're watching my dirty jeans spin around. It's just us and a noisy washing machine. You're wittering on about this games club you're involved with and I'm there thinking, "What the hell am I doing here?" When I'd been on dates with lads before, we'd gone to nice places and they'd fussed over me, paying for things, asking me how I was all the time. It was like that at home too. I'd never had a Big Mac until I was nineteen because Daddy didn't approve of fast food.'

'I never knew that.'

She shrugged. 'It occurred to me that I'd never had a

good time with any of the lads I'd been out with. Not when I thought about it afterwards. They were fun at the time but . . . hollow. It's like the world is fake and you get dressed up to go to all of these places, talk about mundane things and then go home – but it's not real life. The next day, you wake up and reality's dawning. But I was there with you in that launderette and it was really hot. I'd never had to wash my own clothes before – my mum or the maid always did it. I just thought that if you were the type of person who'd dare take a girl on a date to wash her clothes, then you were the type of normal person I'd quite like to hang around with. By the time it was one in the morning and we'd been there chatting for six hours, I knew we were going to get married one day.'

'Keira . . .'

She talked over him, eyes beginning to puff. 'You broke my heart when you left but I'm willing to let it happen again if it means having another go with that lad who could spend six hours talking to me in a launderette.' She gripped his hand tighter, thumb pressing into his skin. 'This is the first Valentine's night that I've spent with anyone since we had our last one together. I've been waiting for all this time for you to walk back into my life.'

Shit, shit, shit.

Andrew could feel the lump in his throat, choking him. He should have cut her off before she'd told him all of that. It was only going to make it more difficult to say what he had to. Slowly, he pulled his hand away from hers, shuffling backwards until they were at opposite ends of the sofa.

'What?' she asked, gulping, surprised.

'I've really got to tell you the truth.'

'What about?'

He held his hands up to indicate the flat. 'This. My office, all of it.' He suddenly felt cold, hairs bristling on his arms, chest tight. 'I chose this over you.'

'Chose what?'

'Everything. The money, this life.'

'I don't understand.'

He found himself squeezing the top of his nose, struggling for the words. 'I know it sounds bad. It's the way your dad speaks, he—'

'My dad?'

Andrew nodded.

'My dad paid for . . . *this*?' Keira kicked her knees up to her chest, hugging them, confused.

'He never liked me and didn't want us to be together,' Andrew replied. 'You didn't speak to each other for a while after we got married and then we thought he'd come round to the idea, at least a little.'

'I know that.'

'He never stopped wanting to break us up. When we went to your parents' house to ask for some money for a deposit on a house because we wanted to start a family, he took me to one side when you were off talking to your mum.'

'You should have said something.'

'He said there was no way he was going to let a scrounger like me have a child with his daughter, that if I was worthy of you, then I'd be able to look after you without coming to him for handouts. He said he'd do whatever it took to break us up before you got pregnant, that he'd destroy my life. He told me he knew people and he'd stop me getting a job. He was going on about my parents—'

'Your parents?'

'He said he'd buy the houses on either side of theirs and rent them out for next to nothing, so the neighbours would drive them crazy.'

'My dad said this?'

'While you were upstairs with your mum.'

Keira reached for her wine glass, downing the remains in one, sucking the final drops from the bottom. She was blinking so quickly that it was as if there was something in her eye. 'Why didn't you tell me?'

'He said I had two options. He'd either destroy my life, or he'd pay me to go away. One way I'd have nothing, the other way I'd still have my life. Both ways, I'd lose you.'

Andrew stretched to take her hand but their shared moment was long gone. Keira snatched it backwards, standing too quickly and staggering slightly. He stood, reaching out to steady her but she pulled away a second time, rushing around the coffee table to the kitchen. She turned on the cold tap, cupping the water in her hands and drinking it down, before dousing her face. When she eventually spun to face him, there was still water dripping from her cheeks and the skin around her eyes was red.

'Don't you think I'd have had a say in it?'

'It's hard to describe. It was just me and him and he said I had to decide within twenty-four hours. If he didn't hear anything, then he'd assume I'd rejected his offer and he'd put wheels in motion.'

'What wheels?'

'To ruin me.'

'You think he could do that?'

Tanjir Ahmed's name bounced to the front of Andrew's mind. 'Yes . . . I don't know . . . he's a rich man.'

'So what? That doesn't make him God. I'm my own person.' She dabbed her face with a tea towel and then flung it to the side. 'Why are you telling me this now?'

'He came to see me yesterday. He'd found out my mobile number and called, wanting to meet in a pub in the centre.'

'Of Manchester?'

'Yes.'

'He never comes up here.'

'I know – but he did. He told me I had to break up with you again, else he'd destroy my life. He showed me things . . .'

Keira was shaking her head slowly. 'Did he offer you money?'

'Of course not!'

'But that didn't stop you last time.'

'It's not like that, it's the way he says things, he—'

Keira lunged at him, thumping an open palm into his chest. 'You're a grown man!'

'I know.'

She pushed him away. 'You said he only gave you two options all those years ago but there was always a third – to tell me, trust me. We were married and that's what you should have done.'

'I know that now.'

She took a breath, stepping around Andrew and pointing towards the endless view. 'But you chose money over me.'

'Yes, but . . .'

Both had tears in their eyes. Keira picked up her bag from the sofa, her heels clattering across the wooden floor as she headed for the door. She stopped, turning to face him. 'But what?'

Andrew wished he could think of something to say that might exonerate him, though there was only the truth: 'But nothing,' he replied, chin sinking to his chest. 'Yes – I chose money over you.'

She nodded shortly, turned, and walked through the door, closing it with a quiet click and striding along the corridor, out of his life for a second time.

Happy Valentine's Day.

37

WEDNESDAY

Professor Geoffrey Steyn was feeding leftover pieces of sandwich to the pigeons when Andrew plonked himself on the bench next to him.

'Nice spot,' Andrew said.

Steyn was wearing a chocolate blazer, with matching trousers and a white shirt. He had thinning white hair swept underneath a flat cap, like a country gentleman out for a lunchtime stroll. He glanced quickly at Andrew, before returning his attention to the pigeons.

'Quite, quite,' he muttered.

'Do you come here often?'

'Pardon?'

'Whitworth Park – do you come here for lunch often? I suppose the weather's been a bit rough recently but sometimes that crisp air is nice and cleansing, good for the soul.'

Steyn started to pack up his lunchbox, pegging Andrew as an obvious park nutter.

'I thought I was going to have to make an appointment to see you,' Andrew continued. 'The university website has your biography, but no phone number. When I called the main reception, they could only give me an email address. My friend and I had to ask a few of the students for directions to your office. Most of them didn't know who you were but we found one eventually. I was going to knock on your door but you need a swipe card to get that far. I was wondering what I should do next when, what do you know, out you pop, flat cap and briefcase, off to go for lunch. It's almost like fate brought us together.'

Steyn peered at him again, eyes narrowing, brow ruffling into a labyrinth of wrinkles. 'Should I know you?'

Andrew held out his hand, nodding towards the city centre. 'Andrew Hunter, I'm a private investigator who works about a mile that way.'

The lunchbox was dispatched back into the briefcase, Andrew's hand remaining unshaken. 'I, er, have to get back to the office,' Steyn said.

Andrew didn't move. 'What was it like to be the first person on the scene when Owen Copthorne and Wendy Boyes were killed?'

Steyn stared at him, thumbs pressed on the locks of his case, frozen. 'Sorry?'

'It was you who got there first, wasn't it? You're the one who said "He shot them both". Before you knew it, everyone was saying it.'

'I . . . who are you again?'

He offered his hand once more. 'Andrew Hunter.'

Steyn ignored it, clipping his case closed and slipping out leather gloves from his coat pocket. 'I told you, I have to head back. I think you might have the wrong person.'

Andrew waited for a few moments, watching a tree close to the park boundary, where a grey squirrel was braving the cold, scuttling across the turf and sniffing for food. Pigeons were still around Steyn's feet, pecking for errant crumbs they'd missed.

'I met a jeweller last week,' Andrew said. 'He owns this little place in town, the type of spot that's been there for years that you walk past every day because no one's a regular buyer of jewellery, well, unless you're Mr T.'

'Who?'

'It's this type of place where you'd go to get something special, like an engagement ring, or your wedding bands. You'd want to go somewhere local where you can trust the guy behind the counter and have a face-to-face conversation, rather than go to a chain where the person serving you is just a glorified cashier. It's called Sampson's, between here and my office, not far from the university. Have you heard of it?'

Steyn stared open-mouthed at Andrew for a moment, before spinning on his heels, almost treading on a pigeon. 'I've got to go.'

'Sit *down*, Mr Steyn.' Andrew glared at him, refusing to let him go, in the way Keira's father had to him. In the way Braithwaite could. Steyn was so confused that he turned in a circle, before focusing back on Andrew and lowering himself onto the bench.

'The owner of Sampson's is, perhaps unsurprisingly, named Sampson – Leyton Sampson,' Andrew continued. 'He seems very talented. He was telling me and my friend all about the repairs he can do, plus he seemed very proud of the fact that he has people mining diamonds directly for him in Botswana. I checked and that's an extremely uncommon thing to happen. Usually, there are middlemen, wholesalers, more middlemen, you name it. It's like any business – lots of people in a line chip, chip, chipping away at the profits. It sounds like he's onto a really good thing – he can undercut his rivals, make more money in the process, *and* provide higher-quality jewels to his customers. It's incredible and so easy to take at face value. Someone says "Botswana" and you almost blank it out. It's just a country somewhere else in the world. Africa? Asia? Maybe South America? Somewhere foreign and they mine diamonds. Amazing. I wonder if anyone has ever thought to question it.'

Steyn rubbed his shoe along the gritted path, making the remaining pigeons strut towards the bushes or flutter away into the skies. 'I don't know why you're telling me this.'

'I'm pretty good on a computer but my friend, well, she's something special. It's natural to her. Sometimes I wonder if she can type faster than I can think. We were looking into Botswana together and what becomes really clear is that you can't do much out there unless you know the language. It's tucked away in southern Africa, wedged between Namibia and Zimbabwe, this huge place. It's more than twice the size of the UK, but with only two million people living there. There are four times more people than that in London alone. If you put Manchester, Liverpool and Birmingham together, that's your two million people.'

Steyn was perched on the tip of the bench, hands pressed together as if praying.

'So there's this enormous country,' Andrew continued, 'where the official language is supposed to be English, yet four out of five people speak Setswana. I've never heard of that but it's easy enough to look up. It's a regional dialect related to the Bantu family of languages, something else I'd never heard of. It's interesting what you can find out on the Internet, though – when you get past the pornography, there's all sorts. For instance, when I was on the university's website, it lists every member of staff, including research fellows, like your good self. Guess what I found under your entry?'

'You don't have to do this.'

'I do, because it's important you understand exactly why I'm here. Under your interests and specialities, it says that, having grown up in South Africa, you speak a dozen languages, including many dialects of Bantu. That left me wondering, what if Sampson's contact isn't some bloke in Botswana on the end of a crackly phone line, what if he's a few hundred metres down the road in a warm university office?'

Steyn stood again, this time turning his back. Andrew watched him take a step and then there was fury raging through him: Iwan patting him on the head; that runt Kevin Leonard taking Gem's money and nearly burning her flat down; his former father-in-law ending any hope he had with Keira, even though he'd eventually told her the truth. Too many people were willing to trample on him but he'd made a pledge to a young girl that he was going to keep. He lunged forward, grabbing the scruff of Steyn's shirt, wrenching him downwards and slamming him back onto the bench.

'You're going to sit still and listen to me!'

Steyn tried to stand again but Andrew shoved him hard in the chest, looming over him.

'*Sit still.*'

'I'll shout for help.'

'Do that. Shout and shout until the police turn up. Let's see what they have to say.' Steyn glared at him, so Andrew leant in closer. 'Do it!'

Steyn started coughing, making Andrew step back. He fumbled in his pockets, pulling out a small orange tub and unscrewing the lid before popping a white pill into his mouth. He was shaking, flapping a pudgy arm but not making contact.

Andrew sat next to him again, twisting to face the professor, who was loosening his collar.

'You can't keep me here,' Steyn said.

'So walk away. I'll head down the road to Longsight police station and have a word with a friend of mine.'

Steyn was out of breath, rubbing his elbow from where Andrew had pushed him down. 'Fine. I'm listening.'

'You're on the site as a senior clinical research fellow and it lists the projects you've been involved with, including that you recently headed a study into post-traumatic stress disorder. It's quite hard to find out anything more about that as you haven't published yet, but I wonder if the name "Luke Methodist" is buried in there somewhere as someone you met. He told his street friends he was looking for help from someone but the medical records are confidential. Then there's the fact that you do a little bit of work away from social sciences, teaching an African Studies module on the side. Bit of extra money, I guess, multi-talented gentleman like yourself. With your background, there's probably no one better. Of course, that means you already knew Wendy Boyes before you saw her dead body – she did her first-year elective with you. I wonder if you told the police that.'

Steyn's wriggle and coat-fiddling gave Andrew the answer he already suspected.

'That Saturday afternoon, when Sampson's shop was robbed, he either called you in a panic, or he came to see you. He said he'd come up with a plan to make some quick insurance money but it had gone wrong because the idiots he was working with had stolen the wrong thing. Perhaps you owed him money or a favour? Either way, he wanted you to sort it. You were a lecturer and these two kids had witnessed the robbery in his shop and were now all over the news blabbing about it. Sooner or later, one of them would work out the wrong thing had been taken. What he didn't realise was that you already knew Wendy, the pretty girl with the wavy black hair who'd been in your module. She'd probably laughed a few times, chatted to her friends, perhaps come to ask you a question or two after the work-shops. She'd stuck in your mind.'

Steyn popped another pill from his pocket, shaking his head furiously.

'Something had to be done quickly. Everyone's email address and phone number is stored on the internal univer-sity database, but that would have left a trail if you'd contacted Wendy from your own phone or email. One way or another, you went to her, asking to meet her and her fiancé, saying you'd seen them on TV. You could have said anything. You wanted their help for a project? Something like that. Meanwhile, you contacted Luke Methodist too – and arranged for everyone to be in the same place at once.'

Andrew paused for breath, to compose himself, to try to lose the edge of fury that was engulfing him. '*You* might have shot them all but maybe it *was* Luke who was disturbed and lost it for whatever reason. Maybe it was his Browning, or maybe it was one bought in a pub. We'll probably never know. Regardless, it *was* you who arranged it. You then contaminated the scene: an anguished onlooker, who couldn't control his stomach. "He shot them both" became fact. What was there to check? And why would people bother when it was so obvious? Then the Evans brothers were arrested and everyone assumed they'd organised it anyway.'

Steyn stood again and Andrew let him. 'I have no idea what you're talking about,' he said.

'So I can go to the police and ask their opinion, then?'

'What is it you want? Money? Are you trying to blackmail me?'

'I've already taken go-away money once. Never again.'

'What then? If you were going to the police, you'd already be there, not harassing me on a park bench while I eat my sandwiches.'

Andrew stood, brushing down his front and pulling up his trousers. He'd lost weight, which was hard to do when spending time with Jenny.

'I just want you to know that *I* know.'

'So what?' Steyn turned to leave but then twisted back. 'Perhaps you should ask yourself one thing, Mr Hunter. *Andrew* Hunter. If this jeweller is as powerful and corrupt as you think, if I'm capable of everything you say, if we can pull all of this off underneath the noses of those around us, what makes you think you're untouchable?'

Andrew put his hands in his pockets, ready to head in the opposite direction. He couldn't force a smile. 'Because, Professor Steyn, you can't harm a man who's already made a deal with the devil.'

38

THREE DAYS LATER

With the slush fest of Valentine's Day out of the way, spring was coming early to Manchester. Sort of. A lone daffodil had sprouted on the edge of a flowerbed, not far from a fountain that wasn't working. It was an obvious hard-ass, showing off to its mates that not even the February chill was enough to scare it. Snow? Bring it on. Frost? A big girl's blouse.

Andrew had his own handful of flowers, some sort of orange and white lilies which Jenny shrugged at, saying they looked 'flowery'. Her level of botanical expertise was up there with his.

Fiona Methodist had been silently standing next to him but now she crouched until she was on her knees and then sat on the dewy grass with her legs outstretched, resting her back against a thick stone slab.

'Is it wet?' Andrew asked.

Fiona was all pointy elbows and knees again, her dark hair bundled underneath the same purple bobble hat she'd been wearing when they first met. 'What do you think?'

'Will you at least take my coat?'

'What will you wear?'

Andrew slipped out of his thick woollen coat and

handed it over. 'I've got a jumper on, I'll live. You look like you're going to freeze.'

For a moment, he thought she was going to argue, but then she took it, slipping her slender arms inside, without removing her own thin jacket. She pulled it tightly closed and breathed out. There was no plume of steam: spring really was on the way!

Andrew nodded, indicating the cemetery around them. 'How often do you come here?' He rubbed his hands together, not wanting to admit he was chilly.

'A few times a week. It depends on the weather. There's not much you can do when it's lashing down, which is most days.'

'How have you been?'

'All right. I got taken on by an employment agency. They know my last name but none of the clients do. When I go to a new place, I tell them I'm Fiona and everyone gets on with it. The girl at the agency has a dad in the army. She sort of knows what it's like, not completely, but . . .'

'I understand.'

'It's not much money but it's better than nothing. I'm still in that flat but if I can keep getting work, then I might be able to find somewhere else.'

'Good for you.'

She tugged her hat down a little further and then dug her hands into the pockets of his coat. 'You'll think I'm weird, but I like it here. It's really peaceful.'

Andrew stood still, listening. He didn't spend a lot of time in graveyards but couldn't argue. Aside from a dog barking somewhere in the distance, a gentle breeze, and the faint sound of cars, there was nothing except their voices.

'The police told me this is what Dad's grave had to be like,' she whispered, her words almost lost to the rustle of the trees.

Andrew stared down towards where she was resting her head, a completely blank gravestone that looked as if it was there holding the spot for when somebody important passed away. Everybody who died was important to somebody, of course, even a person who killed an innocent young couple.

'They said people would desecrate it,' she added. 'It was either have him buried in a different area of the country, have him cremated, or this. I didn't like the idea of burning the body, it seems so . . . *final*.'

Andrew let the moment hang before telling her why he'd called. 'I've got some bad news for you, Fiona.'

She didn't move her head from the stone, but she did close her eyes, breathing in through her nose. 'It wasn't him.'

'I wish I could tell you for sure that's true but I can't.'

She turned to face him, peering straight up, showing the whites of her eyes. '*I* know he didn't shoot them.'

Andrew pointed to the spot on the ground next to her. 'May I?'

She nodded, so he slipped onto the grass beside her, resting his back against the empty headstone. He had no idea what the etiquette in this type of situation was supposed to be but if it was good enough for Luke's daughter, then it was good enough for him. The dew on the grass soaked straight through his trousers but he ignored it, listening to the silence.

'I'm never going to be able to tell you whether your father shot Owen and Wendy. He might have done, but, even if he did, it was because he was under pressure from somebody else.'

'Who?'

'I can't tell you that. You wouldn't know the person anyway. I wish there was a way I could let the world know but it's not going to happen.'

'I'd like to know.'

They sat in silence for a few moments. Andrew gazed towards the horizon, where Beetham Tower soared into the sky. Somewhere near the top was the apartment he'd bought with his go-away money. He'd not heard from Keira since she'd stormed out of there on Valentine's night, but neither had he heard from her father. Was that the last of the Chapman family? Or would Edgar take his revenge at some point when Andrew wasn't expecting it? For now, all he could do was continue with his life.

'Would you like to know a secret?' he asked.

'About my dad?'

'About me.'

'Oh . . . okay.'

'Everybody tells you that hate is a negative emotion, that it builds within you and makes you do horrible things. I've hated someone for the past nine years, longer than that, really. I've loved this girl for what feels like my entire life and her dad hasn't just pulled us apart once, he's done it twice – just because he could. Some of it was my fault and I know I made mistakes – but I also know that if he wasn't there, then we'd be together now.'

'And you hate him?'

'I know it's a strong word. You've been through a lot and dealt with it but you're still young. Young people throw around words like hate all the time. "I hate you", "If you don't get down here this minute, then I'm going to kill you". The meaning of the words gets lost to such a degree that you can tell someone you're going to kill them, and it's like saying you've eaten the last chocolate biscuit. You shrug it off and life goes on.'

'Me and my old friends used to say we hated each other all the time. We'd fall out and then be mates again a week later.'

'Exactly, because *really* hating someone is much more than saying the word. I know he hates me too but that's a large part of what's kept me going for the past eight or nine years. It could have been negative but it wasn't at all. It was what kept me getting up every day. He gave me money to leave his daughter alone, so, because I couldn't have her, I had to force myself to do something worthwhile with the money instead. I enjoyed that seething rage every morning.'

Fiona didn't reply instantly. Andrew didn't know if what he'd said had scared her off, it probably should have done, but she was a tough girl. Sometimes it was easier to tell truths to a stranger.

'Does this mean you don't feel hate any longer?' she asked.

'I don't know what I feel now . . . but it's different. I had my second chance and it's gone again. I think I've been spending all these years hoping that opportunity would come along and, now it's passed, I can try to move on with my life.'

'What does that mean?'

'I don't know yet. My point is that I don't want you spending the next however many years hating some person you don't even know, just because I've given you a name. It might drive you, motivate you, make you want to get up, but it'll get you in the end – just like all those happy-clappy hippy types always say it will.'

Fiona took a deep breath through her nose and blew it out through her mouth. 'Does that mean the person is going to get away with it?'

'It's been dealt with.'

'How? Who by?'

'You're going to have to trust me.'

Andrew reached around the stone and put a hand on Fiona's arm. Even through the material of his coat, she felt so frail. With no parents to look after her, she was a young girl who had to fight the world all by herself. 'Even if I trust you,' she said, 'it's not going to bring him back.'

'No it won't.'

He sat next to her for a while, absorbing the tranquillity, not moving until Fiona was ready to leave. Andrew walked her to the gate that led towards the main road. He offered her a lift home but she insisted she'd walk, so he refused to take his jacket. It was too big for her but, if nothing else, it'd keep her warm on the way back to the city centre. He told her to call him if she ever had a problem, knowing she wouldn't. Fiona was going to create a better life for herself, still believing her father was innocent, even though nobody would ever be able to tell her that for sure. Sometimes a person's truth was more powerful than the actuality. If they believed it enough, then it was true for them, so who cared what anyone else thought.

Andrew watched her walk away and then headed back to the car, slotting into the driver's seat as Jenny put down a copy of the *Manchester Morning Herald*.

'Sorry for being a while,' he said.

'Did she take it okay?'

'Relatively speaking. She'll be fine.'

'Did you tell her the truth about Sampson and Steyn?'

'Sometimes the truth is best forgotten, like with Edie Watkins. Not everyone gets a happy ending.'

'So you're not going to tell Edie's mum where the cats went?'

'No.'

Jenny passed the paper to Andrew, with the front page uppermost that he'd already spent the morning poring over. 'Good.'

'You were right about Owen and Wendy reminding me of myself and Keira,' Andrew said. 'Ever since it happened, it had been at the back of my mind that they were a couple wanting to get married when they were young. Every time I saw their names on the news, I replaced them with ours.'

She pointed to the front page. 'Are you ever going to tell me what you did?'

'Perhaps it's just karma or a massive coincidence.'

Jenny picked up the paper, holding it up for him to see

the front page. '"Uni professor and local jeweller in child porn arrest"? *That's* a coincidence?'

'What do you think I did? Planted it on their hard drives myself?'

Jenny didn't respond. The truth was something he had no plans to share. He had his own demons and, somewhere in her past, she had hers.

'*I'm not a psycho.*'

Perhaps they'd be honest with each other in the future.

Before she could say anything further, Andrew's phone started to ring – Aunt Gem. This time, there were no jokes or threats to ignore.

'Hello,' he said, knowing straight away from her tone that she was in full gossip mode. He mouthed the word 'Gem' to Jenny.

'I'm not disturbing you, am I, darling?'

'No, I'm okay for a bit.'

'I've only just heard the news. It's so awful, dear. I wanted to call to hear your voice.'

'The front page of the *Herald*?'

'No, it's Reg from bingo. He just called, properly shaken up.'

'What's happened?'

'It's his friend's son. You remember that Kevin lad who came round to look at my 'lectrics?'

She mentioned it as if he was an old friend who'd done her a favour.

'I remember.'

'It's just terrible. His father's devastated, so he was on to Reg, then Reg is an old softie at heart, so he got himself all worked up and called me, now I'm calling you. I know I shouldn't have, but . . .'

'Gem, it's fine. I don't mind you calling me. What happened?'

'No one knows. The men are there now trying to figure it all out. Reg heard it was an electrical fire, so maybe you were right about him after all.'

Andrew's ears prickled with danger. 'There was a fire?'

'That's why Reg was so shaken up – he was going on about how it could happen to anyone. One minute you're asleep in your bed, the next, whoosh!, you're off to meet your maker. Poor Kevin. It was only the other day he was round here admiring my teapots, now . . . well . . . I just feel for his father.'

39

Buzzzzzzzzzzzzzz-Buzzzzzzzzzzzzz-Buzzzzzzzzzzzzzzzzzzzzzzzzz-
zzzzzzzzzzzzzzz.

Andrew pressed the button attached to the gatepost at
the front of Thomas Braithwaite's house. There'd been a
pile-up on the M60 and he'd spent more than four hours
driving from Manchester, not knowing if he was doing the
sensible thing. By the time he'd arrived, it was dark and
cold again, with the moon dousing everything in an
unnerving white-blue glow.

The gate didn't open but Andrew could hear footsteps
bounding along the path. Iwan was swaggering towards
him, shoes still shining, suit still clinging. He stopped on
the other side of the gate, accent more pronounced than
Andrew had ever heard it, toying with him.

'Who is it?' Iwan said.

'You know who it is, let me in.'

'Mr Braithwaite's having dinner with his family. He'd
like to be left alone.'

'Open the gates.'

'Believe it or not, I don't answer to you.'

'I'll climb if I have to.'

'Go for it. Watch out for the spikes on top.'

Andrew peered up, knowing he had no chance. There
were no horizontal bars for him to haul himself up on and

he'd never been a good climber anyway. Even if he did get near the top, he still had the spikes to negotiate.

Iwan started to walk away, knees slightly bent, legs wide. He was laughing loudly until Andrew bellowed his name for the third time. He ambled back towards the gate, standing a metre away from Andrew, the thick vertical metal posts between them.

'You shouldn't have come here in the first place. I could see it in you when you buzzed the first time: a wet, pathetic drip of a man.'

'Was it you who did it?'

'Did what?'

'Kevin Leonard.'

'Never heard of him.'

'I want to speak to Braithwaite.'

'That's *Mr* Braithwaite – and nobody comes around here making demands. Nobody. Now piss off before I come out there and make you.'

'Come on then.'

Iwan grinned, scratching his head where there was still a hint of a scrape from where Jenny had sent him sprawling into the gutter. 'Are you being serious? You don't even have your girlfriend around to save you this time.'

'So what's stopping you then? Open the gate – I'm right here.' Iwan glanced over his shoulder towards the house. 'Come on,' Andrew added. 'You don't need to ask his permission for everything. "Please, Sir, can I take a piss?", "Please, Sir, can I shine your shoes?"'

The hulk of a man twisted back to the gate, mind made up. He pressed something in his pocket and the gates started to hum, opening slowly. Andrew stepped back until he was on the edge of the kerb, standing in the glow of the moon, waiting.

Iwan didn't move until the gates were all the way open. He walked slowly, hunched forward, grinning and cracking his knuckles.

Andrew's heart was thundering but that was something he was becoming used to. He waited until Iwan was close enough, reached into the back of his jeans and then pulled out the tyre iron that had been in his boot. Iwan had no chance: he tried to avoid the swinging clump of metal but even the glancing blow sent him slumping to the pavement in a pool of his own blood. Andrew took a moment to check the other man's prone form, making sure his chest was still rising and falling. All those times, he'd allowed himself to be beaten because he'd played fair but Keira's father had taught him that only fools abided by the rules. Iwan had turned up to a fight with just his fists – more fool him.

Andrew wiped the weapon on Iwan's shirt jacket and slipped it into the back of his jeans, hoping he wouldn't have to use it again.

Braithwaite answered the front door a moment before Andrew got there, face creased into a frown as he peered past Andrew towards the open gates. 'Where's—'

'Your monkey's going to be fine, he'll just have a headache in the morning.'

Braithwaite pulled the door closed behind him, stepping onto the driveway, still looking towards the gate. 'I'm having dinner with my family, Mr Hunter, and don't like being interrupted. What do you want?'

'Was it you?'

'Was what me?'

'Kevin Leonard. That's why you wanted his name – it was nothing to do with blacklisting him as an electrician so he never worked for you, it was because you were going to do . . . *this*.'

Braithwaite scratched his chin. His eyes were even bluer in the moonlight, more dangerous. 'Oh, Mr Hunter, what's it like in that apartment of yours? Good views? What's your office like? Your assistant? What did you think was going to happen when you came to me?'

'That was about dealing with Steyn and Sampson.'

'Exactly, so you should consider Leonard a favour.'

'A *favour*? I didn't want this.'

'You said he was a cowboy, that he could have set your aunt's flat on fire.'

'That's not a reason to burn his house down with him inside.'

'If that were true, then why give me his name?'

Andrew was shouting. 'Because you asked!'

Braithwaite remained perfectly calm. 'Come now, Mr Hunter, you knew what you were doing in the same way you knew what the score was when you told me there was a professor involved. I was only interested in Sampson.'

Andrew tried to reply but there were no words. He rocked onto his heels and screamed at the sky, snorting through his nose as he faced Braithwaite, one hand reaching for the back of his trousers. The other man noticed, eyes darting to Andrew's side and back again.

'Don't be silly, Mr Hunter. Some things cannot be taken back.'

'Like house fires.'

'Precisely. I did you a favour. If you changed your mind about what you wanted, that can't be blamed on me. I helped you and you owe me one.'

'I don't owe you anything.' Braithwaite continued to smile narrowly. 'What do you want?' Andrew asked.

Braithwaite pursed his lips together. 'I'm not sure yet. You'll be the first to know when I do.'

Andrew's fingers looped around the tyre iron. 'What if I don't do what you want?'

Braithwaite's eyes twinkled in the light. 'We're all friends – why wouldn't you? I'll have a word with Iwan. I'm sure he's not the type to hold grudges. Now, why don't you let go of whatever you have in the back of your trousers, return to your car, and head home to that lovely flat of yours.'

Andrew's grasp tightened. It wasn't Thomas Braithwaite standing in front of him, it was his former father-in-law. He must have been lying when he'd been talking to Fiona about hate. It was only now he realised it.

'Mr Hunter.'

'What?'

'It's amazing what a person can leave behind. Look at you, all riled up, ready to fight. There'll be sweat dripping from you right now. Hairs that were stuck to your clothes falling onto the floor. Imagine what you left around my kitchen: hairs, fingerprints, all sorts. Imagine what might happen if they ended up at the scene of a house fire . . .'

The air was cold, biting Andrew's throat. 'You haven't . . .'

It took an age for Braithwaite to shake his head. 'No, I haven't. As I said, we're all friends here. I'd far rather we kept it that way.'

Andrew's grip finally loosened. He was locked into a stare-off with Braithwaite again and there was no way he could win.

'Was it you that Sampson called?'

'When?'

'When he realised the movie premiere necklace was coming in, he needed someone who could work quickly. It was the Evans brothers who ended up raiding the shop but I've not found a single thing that shows he knew them.'

Braithwaite showed off his teeth. 'Why didn't you ask me that in the first place?'

Andrew shrugged, defeated.

'Of course it was me he called. Who else was it going to be?'

'So if you were in it with Sampson – if you sorted out the robbery between you – why were you so happy to tell me who he was?'

'Don't you remember my cooking lesson? I don't like mavericks who go off and do their own thing. Those poor kids in the wrong place at the wrong time. If Mr Sampson wanted to do something about it, he should have made a phone call first.' Braithwaite glanced back to the house. 'Now, if you'll excuse me, I'm eating dinner with my family and I'd like to be left alone.' He put one foot on the door-step, before twisting back. 'Mr Hunter.'

'What?'

'Are you familiar with the work of Friedrich Nietzsche?'

Andrew was ready to leave, wanting out of the conversation. 'Not really.'

Braithwaite nodded. 'Well . . . "battle not with monsters, lest ye become a monster".' He paused for a moment, letting it sink in, one hand on the door. 'It's interesting with whom you choose to spend your time.'

'Who are you talking about?'

'Your assistant . . .' He clicked his fingers three times in quick succession. 'She has an *interesting* past, you could say.'

Andrew felt fixed to the spot, not knowing to what Braithwaite was referring.

'I'm not a psycho.'

He opened his mouth, ready to ask, but he could see Braithwaite willing him on, wanting him to be interested. He stopped himself before the words could come out: if he was going to ask anyone, it should be Jenny.

Braithwaite spotted the change, eyes narrowing as he grinned more widely. 'Now, have a good evening, Mr Hunter. In the meantime, look after yourself.'

The front door closed with a solid click and Andrew turned to walk back to his car, the wind suddenly whipping up, fizzing through the trees and sending a chill along his coatless back.

Brrr.

Bloody February.

SOMETHING WICKED

The first book featuring private investigator
Andrew Hunter

Nicholas Carr disappeared on his eighteenth birthday and the world has moved on. His girlfriend has gone to university, his friends now have jobs and the police have new cases to investigate.

But his father, Richard, can't forget the three fingers the police dug up from a sodden Manchester wood. What happened to Nicholas on the night he disappeared, and why did he never return home?

A private investigator is Richard's last hope – but Andrew Hunter has his own problems. There's something about his assistant that isn't quite right. Jenny's brilliant but reckless, and he can't work out what she stands to gain from their working relationship. By the time he figures out who's a danger and who's not, it might all be too late . . .

COMING SOON

NO PLACE LIKE HOME

A gripping standalone thriller from million copy bestseller
Kerry Wilkinson

Craig Macklin was a teenager when his headteacher told him he was heading either to prison or the grave. Instead, Craig left the north of England, saying goodbye to his friends and family to start a new life.

Thirteen years on, redundant and separated from his wife, he returns for the first time.

It's Christmas: markets in full swing, lights twinkling, shoppers shopping, revellers revelling.

Manchester has seen a revolution. The buildings soar higher, the shopping centres sprawl wider. New industries have replaced old and yet, away from the glitter, the tinsel, the hot spiced cider and the enormous inflatable Santa, some things will never change.

Amid the season, there are secrets from which he cannot escape and, when debt-collectors attack his parents' house, Craig realises the teenage hellraiser he left behind might not be so buried after all.